THE DETECTIVE'S WIFE

THE KAT ELAND SERIES
BOOK 1

AVA PAGE

LA JOLLA PRESS

La Jolla Press

1902 Wright Pl, Suite 200

Carlsbad, CA 92008

www.lajollapress.com

Printed in the United States of America

First printing, 2023

Library of Congress Control Number: 2023903812

ISBN-13 (Paperback): 978-1-7372736-6-0

AUTHOR'S NOTE

This book is a work of fiction. All the characters and events portrayed in this novel are products of the author's imagination or used fictitiously. Sometimes both.

DEDICATION

To my Framily,
Thank you for choosing to do life with me. Your acceptance, love, and support are appreciated beyond measure.

You know who you are.

Love,
Ava

PROLOGUE

DROWNING SEEMS like a good way to kill them. The water in my ears muffles the sounds of my little sister, Millie's, Alvin and the Chipmunks' Christmas record. It also muffles my baby sister, Mandy's, cries. The D batteries that run the record player feel like they'll last forever, which is great because we don't have electricity right now.

It's late May, and it's so hot our legs make a sucking sound when we get up from the leather couch, and without electricity we can't even use the box fan to distract Mandy from the sticky heat by making our voices sound like robots. Mandy loves it when I say, "Luke, I am your father," over and over again, even though none of us have seen Star Wars. I pretend I've seen it when my friends ask me. So, I know that's a famous line from the movie.

Without the fan, Millie plays the only album that

makes our baby sister stop crying. She's always crying. To be fair, I don't remember the last time we changed her diaper—maybe yesterday?—and she screamed because her butt was bright red and cracked. It hurt to even look at it. The white stuff that smells like glue that makes her stop crying has been gone for a while now.

We haven't eaten since yesterday's lunch of sliced potatoes made on a hot plate in our roach-infested kitchen. But Mom will be back soon. She always comes back. We're out of potatoes, diapers, and formula. If she doesn't come home soon, I'll call Grandma again. Mom gets mad when I call her, but without diapers, and more importantly, formula, I don't know what to do for Mandy anymore.

Mom named us all M's: Millie, Mandy, and me, Maureen. I would have liked either of their two names better. Maureen sounds older than eleven. Maybe when I grow up, I'll like it more.

I don't like being the older sister, I'm not responsible enough. I hide in the bathtub, and a better big sister wouldn't do that. Through the swishes of the water, I hear the soft chime of the wall clock strike four times. When I first got in, it'd struck once. It isn't fair that I'm hiding in our only bathroom and leaving both my little sisters to fend for themselves. I know it isn't fair.

My legs look like chicken skin as the bathwater gets cold again. There is a patch of light squeezing in from under the door and a little more light from the window placed high above the toilet. I had a candle on before.

The flamed shadows flicked the walls, and it looked like a dance show just for me. Mom doesn't like it when I use a lighter for the candles, but I do it anyway.

The tea light burned out around the time the clock chimed three, and I would've had to leave the bathroom to get another and that would've meant bath time was over. So, instead, I lay in the dimly lit bathtub.

Careful to keep my hair underwater, I pop the drain plug off with my toes and use my other foot to turn the water back on. The hot water rushes back into the tub, starting from my feet, making it comfortable again. I shut off the water and return the plug, all with my feet. I am a monkey.

I lift my fingers and hold them to my face. *Is this what I'll look like when I'm old and wrinkly? Why don't mermaids prune?* I swish my hair back and forth. If I turn quickly enough, I see my thin, dark brown curls twirling around like tendrils of smoke from my mom's Marlboro cigarettes, mysterious and beautiful. Two things I'm not. I close my eyes and I am a mermaid, no longer stuck in this life.

Sometimes Mom makes ringlets with the smoke that slips from her mouth and Mandy claps and laughs. But I hate the way it makes everything smell. And I wish that was the only thing she smoked.

I think about my hair again. *Will this kill the lice? Maybe.* I've tried everything else, and my scalp is raw from scratching. Last week, I ran my hair under scalding water until the water ran cold. I got a few hours of relief, but the itching came back the next morning. I asked Mom for help.

That was a week ago, and the itching hasn't stopped, despite her telling me to ask God for help, which I did, but so far, that hasn't worked. So, I'm trying other ways to kill them. I don't want to cut my hair; it is the only pretty thing about me. The boy who sits behind me in class, Bryan, had lice. He's probably the one who gave it to me. I hate Bryan. He talks too much and blames me for stuff I don't do, like stealing from lunch boxes at recess. His parents shaved his head.

If I complain much more, I know Mom will shave mine, too. Then, she'll tell me the prayers worked because God told her to shave my head. But she won't shave hers, I know this. So, not complaining, and drowning the lice seem as good an option as any. As I lay in the bathwater, the lice are stilled and I don't itch at all. I could lie here, become a mermaid, and live forever, in a bathtub, in our Section 8 apartment.

If I do this every day this week when the new ones hatch, maybe I'll be free of them. For now, I should get out and not whine about the lice that God fixed before Mom gets home and fixes the issue herself with her rusty pair of scissors.

The bathroom door handle rattles. *God, my sisters never give me any peace.* "Leave me alone. I'm in here. I'll be out in a minute."

The door opens anyway and casts a rectangle of light on the ground from the light of the window outside. I pull the bath curtain back to tell my sister to get out, but it isn't Millie. Hands are around my throat before I can let out a scream. Everything goes black, and finally I don't feel any itching, hunger, or sadness anymore. There is nothing.

ONE

THREE YOUNG GIRLS stared back at her from the creased manila folder. The soulful stare of the older girl cracked through her cautious respect for Greg. She bit the inside of her lip and plucked the envelope with the stack of sepia-toned pictures out of his briefcase. She set it on the dining table and pulled the photographs out. *It's just a few pictures. I won't look at the rest.* The paperwork stacked behind the photos remained tucked away.

The girls looked different from one another but also somehow the same like they were half-sisters. They were Neapolitan ice cream: chocolate, vanilla, strawberry. Their matching white shirts were freshly pressed with doily-like collars.

The older brunette teetered on adolescence and was as stiff as their new white shirts. She stood with a board-straight back and challenged the camera with her penetrating stare. Her mousy brown hair was so thin it became translucent at the edge of her shoulders. No haircut, it simply petered out, like it gave up on growing any longer. Her smile barely lifted the edges of her lips.

The waif-thin blonde sister sat on a wooden chair holding the baby. Her closely cropped haircut almost made her look like a boy. Kat wondered if she recently reached the infamous *cut your own hair* milestone, and this was a sullied attempt to fix it. She smiled through her nerves, her bottom teeth showing but not her top.

The baby's cherub-like fingers wrapped around her blonde sister's pointer finger. She was bald except for a few sprigs of fiery red hair spiking out on the sides that matched the rosy hue on her cheeks. The photographer caught the wide eyes of shock at the flash. While it was the oldest who drew Kat in with her stare, the baby looked most like her own daughter, Jillian.

It was probably the last picture of them alive.

Who are they? They look familiar. Kat scanned her memories to untangle the familiarity. Her husband, Greg, was a detective in the homicide cold case unit. So, they were long dead.

Before Jillian left for college, Greg never left his briefcase in the main areas of the house. After work, he'd walk through the door and march upstairs to tuck it away before settling in for dinner. Then, without Kat or Greg's permission, Jillian launched like a rocket into adulthood. Kat hated that word. What did launch mean, anyway? Their daughter still depended on them for almost everything.

She flipped the worn picture over and the one

beneath was a school picture of the blonde. There was a note on the back of the mall picture of the three.

November 2, 2001
Dear Mya,
Surprise, happy birthday! A few weeks ago I took the grand babies for new clothes and pictures at the mall. Don't they look perfect? Maureen insisted she and her sisters match. Of course, Millie was just so excited that her big sister wanted to match. You know Mandy, she was just happy to be there in Millie's lap. This was the only one with Mandy's eyes open.
Love,
Mom

She flipped it back around. Maureen. Millie. Mandy. Despite the new clothes, negligence swam beneath the surface in Maureen's expression. Her mud-brown eyes were older than her years, with an impossible combination of being both beagle-like and angry. Maureen's opposite was the middle sister, Millie. Her bright blue eyes were bigger than any Kat had ever seen. They revealed a new soul, less in tune with her world. Perhaps the age of the photograph dulled the color of baby Mandy's eyes. Because they were the color of a green olive, while her daughter Jillian's were the color of jade.

The sepia tone dulled everything but the penetrating gaze of Maureen's stare. Baby Mandy didn't have freckles yet, but had she lived, they would have smattered the bridge of her nose. She would have covered them with makeup, even though her mother said they were beautiful. Just like Jillian. But Mandy would never get freckles, or hair, or wear makeup.

If they would have lived, even Mandy would have been older than her college freshman daughter. Maybe with babies of their own. She reached into her pocket to touch the ever present piece of cloth she carried with her. A vestige of a previous life. Rubbing it between her fingers calmed her.

She shuffled the picture to the next one in the stack, and immediately wished she hadn't.

TWO

KAT CHOKED BACK the sour taste of bile as she studied the photograph. The oldest girl, the brunette, was naked in a bathtub. Her hair cascaded around her head in mermaid-like tendrils. The flash of the camera caught a ray of light bouncing off the bathwater. She appeared to be peering down from heaven instead of lifelessly at the ceiling. Her mouth hung open, like an angel mid-song, but her dark-ringed eyes were wide with shock. A few specks of black floated in the water beside her.

Kat turned to the next picture. The blonde girl still wore the pageboy haircut from the mall photograph. Her bluish-tinged lips complimented her enormous blue eyes. Her eyes were vacant, representing the husk of a human left behind. The waif-like girl wore a pair of dingy Wonder Woman Underoos, and she, too, stared at the ceiling. The disturbing apartment, which had feces and soiled diapers in the corner, was littered with dirty laundry and other debris. Kat hoped that whatever happened to her was quick. She flipped the picture to the next.

The Jillian lookalike appeared to be peacefully sleeping. Her pallor was paler, and her diaper rounded, like it critically needed a change. The baby's head lay a little crooked, but she remembered from Jillian that babies sometimes slept in surprisingly odd positions. Save the tiny over-loaded diaper, the baby was bare, with a distended tummy and arms and legs that were a little too skinny.

Kat touched the image over the bridge of the baby's nose, where her freckles would've been in a few years. The age of the picture added a brownish hue to what Kat knew were vibrant red sprigs of hair. A heaviness settled into Kat's chest. She shuffled to the first picture again and stared at the trio looking back from the department store picture. Their lights had blinked out before being allowed to shine.

She rubbed the soft piece of cloth in her jean pocket again.

Footsteps entered the kitchen, she spun on her heel and met Greg's wide eyes. A heat crawled up her cheeks like a child caught with her hand caught in a cookie jar before dinner.

"What do you have there?"

She startled at the tone of his voice and the pictures fell from her hands, scattering to the floor.

He snatched the envelope from the edge of the dining room table and crouched, gathering the photographs, stuffing them back inside. The contents were in haphazard order. Her hands wrung as her mind spun about what to tell him as he collected the girls' images. He stood and placed the envelope back in his briefcase, and slid it off the table.

Kat's stomach clenched in a fist. "I'm sorry. They fell on the table. I went to put them away, and well, you startled me." As a police officer, she hoped he didn't spot her thin lie. Greg was a husband first, though, and she'd told plenty of lies to him.

"Katie, I'm sorry. You shouldn't have seen those." He patted her head.

She hated when he called her Katie. To her, it was a child's name, and she wasn't an animal to be patted. Introducing herself as Katie was one of her biggest regrets when she'd re-invented herself so many years ago. She cringed each time he said it. After almost two decades, that was a lot of Katies.

She sighed. "It's a damned shame. Are you working on the case?"

Greg put his fingers on the bridge of his nose and shook his head. He didn't talk about work, but without Jillian, they were running out of things to say.

Finally, he replied, "Kind of. It happened several years ago, but now DNA records have improved some of the investigative techniques. We dust old cases off every now and again for fresh leads. Especially if we have a similar case pop up."

"And?" Kat asked.

"Nothing so far. The mother was a drug addict,

really tweaked out. They brought her in for questioning when she *'found'* the bodies. Less than a week later, she overdosed before her arrest. Addicts don't remember some of the stuff they do when they're high. There was a suicide note confessing to killing her children, and the case was closed."

"Do you think she did it? If she didn't, I can't blame her for killing herself. I don't know what would happen if anything happened to Jillian," Kat said.

His voice dropped several decibels. "Don't say that, Katie. You're stronger than that."

Her mind flickered to her family, and how death changed the fabric of it. Once respected, even revered by society, in a single moment, everything came tumbling down. If anything happened to Jilly, she was certain she'd jump into the grave and let the dirt cover them both.

She tilted her head to the side. "Why do you have the case if she confessed and killed them herself? Why is it re-opened?"

He scratched his red scruff laced with a few white strands. "It's routine, really. After she died, the case was closed. Now, there's another case with some loose connections. Not everyone is the mother you are, Katie."

Was that a compliment or condescension? "What loose connections?" Kat pressed.

Greg zipped his briefcase and rolled his eyes. "Drugs make people do horrible things. Babies are expensive. They need formula, food, and constant care. You know this, Katie. So, it overwhelmed her, and she killed her children. It's not something you'd understand, sweetheart. I'm sorry I left these pictures out. I'll be more careful. Without Jillian here, I've been a little lax." He squeezed her shoulder and rubbed it before disappearing up the stairs to hide the briefcase away in his office. He returned, flushed from his quick errand. "There, all better."

Kat's lips pinched into a frown. She wasn't a child, maybe ten years his junior, but still closer to forty than thirty. What mother would kill their baby over formula and food? Maybe it was postpartum depression? Those thoughts were powerful and haunting as the walls closed in. The idea of a better world without her was not foreign. She changed the subject. "It's Thursday," she said simply.

"I remember. Chase and I are going to the billiards place in a few."

His partner, Chase Weber, was her husband's opposite in nearly every way. His jet-black hair and Greek olive skin made him appear years younger than his nearly fifty, though he and Chase were only seven months apart. He was a forever bachelor and didn't appear to be in a hurry to change his relationship status. He'd slept with half the women in her neighborhood, and at least two in the bi-weekly book club.

Greg said, "Oh, I made reservations for us at Noodleys at four on Monday."

There was no need for a date night on Monday. With Jillian in college, they spent a lot of time alone together and Noodleys wasn't her favorite place, but he liked their Alfredo and their drinks were half-price from four to five. Plus, after nearly twenty years of marriage, he still made reservations for dates with her.

"Sounds good," Kat said. "Remember, I've got my and Ann's combined birthday dinner here on Tuesday as well."

He nodded. "That's right, I forgot."

She glanced at her watch. "It's six-thirty."

"I'll jump in the shower. My date is picking me up in twenty minutes," Greg said, grinning.

He went upstairs, and the shower started a few minutes later. Greg thought her both stronger and sometimes weaker than she was. If anything happened to Jillian, she *would* jump into the grave and let the earth cover them both. Just like her mother.

THREE

KINSHIP AND DRAMA clung to the mothers' forced interactions through PTA meetings, sports, and school events. And with Jillian grown and in college, Kat sat outside that daily circle. The biweekly book club permitted a few chatty hours to catch up. Her chaotic child-rearing days were replaced with reading, rearranging furniture, and trying and abandoning more hobbies than she cared to admit (knitting, playing the guitar, learning to draw, and photography, to name a few).

The striking absence of noise gave her house a hollow quality. There was no toddler pleading for a playdate, tween begging to be driven to the mall, or teen chatting about her latest melodrama. In the thick of it, Kat wished away the exhausting days, but now, through the lens of nostalgia, the monotony of sameness nipped at her. Often, Kat peeked into her daughter's vacant room and saw her bed was tight and crisp. Another reminder of both Jillian's absence and her imprint.

Mandy looked so much like Jillian that Kat had an overwhelming need to see her daughter's face. She Face-Timed her, and her daughter answered immediately. The blue sky peppered with wispy clouds was bright behind her daughter. Jillian's cheeks flushed as the phone bobbed up and down to her cadence.

"Hi, Mom," she said, a tiny ripple of breathlessness the only sign that she quickened her pace.

"Hi, is this a bad time?"

"I've only got a couple of minutes. I'm meeting friends at the library," Jillian said. She wore a v-neck t-shirt with her carrot-orange hair in a messy bun with two sticks in it. She looked like a walking campfire. "Don't you have your book club tonight?" Jillian asked in a breathy reply.

"I do, the Thirsty Thriller Book Club. Try to say that ten times fast." Kat chuckled.

Jillian giggled. "You know what *thirsty* means, right? I've always meant to ask... Did you name it that *on purpose?*"

Kat shrugged. "We drink wine, so it's a nod to that."

Jillian snorted another laugh. "Mom, thirsty means horny."

Kat blushed. "What? Who said that?"

"Literally everyone, Mom. Have fun with the *thirsty* neighborhood ladies. Tell them I said hi and that I can babysit this summer. I've got to go. Love you." Jillian made a kissy face before disappearing from the screen.

"I love you, too," Kat told her, but she was already gone.

Her daughter's laughter rang in her ears as heat rushed to her cheeks. While her daughter laughed *with* her, it stung and it felt like she was laughing at her. College Jillian had a way of making Kat feel like she was in eighth grade again. Then, in a self-fulfilling prophecy, she cringed at herself for caring what her child thought.

There was a quick knock at the door, followed by her friend's familiar voice. "Honey, I'm home..." Camila balanced a cheese tray in one hand, a book under her arm, and carried two bottles of wine in the crook of her other arm.

"I'm here with my contribution." Camila breezed through the door and used her foot to close it behind her.

Kat looked at her own ripped jeans, Prince t-shirt, and red Converse, and back to Camila's floral dress and black kitten heels. There was no dress code for thriller night and everyone else would fall somewhere between them both.

Kat smiled. "You look nice."

"You too," Camila said automatically.

Kat fluffed her messy brown bun. "I got dressed up special for you." She blew a wayward hair out of her face.

They both laughed.

"I just got off the phone with Jilly."

"Aw, how is she? My babies miss her so much," Camila said. It went unsaid that her oldest, Chloe, didn't miss Jillian. They were the same age but stopped talking in junior high school for reasons only the tweens understood. Without siblings, Jillian didn't understand the joys of fighting like wolves one minute and loving each other the next.

"I miss her too," Kat said. She walked to her friend and unloaded the cabernets from the crook of her arm. "Oh, Gen Z stole *another* word from us. According to Jilly, *thirsty* now means horny. We thought we were being so funny with the thirsty for wine, and it turns out we're announcing we're a bunch of horny women in the neighborhood."

"They take everything from us, don't they? Janet will love this. Let's change our genre to something spicy and keep the name." Camila winked.

"Would you read them if they were spicy?"

Camila smirked. "I might try harder to carve out time for those. I'm married, not dead."

"True, true. Let's get this stuff set up." Kat walked toward the kitchen, Camila close on her heels.

Kat poured the Costco fancy nuts into a glass bowl as Camila slid in behind her and put the silver cheese tray on the counter. Camila picked out a few pecans and popped them in her mouth, wiping the salt from her hands on the pleats of her dress. The women looked more alike than sisters. Both had long chestnut hair and sleek bodies. But Camila's affection for makeup was unmatched. She wore a heavy foundation and thick cat-eyed liner. Greg didn't like much makeup, which suited

Kat fine because she found anything besides a swipe of mascara and lip gloss made her look like a clown.

The book club was a strict no-child affair unless the child was still being breastfed. Even then, though, the women often found sitters for a brief respite from their charges, who were vortexes for their attention.

Kat's modest home was the smallest and least expensive house she'd ever lived in. One day, she would inherit more money than her husband could make in one hundred lifetimes working as a detective. Unless her estranged father was one of those people who would donate his wealth to his cat. But he didn't like animals and had never owned one, so her chances were pretty good.

She'd never told Greg of her father's vast wealth. She'd meant to eventually, but then the months became years, and years, decades. Kat planned to cross the bridge after she and her father reconciled or when he passed. Whichever came first. Her wealth had changed and ultimately destroyed her family and every relationship she had as a child. She didn't want Jillian or Greg to change.

Kat turned her attention back to Camila. Tonight she'd catch up on the gossip of the town and maybe sprinkle in some of her own.

FOUR

CAMILA DRAGGED a wooden chair from the dining room. Kat's lips pressed together as the wooden legs scraped across the living room floor. She made a mental note to replace the felt bottoms on the chair. Camila set it in place to complete the circle in the living room. They walked back into the kitchen and Camila dipped her hand again into the bowl of nuts.

Kat said, "Someone is going to have to drop this reading club, or I'm going to have to buy a new chair. This is getting ridiculous."

Without hesitation, Camila said, "I vote for Janet." She wiped a bit of salt from her lip.

Kat snickered. "We all vote for Janet. Last in, first out." Krista, Kat, and Camila all moved into the neighborhood when it was built. Ramona, Ann, and Janet joined years later, with Janet being the latest addition.

Camila shrugged her shoulders. "She's nice enough. But if I hear one more thing about growing vegetables or the benefits of veganism, I'm going to die. She's just so..."

"Crunchy?" Kat completed her sentence, her face twisted into a small grimace.

Camila rolled her eyes. "Like a damn granola bar."

"A *homemade* granola bar," Kat added.

Camila snorted out a laugh.

Kat sighed and bit her lip, a reminder to be kinder. "I feel kind of guilty for lying to her about the brownies. I told her they were vegan."

"I don't care. If she doesn't get high, then she'd be absolutely unbearable. I mean, she's fine with getting high, but God forbid an egg passes over her lips? Come on. I meant to ask. Why is Greg's car still in the driveway?"

Kat rubbed her brow. "He's running a bit late, like always. Chase is on his way. They're going out." She went to the cabinet with the wine and pulled out three bottles of red. Camila opened the two she'd brought to breathe.

Camila raised a single brow. "Chase is handsome, but beneath his charming exterior, I don't see what anyone sees in him."

Hackles on the back of Kat's neck rose to his defense. "He's Greg's partner. I've known him for as long as I've known Greg. And he's a great godfather."

Camila took a small step back and rested her hand against the granite countertop. "I'm sorry, I know you and I don't agree about him. I think anyone who will openly seduce half the neighborhood is sleazy." She wrinkled her nose.

Kat steeled herself in place and crossed her arms. "He isn't married, and he's not forcing himself on anyone." Kat's stomach fluttered a response.

Camila's five children and husband were her life; despite Edward's burgeoning belly, short stature, and receding hairline, she adored him and he worshipped the ground she walked on. High school sweethearts, their marriage was what the neighborhood aspired to. Most Saturday mornings he crouched over their flower beds pulling weeds with the top part of his backside peeking out of his jeans or mowing the lawn in socks and Birkenstocks in summer or white grass-stained sneakers with calf-high socks in spring.

"Well, I hope Chase will be gone before Krista and Ann get here." Camila's face twisted into a smile and again raised an eyebrow. Her smile showed she didn't hope he'd be gone at all. She reveled in his discomfort. Krista and Ann were both married, and they'd both slept with Chase. They were about as similar as salt and pepper shakers.

Krista's hair was so blonde it was nearly white and her stature so thin, a strong wind could knock her over. Ann looked as Greek as Chase, like his less blessed little sister with frizzy hair. She wore thick glasses with a habit of pushing them up the bridge of her Roman nose. Her stout body bore a permanent mom pouch from her three babies. His type seemed to be anyone who might sleep with him. And there was no shortage of options.

Kat changed the subject and told Camila about the pictures that had slipped out of Greg's briefcase.

Camila tapped her finger to her chin. "Hmm, I remember that." She perched herself on the dining room chair at the kitchen table. "That's *The M Girls Murder.* The newspapers thought they were being cute with the headlines with things like *M is for Murder* and *Mom MMMurders.*" She clucked her tongue. "Such a shame."

"God, that sounds terrible. I don't remember it," Kat said. She sat across from Camila and moved the vase of daisies from between them.

Camila turned her head toward the ceiling, combing through her memories for details. "Yes, I was pregnant with Chloe." Her timelines always coincided with who she was pregnant with or how old one of her five children was at the time.

Chloe was born a few days before Jilly. But Kat had been too busy hurling into the toilet to pay any attention to the news. Sad news, like the *Three M Girls* would have plummeted her into a pit of despair.

Kat said, "I guess there was another case like this one, so Greg brought home the file to see if there were leads."

While Kat spoke, Camila's hand fluttered to her pendant, with all of her children's birthstones clinking together. It was a Mother's Day gift from Edward several years ago, and the tackiest piece of jewelry Camila owned, but she wore it every day.

"How awful. I heard the mother did it and then killed herself. Probably postpartum depression or something. I'm so glad I didn't struggle with that with any of my children." She paused and glanced at Kat. "Sorry. I didn't mean it."

Kat waved her apology away and changed the subject. She didn't want to think about the dead girls anymore or postpartum depression. Even eighteen years later, she easily recalled the suffocating, dark thoughts. Though she never thought about killing Jillian. Sometimes, though, she flirted with the idea that Jillian and Greg would be better off without her.

She cleared her mind and asked, "Did you read the book this time?"

"What do you think?" Camila shrugged.

"Do you ever read the books?" Kat asked.

Camila blew out a breath. "Nobody but you even notices that I don't know what I'm talking about. Even if I wanted to read it after, it's too late. I know how the story ends." She ran her long, manicured fingers through her chestnut hair. "But I love being here with my favorite people."

Kat winked at her. "It's our secret. I get it, but I love reading them. It's fun to solve the crime before they do."

Camila cleared her throat. "I don't even like thrillers, but I can't convince anyone to read anything else. Especially you. You figure it out every time. You should have been the detective, not your husband."

Kat's eyebrows knitted in thought. "You're probably right."

The corners of Camila's lips twitched. "Now, if we read something a little more... *thirsty*..."

Kat rolled her eyes and laughed. There was a knock at the door. "It's probably Chase." After over twenty years, a rush of adrenaline skipped her heart forward each time he arrived. She got up and walked out of the kitchen to the front door.

FIVE

THE DOOR OPENED before she'd crossed the room. "Hi, Kat," Chase said. He grinned widely at her, and his eyes crinkled at the edges.

"Well, hi stranger." They closed the distance between them and she kissed his cheek. His hands slid around her waist in a loose embrace. Every time he touched her, she averted her eyes. His magnetic force seduced vulnerable and lonely women like Krista and Ann, and she refused to be one of his conquests. Kat pulled back from him and wiped her lip gloss off his cheek with her thumb.

He raked his fingers through his full, jet-black hair. "How's my Jilly?"

"She's good, adjusting to college. Told us last week that she won't be home for spring break, so I guess it's a good sign that she's adjusting." She paused and added, "Changed her major again, too."

Chase grinned, flashing his crooked incisor, his sole

imperfection, which somehow only made him more charming. "Oh, what's her new major?"

Kat hesitated. "You don't want to know."

"She likes socializing more than studying... so... underwater basket weaving?" He smirked.

"Worse. Criminal justice," Kat said. "Frankly, I didn't think Riverson would offer that degree."

Kat had sat mystified when the acceptance letter returned from Riverson University with a full-ride scholarship for Jillian, the same school Kat's father had tried to get her to go to before she'd left to start a new life.

Chase whistled through his teeth. "Shit, have I taught her nothing? This isn't the job for her. She doesn't want to see what we do. This isn't the job for her," he repeated, his brows knitted together. He had an edge of protection in his voice.

Kat waved her hand, batting off his unease. "It'll change a couple hundred more times. This is her fourth major. She worships you and Greg; she's still trying to figure herself out is all." Kat sacrificed her identity to bear the cloak of motherhood, and Jillian's idolization of her father had her tucking an ugly envy away.

Camila walked in and cleared her throat. "Hello, Chase."

He straightened and tucked a hand in his pocket. "Hi Camila, I didn't know you were here." Despite being the prettiest in the neighborhood, Chase never flirted with her. His charisma seemed to almost repulse her.

"My car is right out front. You're a cop. Aren't you

supposed to be observant?" Her tone was laced with sarcasm.

Kat shot Camila a *cool it* look, and she softened her face and smiled at Chase with an expression that didn't reach her eyes.

Chase looked up the stairs. "Is my date going to be ready soon?"

"In a minute," Greg called down.

Kat laughed. "You know him, still preening and combing the beard. He needs to look perfect for boys' night. We have our usual suspects coming for our book club tonight. Matter of fact, they'll be here any minute."

"Oh?" Chase asked.

"Yeah, maybe you know some of them... Let's see, you know Camila." She gestured behind her to her friend, standing with her arms loosely crossed, smirking. "Who else will be here?" She pretended to think, tapping her finger on her lip.

"Janet and Ramona," Camila said. Chase's face was blank.

Then Kat added, "Oh, Krista and Ann. Do you know any of them?" She returned his wink from earlier.

Chase shrugged and shifted uncomfortably on his feet and called up the stairs, in a more urgent and less friendly tone, "C'mon princess, we gotta go."

Watching him squirm gave Kat a sadistic pleasure. Krista and Ann both reported back to her with every scandalous and delicious detail, which both tempted and filled her with envy. Her love life was about as satisfying as lukewarm diner coffee. When she needed the caffeine rush, it was there, but never quite what she expected or hoped it would be.

Greg said, "I'm coming. Hold your horses, man."

Chase jabbed his thumb toward the stairs and said, "And that's why I call him princess. It takes less time for you to get ready than it does for him."

"It's that beard of his. It takes a lot of grooming. Are you certain you don't want to stay? You would love our neighbors, and we have extra food. Of course, they're all married with children, so I can't set you up with anyone, but they're all really nice women. You'd like them." She eyed him innocently.

Chase's smile turned into a grimace, and his jawline tensed. "Greg, c'mon man. We've got to go." He shot Kat a glance. "Maybe another time."

There was a knock on the door behind him.

"Oh, someone is here. Let me get that." Kat sauntered toward the door.

Chase's eyes slid nervously to the door.

Kat swung it open and Ann stood there in a shapeless gray sweater with hints of cat hair and baggy dark jeans. She held a bottle of wine in the crook of one arm, brownies, and her book tucked under the other arm.

"Hi, Ann, it's so good to see you." Kat opened the door wide to give Ann a glimpse of Chase in the foyer behind her.

Ann straightened and waved shyly at Chase. Her hand wandered to her mouth where she gnawed the side of her nail. Kat silently recounted in her head the details Ann had shared of a particularly energetic afternoon on his kitchen table three months ago. When she was supposed to be out buying groceries for her family. Kat vowed to never eat at Chase's house. He'd never invited them, but if he ever did, she wouldn't eat there. She knew too much about what he did on counters and tables. He was a walking health code violation.

Kat said, "This is Chase."

Ann blushed and tucked a black, wayward tendril behind her ear. "Hi, I think we've met before?" Her voice went up an octave, hopeful.

Guilt punched Kat in the stomach. She wanted to make Chase uncomfortable, but not at Ann's expense. Her friend longed to see him again, but Chase had ghosted her not long after their tryst. His M.O. was never more than a few nights. Simple. No attachments. They were usually married, but he underestimated the longing of a woman lonely in her marriage.

He cleared his throat. "Yeah, I think we've met maybe once before."

She hurried past him and into the kitchen. Kat shot Chase a side glance as she followed her.

Once out of Chase's sight, she spun on her heel and hissed, "What is he doing here? I didn't even shower today..." She lifted her arm and sniffed.

"He isn't staying. Just picking up Greg," Kat said. "He's running late. Again. I'm sorry."

There was another knock at the door and Camila answered. Ramona and Janet stood on the doorstep. Ramona held store-bought cookies still in the supermarket package with a yellow clearance sticker on them, and Janet brought homemade granola in a Tupperware case.

Kat and Ann returned to greet the women. Kat admired Ramona's neon green buzz cut and smiled. "You've gone with green this time. I love it. It really matches your personality and that fantastic dress."

Ramona laughed and touched the fine edges of her hair. A bit of green was still on her skin behind one of her ears from the home dye job. "I figure if I can't have a little fun with the cancer then why even have it, right? I'm going to lose this again, and hot pink is a little cliché for breast cancer. So, next time I'm probably going with purple."

Janet said, "Purple would be lovely on you. Are you using organic dyes? It's so important you don't introduce poisons into your system."

Kat bit the inside of her cheek and shot Ramona a look. Janet was the youngest member of the group, with three children ranging from a baby in cloth diapers to a kindergartener. She planned to homeschool and was an evangelist for veganism.

Ramona glared at Janet. She answered in her booming voice, "Chemo is a lot of poison, but a little more on my head for a few moments of happiness will not kill me. If anything does, the cancer will. So, I'm going to be as wild and crazy as I want while I'm getting through this inorganically." She pushed past Janet and into the house and then focused on Ann. "Did you bring my brownies?"

Her ego more hurt than her shoulder. Janet rubbed

at where Ramona had brushed past. Kat pretended not to see.

Ann nodded. "I did. Tonight's brownies are in the kitchen."

"The chemo is kicking my ass, and I'm not hungry and can't sleep. Those brownies are the only thing that saves me. It's what keeps me coming to our Thursdays. And of course, the company..." Ramona winked at Kat and swirled her dress splashed with blues, greens, and pops of purple flowers. Janet was right, the dress would match beautifully with green or purple hair.

"Thank you," Ann said, blushing for the second time that day. "I made an extra batch for you." She reached in her purse and handed a freezer bag full of brownies to Ramona. "These are a little stronger."

Ramona opened the bag and inhaled. "Oh, I cannot wait to get into these. Thank you so much. You're saving my life one brownie at a time." She tucked her stash away in her purse.

Chase settled on the couch and waited for Greg to come down the stairs. Then he crossed his legs and kicked nervously with his foot. He turned his attention to burying himself in his phone, though he didn't have social media and rarely texted.

The final knock on the door came, and Camila opened the door for Krista carrying a veggie tray. Kat was the host, but Krista was the master of ceremonies. She led the discussion and kept everyone on task throughout the evening to create a book club experience and not just neighborhood ladies getting drunk and high a couple of times a month.

Chase turned and his eyes met Krista's. He stood, taking Krista in with his gray-green eyes. Kat's ribs squeezed tight with envy and she looked away.

"Hi, Krista," Chase said.

Ann's eyes narrowed at Krista.

"Uh, hi. It's Chad, right?" Krista said and opened her blue eyes wider. They were almost opened as wide as the M girl, *Millie*.

He dropped his shoulders and ducked his chin. "No, my name is Chase."

"Sorry, Chase. It's good to see you again." She breezed past him toward the kitchen, and Kat followed. Kat knew she too had gone to his home, and they'd had sex in his Barcalounger. If ever invited, Kat would sit nowhere in his house, either.

"What the hell, Kat? Why is he here?" Krista stammered.

"He isn't staying. He's here to get Greg."

If Krista and Ann figured each other out, it would be the end of her book club. That was one of Kat's only social outlets, and she'd never forgive Chase.

They returned to the living room, and Chase was seated again. Ann excused herself to hide in the bathroom, and everyone stood in awkward silence, waiting for the men to leave. Greg came down the stairs in dark jeans and a white golf shirt. His hair was damp and slicked back, but his red beard speckled with white was groomed.

"Finally," Chase said and stood, leading the way to the door.

"Good evening, ladies," Greg said.

There was a chorus of pleasantries while the women waited for them to leave.

Greg went to Kat and hugged her. "See you tonight, babe," he said before releasing her and following Chase outside.

After they left, a collective sigh of relief rippled through the room.

Ramona said what everyone else was thinking, "Finally. It took them long enough. Now, let's get down to business."

SIX

CAMILA AND KAT retrieved the two bottles of opened wine and glasses from the kitchen. The fancy nuts, clearance cookies, homemade granola, and everything else remained on the counter until the munchies sent them back in from the pot brownies.

Krista sat on the couch with her annotated book on her lap and her back stick-straight. She was president of the PTA, coached soccer, and volunteered at the food pantry. Her oldest son, Gavin, from a previous relationship, lived in California doing something with computers she didn't understand. Her two younger children lived at home, but were old enough to watch themselves.

Months ago, Kat relinquished the coveted recliner when Ramona shared that her cancer had come back; stage three. Her back often hurt from chemotherapy, and the recliner was the most comfortable seat in the living room. Ramona typically seesawed in and out of sleep during book club. She never opened the book but always read it and recalled distinct details that even Krista didn't. She was an eager participant in the book discussion early in the evening before the marijuana dulled her mind.

Ann peeked out of the bathroom and peered down the hall to confirm Chase's exit. Kat gave her a small thumbs up, and she smiled shyly in gratitude as she stepped out of hiding. She went to the kitchen and retrieved her pot brownies, setting them in the middle of the coffee table. While Ann took her usual spot next to Krista, she crossed her arms, making herself as small as possible. She didn't bring her book, but she never did.

Ramona leaned in and grabbed a brownie and immediately popped it in her mouth as she propped her feet back in the recliner, waiting for its effects. Camila and Kat filled the wine glasses and passed them around. Camila handed the last one to Ramona and perched herself on the edge of the couch next to Ann while Kat sat in the winged chair and sipped her wine.

Janet shifted uncomfortably in the wooden chair and placed her book neatly on her lap. Kat was glad for the chair's placement on the other side of the living room. Janet wore patchouli oil instead of deodorant, and chasing three young children under five meant she sweat a lot. Her scent was a mix of musky earth and body odor that curled Kat's stomach.

The women sipped their wine and adjusted in their seats to get comfortable for the evening's conversation.

Ramona closed her eyes. "Ann, your brownies are the best." They hit her quickly with her empty stomach from the chemotherapy. With eyes drooping, she took a long sip of her dark red wine and swished it around in her glass. She hovered her snubbed nose over it, inhaling the tannins. Kat winced at the wine sloshing in Ramona's glass as her eyelids lowered. It was Greg's favorite chair, and they saved for three months to have enough money to pay it off. Kat now understood why people had covered their furniture in plastic in the 1950s.

Ann smiled in appreciation. After her son and daughter started high school, she'd explored her green thumb. An intense woman, she became a certified Master Gardener, but the only thing she cultivated was the marijuana in her basement that she tended under growing lights. They hired gardeners for the lawn and backyard.

Kat took another small sip of the wine. She'd have a couple of small bites of the brownie when they left and be asleep before Greg returned. Her friends would never see her stoned. There were things about her that no one would ever know, not Camila or Greg. Things she didn't even want to know about herself.

Kat said, "So, I've got a very important topic to address. Jillian has brought something to my attention." She cleared her throat with mock earnestness.

Krista asked, "Aw, how is Jilly? Is she doing well in college?" Her voice pitched up and down in a sing-song tone.

"She certainly loves it. I wish we saw her more, though," Kat admitted.

The ladies nodded their heads in empathy.

Ramona asked, "So, what's the very important topic?"

"Well, apparently thirsty now means horny. Thanks to Gen Z," Kat said.

Ramona let out a guffaw. The brownies were already taking effect. Ann's eyes widened and her cheeks turned a shade of pomegranate. Krista smirked and raised a perfectly drawn eyebrow.

Ramona said, "I was wondering when y'all were gonna figure that out."

Janet turned to Ramona. "You knew?" She clutched an invisible set of pearls at her neck.

"Of course I did," she said. "Any teacher worth their weight knows the latest slang. The entire middle school knows. It's funny. I vote to keep it. Shoot, I was hoping we'd read something a little sexier, anyway. It's blood, crime, and murder all the time."

Janet said, "We have to change it." And patted her book on her lap with authority.

"Why? We're married, not dead," Ramona replied, rolling her eyes.

Camila glanced at Kat and mouthed, "*See?*"

Krista cleared her throat. "Let's worry about that later." She cracked open her book to the back. "So," she said, her thin frame leaning over, "did anyone suspect the husband?" Her delicate brown eyebrows perked up in question. They were unnaturally dark for her almost white hair, which drew attention to her dark blue eyes, the color of the depths of the sea.

Janet spoke first. She always spoke first. "It certainly surprised me. He seemed so caring and sweet. Then, boom, in chapter thirty-seven, he's suddenly a serial killer? C'mon. I didn't find that believable. It would be like if suddenly one of our husbands turned into a raging lunatic with a secret love of killing prostitutes."

Camila said, "While not a husband, if it was Chase, we'd believe it." The air in the room pinched. Kat pursed her lips. She hated when Camila stirred the pot. Boredom bred the temptation for excitement, even if at Krista and Ann's expense.

Ramona grinned and laughed as Ann and Krista blushed. Affairs were the worst kept secret in the neighborhood. But Janet looked at everyone, not understanding the unspoken conversation. Ramona's eyes drifted closed again before nodding herself awake for another bite of the brownie. Small bits of brown were stuck in her teeth.

She said, "The husband was a psychopath. It was obvious from the start. Geeze, Janet." And she rested her head back on the recliner. Kat hoped her lime green hair wouldn't stain the cream fabric. They hadn't elected for the scotch guard when they'd bought the chair.

Kat sighed. "These books are all the same. It's always the husband, isn't it? Whoever writes these things has a formula. Why can't it be the wife? Or the crazy ex-lover? The kid? The family dog? Literally anyone besides the husband. It makes these books so predictable."

Camila said, "I know, right?" Her book's spine was tight and a juxtaposition against Krista's well-worn one. It was ridiculous she opened her mouth at all. Krista side-eyed Camila and Camila pressed her lips shut and lifted her glass, taking a sip.

Ann ran a hand through her curly mop of hair. "I don't know, Krista. I suspected the mistress. She seemed to be a real bitch." She narrowed her eyes at Chase's other lover. Kat didn't think they knew, but it seemed they suspected one another. Affairs really were the worst kept secrets.

Krista tapped her thin long finger to her chin, paused, and crossed her lean, pale legs. "The mistress was also a wife, so…"

Kat took another drink, and thought, *this isn't about the book club anymore,* as a heavy silence filled the room. Ramona snored softly.

"Well, enough about that," Kat said. "Honestly, it was a shit book. Want to see a real cold case? I found something today."

Camila and Ann perked up and leaned forward.

Krista shut her book, her notes of no further importance, pushed out her lower lip, and slouched her shoulders. "I guess we're done with the book discussion." She tucked her book into her oversized purse.

Camila and Ann stood to refill the drinks and bring out the snacks, while Kat went to the office and retrieved the briefcase and pulled the manila envelope out. She peeked inside to make sure she grabbed the right one, and the girls stared back at her. She tucked it under her arm and hurried downstairs to the living room. Kat swallowed hard.

It wasn't right to create a spectacle of the three girls to entertain her friends, but they were killed decades ago. No one would know.

SEVEN

KAT STEPPED BACK into the room now charged with anticipation. Even Ramona bobbed her head awake. Kat noted a small green stain behind her head and she bit the inside of her lip. It looked like the same shade as the sneakers Edward wore when mowing the grass.

Like a thriller novel, Kat teased out the suspense. She waved the manila envelope in front of them. "This slipped out of Greg's briefcase earlier. Do you ladies remember the Three M Girls?"

The women's eyes grew wide as they abandoned their snacks. *What harm could a bunch of chattery neighborhood women do to a cold case, anyway?* she thought.

She set the manila envelope on the table. "Before we open it, what do you remember about the case?"

Ramona was now fully awake. "I remember they all had names that began with M and the mother murdered her children, and then she killed herself. I think her name began with M, too."

"It did," Kat confirmed. "Her name was Mya."

Ann tucked her dark hair behind her ears and pushed her glasses up the bridge of her nose. "If she murdered her children, why is it considered a cold case? Aren't cold cases ones that *aren't* solved?" She rubbed her fingers absently together and glanced at the manila envelope sitting like Pandora's Box in the center of the table.

"They're investigating a link to a similar case," Kat said. "Something more recent."

Janet took a small sip of her wine. "A similar case? I don't remember hearing about it." She leaned back in the uncomfortable wooden chair and glanced nervously toward the door.

Kat shrugged. "Me either, but that's what Greg said when he found me looking through the photographs."

Camila interrupted, "I can't imagine how any mother could kill her child. If you don't want them anymore, put them up for adoption. It's as easy as that."

Kat bowed her head and absently put her hand over her pocket where the bit of fabric was nestled. It wasn't *easy* at all. Simple didn't equate to easy. She changed the subject and picked up the envelope. Kat withdrew the picture of the girls alive and handed it to Ramona to pass around the room.

Ramona said, "Krista, this girl looks like your daughter." She handed the photo to Krista with her forefinger above the blonde girl's face.

"She does," Krista agreed. The wide blue eyes were as big as Krista's oldest daughter, who was a senior in high school.

"And this one could be one of yours, Ann," Krista said. She handed the photo to Ann.

Ann gulped. She took the photo and peered at the brown-haired girl with the sad eyes. Indeed, the oldest girl looked sullen, like Ann often did. She quickly handed the photo to Janet, who passed it back to Kat without looking at it.

Kat took the picture and said what everyone else was thinking. "And this little girl, she looks like my Jilly." She touched the baby's face and laid the photograph in the center of the coffee table. The women let out a chorus of solemn agreements. She scanned the contents to see what other information she could draw out before the crime picture grand finale. "Looks like they did some DNA gathering here."

Janet crossed her legs. "I wonder if people banked cord blood, would our DNA be in a database somewhere?"

"I don't know, I'd imagine so," Kat said, keeping her eyes on the paperwork. "But I doubt this family would have done that. She was a drug addict. I can't imagine she came from a family of means."

In a desperate attempt to change the subject, Janet asked, "We banked our cord blood. Did any of you?"

Ramona and Ann nodded. But Camila, Krista, and Kat shook their heads. Camila said, "It was too expensive, but I wish we had."

"Well," Ramona said, "cancer runs in my family, so we thought it was worth the expense. I'm glad we haven't needed it for them." She knocked on the wood to protect her children from her fate.

"I wanted to," Kat said. "But Greg thought it breached privacy, and it was too expensive."

Ann said, "If someone uses my DNA to catch someone in my family who is a serial killer, then good. I have nothing to hide. So, privacy doesn't much matter to me." She took a long sip of wine.

Kat rustled through the papers and let out a whistle. "Well, well, well, look at that." The women leaned in as the room fell silent. "Like I thought, the three girls were half-sisters. Different fathers."

Ramona clucked her tongue. "That was already obvious, wasn't it? Look at them."

Camila played with her necklace. The gaudy jewels of her children's birthstones clanked together. "I wonder where the fathers are now. How does someone survive something like this? Losing a child? It would drive you insane."

Kat thought of her mother and agreed. Her brother's death tore her family asunder. "Maybe it's different for fathers, though," Kat said.

"What else is in that envelope?" Krista asked, her eyes gleaming with curiosity. Krista's passion for crime shows and podcasts was unmatched. Once, after too many glasses of wine, she confessed to Kat that she was jealous she married Greg. She longed for conversations of cases, and danger. He rarely talked about work, but Kat never told her that.

She thumbed through several pieces of paperwork and glanced at her watch. Every time the women came over, the hours slipped by quickly. She opted for the crime pictures and suicide note.

EIGHT

KAT PULLED out a photocopy of the note attached to the photograph. The typed letter bore no signature.

To whom it may concern,

I'm so sorry for everything I've done. I didn't mean to hurt my children, but I just did. Everything is so hard, and terrible. I couldn't leave my babies in a world like this. It wasn't fair to them. I've messed up everything in this life, including my children. I cannot leave them in a world without a mother.

Please forgive me, I'm sorry.

Mya

"That looks like a photocopy of the note. I wonder where the real thing is?" Krista asked.

"I am guessing it's in an evidence room somewhere, right? Can they get fingerprints off of paper?" Ann asked, turning to Kat.

Kat shrugged her shoulders. "Just because I'm married to a detective doesn't mean I know." She laughed and sipped her wine. She removed the paperclip and examined the picture behind the note. It was a picture of the note found inside a typewriter.

"Typewriter?" Ramona said, incredulous. "She typed the suicide note for her children on a typewriter?"

"Well, it was a long time ago. Computers weren't commonplace then," Kat said.

Ramona rubbed her chin and took another bite of brownie. "God, I can't believe it was that long ago. Time is funny. Sometimes it feels like it goes so fast, and other times it drags along."

"Can I see the note?" Ann asked. Kat handed it to her. "It seems so... impersonal, right?"

Camila cocked her head to the side. "It certainly does, like who would type a suicide note on a typewriter and leave it there? And the '*To Whom it May Concern*' seems like the person writing it doesn't even know who Mya would apologize to. She doesn't even use the names of her children. And she says she refuses to leave them in this world without a mother, but she killed the children first, then went to the police, and then committed suicide?"

Kat said, "Something isn't right about this." She pulled the pictures of the girls out and fanned them face up on the table. No more delays and dragging the paperwork out one at a time. Kat tracked Greg's phone, and he was still at the billiard hall.

Janet gasped. Ann picked up the picture of the oldest girl in the bathtub. "That poor, poor girl."

Krista picked up the picture of the middle girl who had markings on her neck and big blue eyes. "She looks like she died afraid."

Janet said, "I'm going to be sick." She scrambled to her feet and darted to the bathroom.

The women rolled their eyes after Janet ran off. They stacked the pictures neatly in the middle of the table, and Kat gathered them and tucked them safely back in the envelope. Ramona hoisted herself from the recliner and tucked her feet in her sneakers but didn't tie them.

Krista stood first. "Okay ladies, I've got to go. My husband will be home soon, and he just got back from being out of town. It was so nice seeing everyone."

Then, one by one, all the ladies rose. Camila said, "Put that stuff back in Greg's briefcase. Let's leave the detective work to the experts." She looked at Krista. "What's next month's selection?"

Krista said, "Oh, with all of this..." she gestured to the envelope, "I nearly forgot. It is *The Killing Cargo Jane*. It's actually about a case where a mother kills her children."

"Great," Ramona said. "Kat, read that and figure out who done it and we'll chat about it next month." She smoothed out her dress and bent to grab the book she'd flung at her feet.

Kat stacked the photos and note in the same order she'd found them, but Greg had hastily put it away himself, so she doubted he would notice, and tucked the envelope under her arm to take upstairs.

Janet emerged from the bathroom, her complexion ashen, and gathered her purse. As they left, Kat pulled Janet to the side gently by her arm. "We don't talk about what's here. Not even pillow talk with your husband. Understand?"

Janet nodded, and Kat wondered if it would be the last time she came and sat in the wooden chair with the others. After they left, she nibbled a corner of one of the pot brownies. Ann slightly undercooked them, which was Kat's favorite. It made it hard to resist having more than she should have. Kat went back upstairs to return Greg's briefcase. As she lay down, the girls' faces remained imprinted on the back of her eyelids.

Especially the Jillian lookalike.

NINE

THE NEXT MORNING, Kat nursed a headache but woke to the smell of coffee. She didn't hear Greg return from billiards the night before, but she never did when she ate some of Ann's brownies. Each batch was stronger than the last. Before she went downstairs to greet Greg, she scrolled through the news on her phone. A story of a mother who killed her infant daughter was splashed across the headlines.

Arlington Woman Killed her Infant Daughter, Then Herself in Murder/Suicide, Say Police

ARLINGTON - A 33-year-old Arlington woman killed her six-month-old daughter and then herself in their apartment, police said Wednesday. Officers went to the 1200 block of Greensborough Circle at about 7 p.m. to respond to a call from a neighbor.

Once inside, they found Beatrice Richards and her daughter Amelia unresponsive, police reported. "Based on the preliminary investigation, this is a homicide and suicide," police said. "There were no signs of forced entry. The public is not believed to be in danger."

Anyone with information regarding the case is urged to call Arlington Police.

If you or someone you know is considering suicide, please call the National Suicide Prevention Lifeline at 1-800-273-TALK (8255).

Kat rubbed her eyes and examined the picture of the mother and daughter attached to the article. The mother was smiling and her towheaded baby propped on her hip. Her daughter's fat rosy cheeks gave her a chipmunk appearance as she grinned at the camera. Six months, and the baby's head was turned instinctively at the camera for a picture as if a lot of photographs were taken of her during her brief life.

Kat put a bra on under her sleep shirt, tucked a hand in her sweatpants pocket, and let her fingers wander to the small patch of fabric she kept as a reminder of how easily things are lost. The tiny piece of fabric brought with it a sense of impermanence and gratitude as she rubbed the nubbly piece between her fingers. The coffee beckoned her downstairs.

Glancing at the living room, everything was put back together. The snacks, glasses, and wine bottles were gone, and the wooden chair tucked neatly back at the dining room table. Her husband sat at the kitchen table, showered and dressed for his Friday in a casual white button-down shirt and navy slacks. He wore cologne that still made her heart skip a beat.

"Good morning, sunshine," he said and smiled at her.

She rubbed her temple to ease her pounding head. Stretching her arms overhead, she opened her mouth wide for a deep yawn. "Good morning. Thanks for picking up after us."

"Of course. You ladies come in like a tornado." He shook his head and smiled like he'd cleaned the playroom at a daycare.

Kat grinned through a grimace. No use getting irritated at every condescending remark and taking things the wrong way. Two decades of marriage and she'd simmered her hot buttons of annoyance down to a dull ache. It was one less thing she'd have to do today. Now, she had exactly zero things on her list. "Why are you ready so early?"

"Early? It's eight, the day is half over. You sleep in after your thriller night every time. I've got to get to work in a few minutes. My car is still in the shop. Chase is swinging by to get me. I can't wait to have mine back. I'm tired of being on his schedule. You never know whose bed he's rolling out of." He smiled wryly and took another sip of coffee.

"Tell me about it," Kat said. Eight was late to sleep in, even after a thriller night. At the next gathering, she vowed to take a smaller nibble from Ann's strengthening concoction.

"Oh? Who did he sleep with this time?" Greg's brows perked up at the question.

"Huh? Oh, no, I meant in general," Kat said as she wandered to the cabinet. Greg was not privy to the girls' book club conversations. Something deeper than spousal privilege protected those interactions. She poured a cup of coffee in her mug they'd bought from the Grand Canyon the year before. It was Jillian's last vacation with them before she ventured off to college. Kat's feelings still stung from Jillian's spring break cancellation. Kat pretended not to care, but they would have to make phone calls for refunds for the cruise they booked as a surprise.

"I saw this news story." She tilted her phone to Greg's face, showing him the headlined story. His face illuminated a bluish hue by the artificial light. He took the phone from her and held it back and squinted. Without his reading glasses, his arms were nearly straight to read the screen. She sat beside him.

"Mmmm, yes, I knew they'd run it soon." He passed her phone back.

"Is this why they re-opened the other case?" She put the coffee to her lips. It was still too hot, so she blew it instead.

"It is," Greg said.

"But why? Why do you think it's related?"

"It's probably nothing, just a drug addict going out with a bang. It's terrible that she took her baby, too. If someone wants to kill themselves, fine. But leave the child to someone else, geeze, it's not that hard. Like I said before, there are a few tangible links that need to be reviewed." Greg's tone clipped his words, indicating he didn't want to continue with this conversation. She let the words settle between them.

"But I saw pictures of the mother, Beatrice. She didn't look like a drug user. I mean, I don't know if they have a certain look. I feel like they do." Kat bit the inside of her lip.

Greg's forehead wrinkled. "Yeah, that's been bothering me, too. She didn't seem to be the type. But there are some other links that need to be flushed out."

"Like what?" she asked, failing to control her curiosity.

Greg's mouth turned into a line. It was the same expression he gave Jillian when she tried to be more adult than she was. "Now, Katie, who's the detective here, you or me?"

"Sorry, I was just curious," Kat said. Embarrassed, her cheeks grew hot.

"Anyway, what book are you ladies reading next month?" he asked, but was back into his phone, scrolling through his social media feed.

"Green Eggs and Ham," Kat answered.

"That's nice," Greg said, and patted her hand.

Kat had changed a lot from when he met her at eighteen. However, he still treated her like she was that girl running from home with a fake ID in a bar, barely old enough to sign a document. Her frustration heightened as she tried to even the imbalance of their decade age difference. He remained impervious to her growth despite over two decades of life together and raising their child. Despite trying to become Kat, he pigeon-holed her as Katie. At eighteen, that was charming, but now she cringed each time he said it. And saw it for what it was, a complete disregard for what she wanted.

He glanced at his watch. "Chase is going to be here soon," he said and went upstairs to the bathroom to finish getting ready.

The Three M Girls conversation was over, but for her, the questions remained. These cases may have been alike, but also not alike at all. Her detective husband chalked both women up to drug addicts who killed their children on a whim. Something wasn't right.

TEN

SHE LINGERED in the kitchen until she heard the bathroom door click shut. Then she tiptoed upstairs to the office next to their bedroom. He wouldn't be gone long, so she needed to work fast. She coughed over the unzipping of his briefcase. Quietly, she opened the first envelope and pulled the stack of papers and photographs out and snapped a picture.

The shutter on her phone cut through the silence as it captured the image. Alert like a prey animal, she snapped her head to attention on the door and froze. Placing the papers on the desk chair out of sight, she side-winded away from the desk. Her mind clicked in place, her excuse, SnapChatting Jillian from the office for better light.

She watched the door a moment and heard the water running in the bathroom, then the electric toothbrush. Ninety seconds. She retrieved the stack of papers from the chair for the Three M Girls and spread them out on the desk. She took photos of every piece of paper. Kat would sort through them later. She put the pictures in a hidden album on her iPhone.

There was a second envelope. The second case. The envelope for the fresh case was thinner, but only one child died as opposed to three. She poured the new contents across the desk and snapped pictures. She scanned the titles of the documents as she took the photographs: toxicology, DNA testing, police report, and pictures of the scene. She snapped pictures of all of it. *Why paper files?* She tried not to look at the baby lying on the floor. There wasn't time for shock, contemplation, or hesitation.

Both cases contained troubling elements.

What would cause a mother to kill her children?

Was it postpartum depression?

Why were they studying the case for similarities?

It had to have been more than a suicide note.

During Kat's bouts with postpartum depression, she recalled the dark thoughts that clung to her like static, but she never considered choking the life out of her baby.

She heard the front door click open. "Honey, I'm home," Chase's playful voice called from the base of the stairs. Kat shoved the paperwork back in the envelope, then the briefcase. For a police officer, Greg was blissfully unobservant. She didn't worry much about anything being in the wrong order. He never recognized when she cut her hair or wore a new dress. But it was also a blessing that he hadn't noticed she'd put on a few pounds since they were married. She zipped the briefcase, slipped out of the office, and peered down at the foyer.

"Hi, stranger," Kat said, her tone friendly as she descended the stairs.

"Kat, you look like a trash panda," Chase said. He smiled and winked.

She moved her hands to her eyes. Kat hadn't seen herself in the mirror yet, but assumed they were ringed with dark black circles from makeup and sleeping, both stoned and buzzed. "I just woke up. Is it that bad?"

He laughed. "Yes, yes, it is." His shoulders were relaxed, and he wore a button-down shirt with the sleeves half-rolled up. Chase and Greg both kept ties and jackets at the office in case official business cropped up. But she hadn't seen either of them in a tie in years. They looked like a couple of frat guys that grew up and were comfortably heading to golf, not the precinct to find rapists, robbers, pedophiles, and mothers who killed their children. He was far more relaxed now that a couple of his ex-lovers weren't ready to start a cat fight in her foyer. He smelled like Irish Spring and his cedar cologne.

"God, tell me how you really feel," she said, rolling her eyes, but she grinned at him.

"I always do." He winked again.

Against everything she knew was right. When he winked, a brushfire raced across her nerves in response. *Damnit, he's charming.* "Must have been a little too much wine," she said, rubbing her head.

"Or too many 'brownies.'" He made air quotes around the word brownies.

"No, it was the wine. Have you had any lately?" she asked innocently. Two could play this game, and if he wanted to play Checkers, she'd play Chess. If Chase wanted to talk about her brownies, she'd bring up the night he sipped a little too much wine with her.

He blushed and looked at his feet. On that night many years ago after a couple bottles of wine he'd gotten so close to her she felt his heat. He'd leaned into her and said, "I love you. I've always loved you." His breath had warmed her face, and she wanted nothing more than to fall into his arms.

Kat had pretended he meant it differently. "I have always loved you, too. You're Jilly's godfather and will always be a member of our family."

He'd wrapped his arms around her waist and pulled her to him. It had taken the breath out of her and she'd wanted him, too. "You know that's not what I meant." He'd leaned in and tried to kiss her that night.

She'd wanted to kiss him, but instead, and equally as passionately, she'd slapped him across the face, hard. She'd watched in horror as the red of her handprint had blossomed on his face. He'd looked at her with an apology in his watery eyes, but said nothing and walked out the door. Like the other secrets Kat had locked away, she'd never told a soul.

She heard footsteps upstairs and looked up.

Greg appeared at the top of the stairs, with his brief-case in hand. His red hair was deeply parted, showing off his widow's peak on the right. She hated the name widow's peak.

"Do you have something you want to tell me, Katie?"

Kat's palms sweat. *Did he notice she went through his bag? And would he face off with her in front of Chase?* If there was a hole to crawl in, she would have burrowed beneath the earth.

Greg said, "You're not going to tell me what time to be home for your birthday dinner? Your Rosacea is acting up, again. Your face is really red."

She blew out a sigh. It wasn't the Rosacea heating her face, but was glad to have an excuse. "Ha, I was going to text you later."

"Yeah, right, you forgot again, didn't you, my little trash panda?"

He eavesdropped on Chase, calling her trash panda. She grimaced and used her shirt sleeves to wipe some of the black smudges.

Chase shifted uncomfortably. "Now, now, leave Kat alone. After thriller night, she's always a bit out of sorts. Happy birthday, Kat. I'm also terrible with dates." He kissed her on the cheek.

Kat laughed. "Well, I guess if I don't bother with birthdays, maybe I'll never age?"

Chase's eyes grew solemn. "Aging is a lot better than the alternative."

Greg went down the stairs and came to her and tussled her hair as he picked up his phone from the table behind her. "Oh, Chase is the philosopher today, isn't he? He gets like that when we have a case with dead children. Don't ya? Speaking of the case, I've got to be careful. My curious little wife picked through the case file yesterday." He wagged his finger at her as he said the words.

She crossed her arms over her chest and jutted out her bottom jaw. "I did not. They fell out of the briefcase," she stammered.

Chase pivoted the subject back to Greg. "Why do you still work by paper, anyway? Damn, Greg, you're the last one to bring the 'files' home." Again, his arms raised to make an air-quote gesture.

"I enjoy having the papers to thumb through and the pictures to inspect. I hate screens." He shrugged.

Kat's mouth was a line. *Why did he do that? Say things to embarrass her when Chase was around. Did he mistake their deep friendship for something more? Was it something more?*

Greg leaned in. "Aw, don't be mad, Katie, I was joking. Having a little fun." He pinched her chin and kissed her cheek where Chase had, like a dog marking his territory, and followed Chase out the door.

ELEVEN

KAT WENT to the bathroom and stared into the mirror. "I look like a linebacker," she said to her reflection as she wiped at the marks with a make-up remover and splashed warm water on her face to loosen the stubborn dark smudges. Her chaotic hair fought valiantly against the brush. Giving up, she combed out the sides and styled it in a passable bun.

She went to her bedroom to take off her pajamas and get dressed. Her unwashed jeans felt loose in the right spots and the light gray cable-knit sweater felt more like a blanket. Kat fished the swatch of fabric out of her sweatpants pocket and slipped it into her jean pocket.

She went down to the kitchen and sipped her black coffee, now cool enough to drink, and drummed her fingers on the dining room table. A year ago she would have been planning the team dinner, making Jilly's lunch, or arranging a shopping trip for her daughter's spirit bag before the game. Her hobbies, interests, and time wound so tightly around her daughter's journey to adulthood that she hadn't considered the indelible imprint Jilly would leave behind. Parenting was the saddest job of all. In raising her child, she rendered herself obsolete.

Before Jillian and Greg, she was someone else. But that person was gone. Her penance was a life of caretaking of others. But now her daughter was gone, who could she care for? The victims of unsolved crimes seemed a good place to start. The pictures in the briefcase were a gift to finding a purpose again. She refreshed her coffee cup, grabbed her laptop laying on the side table, and brought it up to Greg's office to view the pictures on his larger monitor.

She opened the *Budget* file where the pictures were hidden and clicked print and the office machine fired up and went to work. While she waited, Kat double-clicked on the folder and examined the newest case.

The crime scene for the new baby was near identical to the first set of murders, except the little girl's eyes were closed. Beatrice was not with her. Amelia wore a pink zipped onesie sleeper, and her cheeks were round and cherub-like. Kat clicked to the next picture, and on the printer there was a note. The note read:

To whom it may concern,
    I'm so sorry for everything I've done. I didn't mean to hurt my child, but I just did. Everything is so hard, and

terrible. I couldn't leave my baby in a world like this. It wasn't fair to her. I've messed everything in this life up, including my child, and I refuse to leave her in a world like this without a mother.

Please forgive me, I'm sorry.
Beatrice

As she read it, her printer beeped its notification that its job was complete. She gathered the small stack and thumbed through the pictures. At a glance, the newest crime scene looked nothing like the Three M Girls' apartment. The house was just a few streets from them. Beatrice lived in an upper-middle-class neighborhood in the same school zone as Kat. Amelia would have been a Wolf at Williams High, like Jillian. Perhaps, in a few years' time, she may have been among the throng of children who clogged the neighborhood streets for the annual homecoming parade in November. Maybe she'd play the trombone in the band, or shout school spirit in her cheer uniform, a quiet girl on the student government float, or a proud student spectator with her gaggle of friends.

She read the police report:

My partner and I were dispatched to the house to perform a welfare check after a neighbor (Meredith Davidson) stopped by as planned and no one answered the door. She looked through the door to see her neighbor lying on the floor with her child. Upon arrival, the door was not locked, and I saw the woman approximately in her thirties and an infant on the floor through the top glass of the front door. Neither appeared to be moving. We knocked and announced our identification and arrival. There was no response from either party. My partner radioed for backup and an ambulance, and my partner and I entered the premises to check on the occupants.

As we approached the adult female, I observed she appeared to be seizing and experiencing a medical event. She was dressed in a robe and had wet hair. My partner donned medical safety gear and assessed the adult victim as I checked on the infant. The female infant was pale in pallor and cooler to the touch, eyes closed, and unresponsive. There was bruising on her neck and it may have been broken. Called in for coroner support.

Attended to the female adult, and she was still warm with a weak heartbeat. Her breaths were shallow, and she whispered repeatedly "Ma-ma." Seizing intensified and paramedics arrived and transported her. Adult female expired en route to hospital.

Neighbor witness arrived at the door. My partner approached and asked if she saw anything of concern besides what was in the original welfare check request. She remembered nothing suspicious. She reported an adult male lives at residence, but home was cleared and no one else was home. His car was also not in the driveway. Neighbor advised she called the male's workplace, but he did not answer. She also called the woman's mother.

As we were processing the scene, a woman who identi-fied herself as the mother of the adult female approached. She stated her name was Viola Johnston and her daughter was Beatrice Richards. Ms. Johnston attempted to access the active crime scene. She was later transported to the hospital for shock.

The residence appeared tidy, and neat, no signs of robbery or forced entry. No signs of neglect of the infant. During the initial search I located a suicide note on the computer printer and entered it as evidence. Called homi-cide unit for further processing.

Signed: Officer Jerome Blinks

The department was over a few hundred strong, and Officer Blinks was not a name she recognized, but he was from the same police department as her husband and Chase. The similar suicide note was the link Greg had alluded to but didn't share. The only difference between Mya's suicide note and Beatrice's was the plural use of child and children.

Amelia seemed to have died in a combination of Millie and Mandy's death. *Strangulation and a broken neck?* She searched the internet to find out if the original suicide note was released. She couldn't find any infor-mation on it. How would anyone know what the orig-inal suicide note said? Unless it was a person related to the original crime.

Kat googled Beatrice and stumbled on her social media profile. She posted pictures of her daughter often.

It said she worked at a major consulting firm and in her professional social media profile she wore a business blouse and a pearl necklace that aged her at least ten years. She hardly looked like the drug addict Greg suggested she was. She thumbed through the report to find the cause of death. A fatal dose of morphine.

TWELVE

KAT NAVIGATED BACK to Beatrice's public profile, and there was a picture of the happy family. A man, who she guessed was the father, looked to be about forty-five, his blond hair mottled with hints of whitish gray on the sides. He looked a few years older than Beatrice, but not creepily so. His arm encircled her waist as she tossed her light brown hair back and laughed. They both wore the obligatory white linen shirts and khaki pants, standing on an unnamed beach. In his other arm was the little girl, Amelia, whose legs wrapped tight around the man, and her thumb jammed in her mouth, staring at the camera with wide blue eyes. She wore a white bonnet that covered her blonde hair and shaded her face from the sun, though her cheeks were pink. Her chunky legs peeked out from the bottom of a fluffy white dress.

Kat clicked on the father's profile. *Evan Richards*. The news story was fresh and his profile was still live. His profile picture already had thousands of comments and climbing. She wasn't the only amateur sleuth. Kat opened the comments and read.

Murderer.

Baby Killer.

Burn in hell.

Something smells fishy - you were the only one to live?

She scrolled through the condemnations, all people who didn't know Beatrice or Amelia looking for a place to express the mob's projected fear and anger. She stopped reading. The news story left out the morphine and suicide note. If Evan was innocent, the media would bury a poorly worded retraction in the back of the news, leaving any life he patched together after this tragedy plagued in doubt and tattered. *If it bleeds, it leads*, thought Kat. The media added blood to shark-infested waters, causing a frenzy but giving them no actual meat. Today it was Evan Richards, but tomorrow, a fresh dumping of news chum would distract the readers to the next human tragedy.

Kat scrolled through the pictures in his profile, and only Beatrice and Amelia were in them via being tagged by her. Like there was no life before the two of them. Kat clicked on his friends and found he only had twenty-nine. Flipping back to Beatrice, she had thousands and often tagged Evan in them. Kat's research was interrupted by a text.

Camila: Coffee?

Kat gulped the last of her first cup of coffee and replied.

> Kat: Sure, I have some stuff to show you. My place?

> Camila: Be there in ten minutes, just dropped Horace off.

Camila's youngest child was six and named after Edward's father who died during her final pregnancy. *The poor fella would need to make up for his name with heaps of personality, money, or good looks*, thought Kat.

Kat didn't finish reading the paperwork, but needed a place to stash the documents. She placed them in a large envelope from Greg's desk drawer while she waited for Camila. Taking the pictures of his files was a deliberate act of betrayal, but her curiosity overshadowed her guilt. She wished she had the 'hidey hole' in this house like the one from her childhood home. It had been in her brother's room, under the floorboard, next to his bed. The two would keep their treasures there and leave gifts for one another in it. After her brother was killed, she'd visited it a few times before she ran away to see if he'd sent her a message from beyond. He never did.

Ten minutes later, she jumped at a knock at the door. She tucked the envelope under her arm and went down the stairs as Camila let herself in. She held two cups of coffee from their favorite coffee shop in a small coffee holder and two small brown bags with grease-stained bottoms.

"I was about to start another pot of coffee. You didn't have time to actually go to a coffee shop and get here," Kat said raising an eyebrow at her.

She smiled and breezed inside. "I ordered it before I texted you. I got our favorites and some croissants." She shook the brown bags at her, and Kat grinned broadly. The women sat on the couch. Kat placed the envelope at her side and Camila handed her a brown bag with her croissant and the cup of coffee.

Kat took a long sip. It was a honey latte, and the sweet honey finish comforted her. "I haven't ordered one of these in a while. That's so good."

"Right? I figured we'd treat ourselves," Camila said. She wore a pair of jeans, Converse white sneakers, a t-shirt from Horace's school, and a slicked-back ponytail with her face bare.

"What for?" Kat asked and took another sip.

"Your birthday?"

Kat smiled. "I think everyone remembered it's my birthday except me."

"Maybe you don't want to remember because you are a step closer to forty," Camila said.

"I've still got a couple of years to go. How does it feel being over forty?" She nudged Camila with her elbow.

"Just like my thirties, with a few more aches and pains, a wrinkle here and there, and some white hairs." Camila grabbed her back and hunched over like she hurt. She straightened and snickered.

Kat opened the bag and put her nose inside and breathed in deep. The yeasty smell made her mouth water. She reached in the bag and tore off a corner of the buttery croissant and placed it on her tongue. It nearly melted with the warm butter and thin layers of dough. "Oh, these are fresh."

"Mmhm," Camila agreed as she took a bite of hers. She crossed her legs and leaned in. "So Krista and Ann were about to come to blows over Chase last night."

"I know, right? Thank God for Ann's brownies. Her very strong brownies..."

Camila said, "And for what? No one is going home with him. Now they have ruined marriages because of him." She took another bite of the croissant and sipped her coffee.

"Now, that isn't fair. It isn't Chase's fault. He's not the one who's married."

"He isn't, but he knows they are. Married with children." Camila set down her coffee and rolled her pendant between her fingers.

Kat bristled. "That's right, *they* are married with children. *He* is single and unattached. They knew what they were getting with him. Something... uncomplicated."

Camila sighed. "Well, he chooses vulnerable women who are bored, but are content enough to stay with their husbands. Then he doesn't have to worry about anything. It's safe and reckless at the same time. He doesn't care about either of them. He doesn't care about anyone but himself."

Kat sipped her coffee and said nothing. Her mind wandered again to when he confessed his love for her.

Chase was a lot of things, but one thing he wasn't, was a liar.

Camila changed the subject. "How do you think Ramona was looking?"

"She was in good spirits. Whenever she has the energy to dye her hair, she's doing a lot better. I look forward to seeing the purple. That'll be great on her."

Camila nodded her head in agreement and she cast a glance at the envelope at Kat's side. "Now, what is it you were saying you wanted to show me?"

THIRTEEN

KAT PLACED the bag on the table and picked up the envelope. Her finger left a small imprinted grease splotch on the corner. She fished through the contents and pulled two pieces of paper from it and sat them on her lap, and spilled out her confession. "I couldn't let it go. I took photos of the cases. Then I printed them."

Camila's eyes widened as she glanced at the face-down papers on Kat's lap. "You did?"

"I know. I know it isn't my place. But there's something that is weird." She turned the photocopies over and handed them to Camila.

"What's weird?"

She bit the inside of her lip before hurrying on. "Well, Greg said the cases are linked. I mean, the suicide notes are similar, but why reopen a case when it was closed? How would they have known to reopen it? There has to be something more."

As Camila examined both photos, Kat opened the

envelope and placed the rest of the papers on the coffee table.

Camila finished reading the notes, put the photocopies back on the table, and her hand again absently went to her pendant, holding the tiny jewels of her children's birthstones in her hand. She rolled the rainbow between her fingers as she spoke. "The notes are almost exact."

Kat nodded in agreement. "Yes, even how they were delivered. On a typewriter and a computer, I mean, of course, because of the twenty-ish years between them. I checked online, and they didn't release the Three M Girls' note. At least, I couldn't find it anywhere."

"Maybe it was on one of those crime podcasts? They could have done a freedom of information act request or something?" Camila asked.

Kat put her finger to her chin. "Maybe."

Camila said, "With the unsolved case of three dead babies, that would have captured the crime-fighting and bored public." She chuckled and took a small bite of her pastry.

Kat drummed her fingers on the coffee table in thought. "But that's the thing... it wasn't a cold case. It was a solved case, remember? Until this fresh case came out. There is nothing in the media about the links between these two cases."

Camila nodded and washed down her pastry bite with a small sip of her latte. "Right, I never considered that."

"I was thinking, Greg said there were other links. I'm

trying to figure out what they are. The answer has to be in here somewhere." Kat gestured to the scattered papers on the coffee table.

Camila popped the last of her pastry into her mouth and leaned back into the couch.

Kat scanned the documents, and her hand trembled over one of them. "Damn. There it is."

"What is it?" Camila asked, placing her coffee on the table.

Kat handed her the picture of the report, and Camila scanned through it. "I don't understand? It's a DNA report, so what?"

Kat handed the papers to Camila. "Read the report for the second child, Millie. Specifically, the father's name. Then read Amelia's father's name."

"Well, I'll be. These two girls were sisters? Twenty years apart?" Camila asked.

Kat whistled through her teeth. "Half-sisters. The father's name is Evan Richards. I researched him earlier based on the second case. I don't remember seeing his name in the news for the first one, and I don't think the news story said either, because the articles I read didn't cover it. They'll figure it out, though. And probably soon."

"So you think he killed two families?" Camila asked.

"I mean, he's a good place to start. We've read enough thrillers to know it's always the husband, isn't it? So we should look into that."

Camila straightened her back. "Kat, you're scaring

me. This is a good starting point for *Greg*. That is what you meant, right? Right?"

Kat chattered on without answering. "If we interviewed the parents of Mya and Beatrice, we could say there's more media on the case and that we have a few questions. An exclusive story or something. We don't have to talk to Evan Richards..."

Camila's brows gathered in concern. "You're not seriously considering talking to people? What would you say? No offense, but you aren't qualified for this. You aren't a member of the media or a police officer. You're just a... mom."

The words stung Kat, but she pressed on, "What's stopping me from being an independent reporter? What gives the cold case podcast people authority? Who gives freelance reporters authority?"

Camila set the papers down and faced her friend. "For one, they don't have access to documents that aren't public. This seems like a cheat. And unsafe."

Kat tapped her finger to her chin, ignoring Camila's cautions. "I'm curious to see how the two cases relate. Greg was dismissive of the two cases being related."

Camila said, "You know I love you, but I have to say it. You're not a police officer."

Kat sighed. "I know. I'm not talking about confronting anyone dangerous. If I had context, I'd plant the idea into a conversation with Greg. He said it was probably a coincidence, but there's no way he believes or should believe that. Maybe he has too much on his plate, but this case isn't getting the attention it deserves." She crossed her arms.

Camila shook her head vehemently. "It isn't your job to figure out. This is for the cops. You and I are just stay-at-home mothers."

"Well, one of us is. My girl is in college. And we've always been more than that," Kat said.

Camila sighed. "Maybe you should study criminal justice. God knows you love it. Get the right tools to do this. Don't go picking through your husband's files and try to be Nancy Drew."

Kat lowered her head. "It was a dumb idea. I'm sorry I brought it up." The heat crawled into her cheeks, and she wanted the conversation to end. Camila would not help her, no matter how she pleaded. She made one last attempt. "I mean, those pictures, and those babies. It's so sad. If the mothers didn't do it, and no one pays for their crimes—" Kat's voice broke and she couldn't finish her sentence.

Camila shifted in her seat. "We have children of our own. Responsibilities of our own. I don't even have time to read our books for the thriller club. This is dangerous, and I can't risk my life for these kids. They're already gone. It may sound crass, but nothing you or I can do will bring these girls back. My kids need me, and Jilly and Greg need you."

Kat turned her eyes away from Camila. As a mother, Jillian had demoted her from a vital organ like the heart to an appendix. No one knew what it did, it was likely an ancient relic of evolution, but its sole use was to cause trouble if it became infected.

Camila said, "Kat, I know things have been difficult with Jilly going to school. This is interesting, but it's also dangerous. If they weren't killed by their mothers, then there's a killer on the streets. We have children and responsibilities." Then, like she pulled the thread within Kat's chest, she added, "Just because Jilly is in college, doesn't mean she doesn't need you anymore." Camila placed her hand on Kat's.

Kat tried not to pull away from the heat of her friend's hand. She left her hand lingering as long as she could bear and gently withdrew it and tucked a stray hair that fell from her bun behind her ear. She gathered the printed papers and put them in a pile. "You're right. I will look for anything to pass the time. I'm bored."

"Maybe volunteer at the animal shelter, or a retirement facility? Or spend time at the food pantry with Krista?" Camila suggested.

"Ugh, you're sounding like me when I had a sullen and bored teenager on my hands. Now I know how she felt."

Camila's shoulders sagged. "I'm sorry. I'm just trying to help."

"No, I know. I know. I appreciate it. I enjoy the free time, and I don't. It's hard to explain."

Camila smiled. "Sometimes I wish I had that kind of time, but you're right. It would be bittersweet. It would mean my babies have flown the nest." She added, "I'm sorry, that wasn't sensitive."

"No, it's fine. I have to get used to it. They aren't meant to stay with us forever," Kat said. She unconsciously put her hand over her pocket where the small piece of fabric was.

Camila finished her latte and stood. "Alright, I've got to get to the grocery store or we are going to be eating air for dinner tonight."

Kat put the pile of papers in the envelope, tucked it under her arm, and stood. "I'm going to get rid of these and talk to Krista about the food pantry."

Camila smiled ruefully and hugged her friend. "Happy birthday, Kat."

As Camila left, Kat walked back to the office to shred the papers and forget the entire ordeal. She looked at the picture of the dead Jilly lookalike and instead spread them out on the desk. Kat scanned the pictures she took of the paperwork. She knew what she was looking for. The first interview with Evan Richards. He had an alibi, which placed him physically fifty miles from where Mya's children died. The only issue with the alibi was the person who gave it was his mother, but mothers would do a lot for their children. Even lie.

FOURTEEN

SHE SAT at Greg's desk. It reminded her of her father's. It's large mahogany top too big and bulky for the computers of today, with a seat so vast she couldn't sit comfortably. Kat opened her calendar app and set a reminder to ask Krista about the food pantry volunteer positions. *For my birthday... I'll read the cases,* she thought. *Tomorrow, I'll move on with my life and forget this ever happened.* She re-opened the file and read.

The ME ruled Mya's death suicide by a purposeful overdose of heroin. Judging by the condition of the crime photos, her life had been in disarray for some time. She searched for Mya Walton on the internet to learn more about how she lived, but there wasn't any social media back then to provide a window into people's lives when Mya died. She searched for clues the internet may still hold on the secrets to a random woman's actions and death from twenty years ago. Her eyes widened at the results. Various news stories were returned, but one of them reported an extra piece of information she hadn't known before:

Mya Walton may have become depressed because of her family's fall from grace. Once a prominent family, her father's, Peter Walton, business declared bankruptcy, leaving the heiress penniless.

Heiress? Via her father's business? Heiress wasn't a word tossed around lightly by the media. They reserved it for the elite few. The sprinkles on the upper crust of society. She googled Peter Walton. He invented and owned a car part business she didn't understand and had little interest in investigating. However, it failed spectacularly. It caused multiple accidents. Serious accidents, killing or maiming dozens of people. He was a defendant in a class action suit and the family business never recovered. Kat scanned the articles on the car part and found multiple families interviewed who'd lost loved ones.

Kat read in the file that Mya had a sizable, but not obnoxious, life insurance policy of one million dollars. Twenty years ago that was a lot, but still, for being labeled an heiress, it would have been expected she'd have some protections for her children. But in the event her children died, it went to her parents, Mariah and Peter. *Motive.* Kat thumbed through the file for the parents' alibi and found that they'd been celebrating their anniversary in Hawaii with many witnesses and a flight manifest while their grandchildren were killed. They were back in town for Mya's death a few days later.

The DNA reports identified the father of the oldest M

girl, Maureen, as Art Short. Kat researched him, and a mugshot came back, which seemed promising. He had several run-ins with the law: robbery, larceny, and some drug offenses. She clicked on his latest picture. Aside from the hard life he'd lived, as evidenced by the missing teeth, sunken cheeks, and grayish complexion, he shared some characteristics with the young Maureen. Her big dark eyes were his, and they both bore small clefts in their chins. There was no evidence in the file that Art Short took part in Maureen's life. Kat scrolled through the results and sighed. He was a dead end. A literal dead end. She stumbled upon his obituary.

There was no reference to the baby, Mandy's father. Kat wondered if he was aware the baby existed. Maybe it was better to not know she had ever lived than to grieve her loss. She scanned the birth certificates of the girls in the case file, and Mandy was the only one with a blank line for the father.

She inspected the birth hospital records for the girls. Mya birthed large babies. Maureen was born at seven pounds and twelve ounces, Millie weighed in at eight pounds even, and Mandy was the biggest of all at eight pounds and two ounces.

Hmm, that's odd. I thought babies born addicted to drugs were usually underweight. Maybe Mya wasn't always an addict? Maybe that was something that happened to her after the baby was born, or after the bankruptcy.

The pictures of the home and children showed severe neglect, but perhaps it happened quickly in the span of Mandy's brief life.

She shuffled to the next piece of paperwork and it was another suspect, Terri (TJ) Jenkins. TJ was the one who supplied the lethal dose of heroin to Mya. She reviewed the case and was taken aback because TJ was a woman. She had blonde long hair, hazel eyes, and looked like anyone Kat might see on the street or invite to the neighborhood thriller book club.

She googled TJ and Three M Girls and found her on page three of the results. An anonymous source turned her in for questioning. When they brought her in, she confessed immediately. However, the rookie arresting officer never read her the Miranda Warning before eliciting the confession. TJ withdrew her confession, and she walked. She'd kept her nose clean since. Well, she hadn't been caught doing anything, at the very least.

Kat flipped through the persons of interest in the fresh case. Beatrice's autopsy showed she also died of a drug overdose. However, the drug of choice was morphine, not heroin. Kat searched for a link between Beatrice Miller and Mya Walton beyond Evan Richards, but TJ was only a supplier for Mya. Unless she also peddled morphine, which Kat doubted.

She went online and researched the first grandparents, Peter and Mariah's, information and jotted it down. *They live on the way to the grocery store. What am I doing?* She stood, rubbed the tiny cloth in her front jean pocket, folded the paper with the address and phone number, and slid it into her back pocket. *I'll keep it with me, just in case.*

If anything were to happen to Jillian, she'd cooperate

with whoever would help or bring attention to the case. *The parents deserve closure*, she thought. Kat's unique position of time and access to the files could deliver it. She promised herself she'd only talk to the parents and would steer clear of the probable killer, Evan, and the drug dealer, TJ.

Before she talked herself out of it, she pulled the scrap of paper from her back pocket for the Waltons and dialed the number.

"Hello?" a man's voice answered.

"Hi, I'm... Camila O'Brien, a reporter for the local newspaper." She froze. She hadn't thought this through. There was no backstory. Kat failed to identify the newspaper and she'd spit out Camila's full name instead of her own. Kat kicked herself.

On the other line, there was a pause. Then his voice returned, cautious. "Okay, what can I help you with?"

"It's about Mya Walton. We understand there's been a similar case, and there is an investigation into whether they are linked." Kat wondered if, when the police reinvestigated a case, they told the next of kin. She didn't know, but she doubted it.

There was silence on the line, and a muffled whisper, confirming her suspicion. Then, a female voice came on the line. It was shaky with age and grief. "This is Mariah. Have you finally found out what happened to our Mya and our grandchildren?"

Her pain was palpable, and the crime was decades ago. Kat cleared her throat. "No ma'am, not yet. The police are investigating some links, and I'd like to come over and interview you if it's possible. Are you available this afternoon?"

Mariah rattled off her address, and Kat didn't need to write it down because she was staring at it in front of her.

She hung up the phone, put the note back in her pocket, and thought, *What have I done?*

FIFTEEN

KAT SHOWERED and dressed in slacks, a floral blouse, ballet flats, and a necklace. She applied mascara, blush, and lipstick and pulled her long, still wet, brown hair back into a slick bun. She gazed at her reflection and went to Jillian's room to find a pair of her blue light glasses that she didn't need. The glasses were wire-rimmed and made her appear closer to her age. She assessed her reflection and considered if she looked official enough to be considered a reporter. It reminded her of the days she'd play dress up with Jillian.

She rummaged through Greg's desk for a legal pad and slipped it into her large purse. *Maybe they need someone to listen,* she thought. *I'll listen to their stories of the Three M Girls and know they aren't forgotten.* She knew she was justifying her curiosity, but it was too late. She wasn't a police officer, but she knew what it was like to be a mother, and what happened to a family when a child died. In no world could she understand what it would be like to kill a child on purpose and the collateral damage that it would inflict on the family.

She climbed into the car, and the engine rumbled to life. Greg drove the car last, and the seat was too far from the pedal. She scooted the seat forward so far her elbows rested on the wheel. Dangerous or not, it felt the most comfortable and in control of the vehicle. After what happened to her brother, Duncan, she drove as sparingly as possible. As soon as she started the car, Greg's radio station played *The Freshmen* by Verve Pipe. It used to be her favorite song and she would listen to it on repeat. Her heart immediately sank, and she turned off the radio and hit the steering wheel hard with her hands. She peered skyward through the windshield.

"Duncan, are you trying to talk to me? Should I stop? Or are you telling me to keep going and find justice for these children? If I get enough information, I promise I'll give it to Greg for him to take a second look..." She reasoned with the air, and the ghost whom she knew sat next to her didn't respond. *Maybe I'm doing this for myself and my unresolved wounds.* Kat brushed the thought out of her mind and left the radio off.

Instead of heading to the grocery store, she turned left toward the gated community where the Waltons lived. Apparently, bankruptcy treated them better than most. The newspaper article painted the Waltons as destitute, but the part of town they were in was outside of Kat's current tax bracket, but below the tax bracket she was born into. Still, they were hardly as penniless as the media suggested. There was a guard at the gate as

Kat pulled in. Her car would be the only Hyundai in the neighborhood unless they gave children starter cars. Kat wished her parents had been wise enough to give her brother a safe starter car, instead of the one that killed him.

The guard was probably eighty and glanced up at her from a crossword puzzle book. "Hi, I'm K... Camila O'Brien."

He smiled at her, showing off his impossibly white dentures. "Hi, the Waltons called you in." The guard waved her in and hunched back over his crossword.

She pulled in front of their house and parked. The brick sidewalk wound its way through perfectly trimmed bushes, lights, and two potted plants that flanked a stone entrance portico to their doorway. From the outside, it looked like an impossibly large but cheery home. Not a home of people who were suffering from devastating grief and loss. Kat's mind spiraled.

Maybe they're okay after all? I don't belong here.

She restarted the car and put it in reverse. Kat looked up one last time and met eyes with an older gentleman peering out his living room window at her. He now had a name, phone number, car make and model, and could identify her. There was no turning back. "Shit," she muttered and put the car back in park. She checked the rear-view mirror for lipstick on her teeth, knowing his eyes were on her from the window. The Three M Girls weren't in the news story at all. Kat fished the notepad and pen from her purse, looked up at the window again, and his face wasn't there.

As she walked down the passageway toward the door, her stomach clenched, and she put her hand in her pocket to touch the fabric, bolstering her strength. Kat hadn't planned through her story, but something compelled her to find out more. Her boredom now involved dragging a grieving family back into their decades-old trauma. There were no guarantees her curiosity would change anything.

Before she knocked, the man opened the door to greet her. According to the documents, he was the same age as her father, whom she hadn't seen since she ran away at eighteen. She wondered if he looked as broken as the man standing in front of her. The bags under his eyes hung low, packed tight with grief and loss.

"Hi Mr. Walton, I'm Camila O'Brien. We spoke on the phone?" The ease with which her best friend's name slipped out of her lips nicked at her conscience.

"Yes, yes, come in," he said. He opened the door wide, and she followed him in and the door latched closed behind her.

SIXTEEN

THEIR HOUSE SMELLED MUSTY, as if sorrow had a scent. Like the entire structure was stuck in a time before Mya and her girls' deaths and the air and the people hadn't moved a day since. The old man turned to her and extended his hand. Her hand was slick with sweat, and she hoped he was polite enough not to say anything.

Mr. Walton said, "I was surprised to hear from anyone after all these years."

"Thank you for seeing me." Kat glanced around their living room. Pictures of Mya and her children cluttered every surface and wall. It wasn't the Mya from the crime photos, but a vibrant blue-eyed woman with hair teetering between brunette and blonde. Some called it dishwater, a terrible name for a beautiful hue.

Peter watched as she scanned the pictures in the room and explained, "We've kept our home the same since they passed."

Kat gulped but didn't answer. Her face flushed as she fumbled in her purse for the notepad to do her pretend job. In their shoes, would she wallpaper Jillian throughout her home, or try to erase her and outrun the sadness of her loss. She didn't need to wonder. Kat faced that very question before, and she'd run as far as her legs would take her. Never turning back. At eighteen, she wasn't wise enough to know there was no outrunning the loss. The dead refused to be erased. They visited in unexpected ways. Like the song on the radio.

Kat walked up to the mantel and pointed at a picture. "May I?"

"Of course," he replied. Peter held the picture, briefly touching his daughter's face before he placed it in Kat's hands.

She took the plain wooden frame from him gingerly and stared at Mya. She wore a white polo shirt and khaki pants. Her hair was tied in two blondish-brown pigtails, and she grinned at the camera, missing her two front teeth. The middle blonde child, Millie, favored the young Mya most.

Peter rubbed his palm over his heart, like he could heal the brokenness. "She's in Montessori School there. So bright and full of life." He blinked and turned away from Kat.

The photo showed no sign of her tragic fate. She set the photo back on the mantel and glanced at another photo. Mya holding her oldest daughter, Maureen, and her mother by her side. She and her mother stood shoulder to shoulder, and they both beamed with happiness. Mya's face was clear of sores and her body, fresh from giving birth, didn't look like the emaciated one from the photos burning brightly in Kat's mind.

Peter sat on the emerald green sofa and gestured to the recliner, and Kat sat and put her notebook in her lap. He said, "Why would you write about our daughter and granddaughter's case?"

Kat cleared her throat. A simple internet search would prove to them she was a liar and no independent reporter. She hadn't practiced what to say. "Well, every once in a while a cold case is re-examined with the emergence of DNA and other cases."

But it wasn't a cold case, she thought.

"Oh," he scratched his long white well-groomed beard, "I see." He crossed his legs and looked up at the stairs. Kat followed his gaze and a woman with glassy hooded eyes and white hair pulled tight into a ponytail stood at the top. She looked smaller than the photos on the mantel. Like grief had shrunken her.

As she descended, the same shaky voice Kat heard on the phone said, "Hello, I'm Mariah, Mya's mother. You're looking into what happened to our daughter and our grandgirls, is that right?"

Kat adjusted in her seat and stood to greet Mariah. The Waltons were not ones for small talk, and Mariah's beady eyes stared straight through her. She held out her small bony hand, and Kat took it in hers. She wondered if Mariah detected the lies sloughing off of her.

"Yes, that's right."

Kat sat in the recliner, and Mariah sat opposite her on the sofa with Peter.

A teakettle whistled from the kitchen, and Peter stood. "I am afraid it will be awhile. We love nothing more than talking about our Mya. After so many years, people stopped asking. I'm afraid you'll be here a minute. I'll get everyone some tea."

Kat smiled, and Mariah leaned back on the couch to begin.

"I know, by the looks of everything here," Mariah gestured to their upper-middle-class home, "it's hard to believe our daughter became an addict. People think addiction won't affect their families. But that is simply untrue. Everything can appear *normal* on the outside when it is anything but."

Kat looked at her legal pad, unable to bear her mournful eyes any longer. She scribbled *drug abuse*. A fact she already knew.

Mariah said, "People turn to drugs for all different reasons."

"Do you know why Mya did?" Kat asked.

Mariah closed her eyes like she replayed the memories. "Mya was always a bit of a free spirit." She opened her eyes again and leveled them at Kat. "By today's standards, she'd be normal, I guess. Back then, though, she was a rebel."

"How so?" Kat asked.

"Mya always followed the beat of her own drummer. She didn't comply with society's standards. At seventeen, she was pregnant with Maureen."

"That must have been difficult for everyone," Kat said, her memories entangling with Mya's and she bit her tongue to stop herself from crying.

"It was, but also it was such a joy to have Maureen. She was a serious girl. Her father was a boy named Art Short. He was the opposite of serious." Mariah chuckled. "Mya met Art when she was a senior in high school and he'd dropped out of college. He drifted into town and swept our daughter off her feet on his motorcycle. Just as quickly as he drifted into town, he drifted right out."

"Motorcycles and teenage girls are magnets," Peter remarked as he came in and handed a teacup to his wife, then one to Kat. "Art was a nice kid, but directionless. Running full-steam into the fog. He wouldn't be tied down to a family. He found some trouble with the law. Ultimately, it was that same motorcycle that killed him, I'd say, about five years ago." He retreated to the kitchen for his tea.

"I'm sorry," Kat said to Mariah.

Mariah batted the thought away. "It was a long time ago. I only saw him once at the back of the room when they put our babies in the earth. Anyway, then Mya met Evan Richards." Mariah spit out his name like poison had touched her lips. "Their relationship was all drama, up and down all the time. He got her pregnant and left. So, at that point, Mya had two children and zero fathers in their lives. It was sad for Maureen and Millie." Mariah picked up the last picture of the girls, the one that had a copy in the crime file, touched the girls' faces, and put it back on the side table.

For something to do Kat scribbled on her pad, *Evan Richards, father of Millie*. Another fact she already knew.

Peter came back in and sat on the recliner and sipped his tea.

"What about Mandy's father?" Kat asked.

Peter said, "Ah, yes. That was Jesse. They got serious really fast. He left months before Mandy was born. I'm not sure he even knew Mya was pregnant. We never met him. We were dealing with a lot of things and watching the two older girls often. His name isn't even on the birth certificate."

"What was his last name?" Kat asked and adjusted her blue light glasses.

Mariah and Peter looked at one another, and she responded, "You know, it never mattered, but I think his name was Jesse Martin, if I recall. After he left, we checked him off as another deadbeat. She was so unlucky in love." Mariah patted Peter's knee, and he smiled ruefully into his teacup and blew the steam.

"Do you know where he is?" Kat asked.

"No idea. I don't even know if he knows Mandy ever existed. Or that Mya is dead," Mariah said.

Kat noted on her pad, *Jesse Martin, Mandy's father*. This was the first bit of information she had gleaned that wasn't in the original file.

"Around that time we were..." Peter said.

"Pre-occupied. And we didn't pay as close attention as we should have to Mya," Mariah said.

"What was it that pre-occupied you, if you don't mind me asking?"

SEVENTEEN

PETER'S SHOULDERS ROUNDED, and his hands clasped the teacup in his lap. His lips pursed tight.

Mariah answered for them. "We had some setbacks. We claimed bankruptcy, and there were lawsuits. I returned to work as a hospice nurse to help financially." She patted her husband's knee gently.

Peter locked eyes with his wife, and his jawline jumped. "I'm not keeping anything from the media, Mariah. Not this time. We will get justice for Mya, Maureen, Millie, and Mandy."

Kat watched a conversation of tics and glances spoken between the two unfold. A private language developed over the course of a long marriage. Mariah bobbed her head in silent agreement.

Peter turned back to Kat. "We went bankrupt because of my business," he said flatly. "My invention hurt many people, and we lost everything. We received death threats daily. So we were preoccupied with everything that entailed."

Kat noted in her journal - *death threats*. "Were any of the threats credible? Or investigated?"

Peter shrugged. "We had a few pieces of mail, and people came past the house. We were social pariahs for a while. I was so embarrassed, we dealt with it privately and never reported it."

Mariah continued the story like Peter turned the page and handed her the book open at a different chapter. "We financed Mya's lifestyle until we filed for bankruptcy. She was angry with us for what happened." Mariah threw her arms up in exasperation. "At some point, Mya turned to drugs, and we don't know why. Her and that boy Jesse broke up right when we were having financial issues. I wasn't paying close enough attention to the signs. She was such a wonderful mother with her two girls before Mandy was born. Really, she was. But no one remembers that part of her life." Her bird-like eyes softened. "They only remember how they died." Her voice choked out the words. "They weren't the Three M Girls, they were Maureen, Millie, and Mandy, and their mother Mya; but I guess that was too hard for the media to remember."

Kat scribbled on her paper: *bankruptcy, drug use after bankruptcy*. The palpable pain inside the house suffocated her. "When you noticed she was struggling, what did you do?"

Mariah said, "We didn't figure it out until she had

Mandy and I went to her house and found... evidence." Her voice hitched in her throat.

"I see," Kat said.

Peter's hand cupped Mariah's knee. "It's okay. Mandy was a healthy, robust baby."

Mariah nodded. "Yeah, I know." Her chin scrunched up, and a single tear slid down her face. "Mandy cried a lot. Like I said, I'm a nurse, so I recognize withdrawal when I see it. I watched her closely after I found the evidence of what Mya had done. Mandy was irritable for the first couple of weeks. But she wasn't underweight at birth, and didn't have serious side effects, like seizures. I snuggled her a lot. I told everyone Mandy was colicky because I was ashamed." Mariah's hands fluttered to her lap and her fingers intertwined. "She wasn't so bad that she had to go to the NICU. It's something I've learned to forgive my daughter for. It was a horrible mistake. Horrible. But aside from the crying for the first few weeks, she was a healthy little girl. Mya felt terrible about it. She was a wonderful mother, but never overcame her addiction." She swallowed and added, "It's a disease, you know."

Kat scribbled, *Mandy healthy, but withdrawals. Late-stage pregnancy drug use.*

Peter said, "We put Mya in out-patient and in-patient facilities. We tried everything." He patted his wife's shoulder. "My wife took good care of our grandchildren each time Mya tried to get help, but her addiction put us deeper in debt. We couldn't afford it, but we thought it could save her life. We set up counseling, cut her off financially, and that's how she ended up in that God-forsaken apartment. Mariah picked up our grandchildren whenever she'd let us. We were going to watch her fail and foster her children. Hoping her rock bottom would finally get her sober. Maureen didn't want to leave her mother, so we waited too long."

Mariah said, "We should have done more. I picked up a lot of shifts to help financially, and my schedule was pretty full. Honestly, some days I was too tired to get the girls." Her voice cracked and trailed off, and Peter put his arm around her.

He rubbed his wife's back. "It wasn't your fault."

Kat felt a piercing guilt for tearing open the delicate covering on their gash of a wound. She glanced at the door.

Peter put his hand on Mariah's and whispered, "It's okay."

Mariah wiped away a tear and said, "We were hopeful it was another one of her phases. To deal with the abandonment from the girls' fathers. Mya knew we'd take the children and she would never, ever hurt them. I'm sad for my youngest granddaughter. She never got to experience the mother that Maureen and Millie did. Maureen finally agreed it had gotten too bad, and it was time. I was working with a lawyer and social services to take temporary custody of them. Just until Mya got better. Over the last few months of her life, she lost her friends and tried to push us away, too. It got to where I had to plead with her to take the children, buy groceries, or swing by. I was probably too judgmental, and she was tired of my nagging."

Peter said, "When the police went over everything with us, they said it was probably postpartum depression or a psychotic event that caused her to do it. But who would address a suicide note to, *To whom it may concern*?"

"That bothered me, too," Kat said.

"You saw the note?" Mariah asked.

Heat flushed up in Kat's face. "No, I'm sorry. I meant that *would* bother me, too. What else did the note say? Did you see it?"

Mariah's face went to stone, and she recited the note contents from memory. The way she shut down reminded Kat of her mother when her brother Duncan died. Losing a brother was terrible and impossible to comprehend, but the mother's life was destroyed. It was like a shattered plate, no matter how much was done to glue it back together, its function may be restored, but it would never be the same.

Peter said, "Mya remembered nothing about hurting her girls. And I believed her."

Kat changed the subject. "How did you see the note?"

Peter said, "They brought us in for questioning. Asked us what we knew about Mya, her drug use, and our grandchildren. They showed us the note. That's when we knew."

"Knew what?"

Mariah finished Peter's thought. "That our daughter

didn't kill her children. She may have killed herself, but never her children."

Kat addressed the next delicate question. "Did anyone stand to gain financially from Mya and the girls' death?"

Peter shifted in his seat, and Mariah shot him a glance and looked directly at Kat with a challenging stare. "What do you mean by that? Did we get rich off of our daughter's and grandchildren's deaths? Is that your question?" Mariah crossed her arms and glared.

Kat froze and stammered, "It's, it's just a question about anyone who may have stood to gain financially. I didn't mean you in particular, Mrs. Walton."

Peter answered, "We inherited one million dollars. It should be public record." His voice took on a cool tone. "But that was a life insurance policy we had in the event she died before her babies. We did not expect to bury all four of them."

"We were in Hawaii as our grandchildren were being killed, if that was your question," Mariah said.

"It wasn't my question at all. This is a general question asked of all cold cases. I'm sorry, perhaps this interview is over," Kat said, and shut her notebook.

Peter said, "No, no. We're sorry. We gained financially from their deaths. But I would give my life to get them back. The insurance payout was because we lost everything. It should have gone to her children."

"I'm sorry," Kat said. "I understand this is so hard, and I meant nothing by any of my questions." Her chest tightened and her eyes slid to the door wishing she could bolt and never look back. Kat kicked herself for giving Camila's name.

Mariah's icy glare softened slightly. "Someone killed our family. So, what's next?"

Kat hadn't planned for the question. She re-opened her notepad and scribbled a few meaningless words down. *They don't believe Mya killed the children* to give herself some time to think. She paused and considered them, contemplating her next words. Before they came, Peter asked, "Why did our family's case get re-opened?"

Kat cleared her throat. "Well, there's a recent case that has some similarities to Mya's."

"Oh? Similar like how?" Mariah asked. "Were more children killed?"

"Unfortunately, there was a child who died. And a mother."

Mariah's back straightened. "How is the case similar?"

"The suicide note, and DNA," Kat said.

"We can go to the police station. Tell them what we know?" Mariah offered.

"No," Kat responded too quickly. "I have received this information from an anonymous tip inside the police department, and we're doing an exclusive story."

"So?" Peter asked. "Did you get more information to help? What more can we give you or do for you?"

Mariah perched on the edge of her seat and both she and Peter stared at Kat, waiting for her answer.

Kat tapped her pen against her knee. "I have a better idea of who Mya was. It's helpful." That wasn't an answer, but she'd run out of things to say. "The detectives are investigating leads." It was true. Her husband had the file, and he was a detective.

"What was the DNA link?" Mariah asked.

"Millie's father was also the father of the girl in this case."

Peter's mouth fell open, and Mariah's went into a straight line. She said, "Evan did it."

Peter's eyes were wide with shock. "Did he kill Beatrice and Amelia?"

"How did we miss this in the news?" Mariah asked.

Kat straightened. "Did you know Beatrice and Amelia?"

Mariah put her teacup on the coffee table and crossed her legs. "We met them a few times, and I think the baby, Amelia, once. Beatrice knew what happened to our family and wanted our families to meet before she built a life with Evan. Our warnings fell on deaf ears. That poor, poor baby." She crossed her arms over herself and rocked gently.

Peter put his hand around his wife's waist, and she leaned into him. "I'll order flowers."

Kat slipped the pad of paper with the notes with very little new information inside her purse and stood. She wiped her sweaty hands on the sides of her slacks. Compulsively, her hand touched the outside of her pants where the tiny piece of fabric lay.

She wanted nothing more than to escape their time capsule of sorrow. She'd already said too much, but nothing more about Beatrice and Amelia than what was publicly available by reading the headlines. There was a flutter of guilt as she witnessed their realization that Evan probably killed a second family.

She swallowed hard. "I really should be going."

Mariah and Peter stood, and Mariah held her hand out to Kat. "It was so good to meet you, Camila. Promise me one thing?"

"What is it?"

"Get that son-of-a-bitch," Mariah said with a vehemence Kat did not expect.

Kat stepped back and said nothing.

Peter said, "We'll be in touch."

EIGHTEEN

PETER CLOSED the door behind Kat, and she quickly walked to her car. She navigated out of the gated community, the grocery store completely forgotten, her mind on auto-pilot as the car steered itself home. She drummed her hands on the steering wheel and let her mind wander to Mariah and Peter and the strange interview.

How powerful a grandparent's love was. One Jilly was denied, purposefully, by Kat. Greg didn't know that her father was alive either. She faked both her mother and father's deaths not long after she met Greg when he was on a six-week reserve deployment. While her mother was long dead, that wasn't what she'd told Greg when she stumbled into him at the bar with her fresh fake ID.

So, when he deployed with his unit, she emptied the contents of the barbecue into a couple of thrift store jars and set them on the mantel. When he returned home from his military deployment, she told him her parents died in a crash, and she'd settled their estate. She didn't want to trouble him on his deployment overseas and affect his focus. He held her tight and admired her for her strength.

Initially, Kat was sure it was for the best, but seeing the pain and care on Mariah and Peter's faces, now she wasn't so sure. As Kat grew in her motherhood, she understood a grandparent's love was shaped differently from the love of a child. A guilty pleasure washed over her as she nursed the dark recesses of her conscious and relished the vindication in stealing joy from her father. Robbing him of dignity or happiness as he withered away tickled her more than she wished it did.

But stealing even an ounce of happiness from her daughter felt inexcusable. She thought of the scrap of fabric in her pocket and remembered exactly why he'd never know Jilly and she'd never be sorry for it.

Jilly wasn't any luckier with Greg's side of the family. His parents died before they met. The state passed him from foster home to foster home, and Greg didn't talk about his childhood. At eighteen, he aged out and enlisted in the military, then the police force, and stayed in the military as a reservist.

Greg and Kat were both only children with nothing but one another to buoy each other up and build a life. Jilly never knew the love and chaos of cousins, aunts, uncles, or kin. There was only so much Greg and Kat cobbled together with good friends and godparents. But friends didn't stay in one another's orbits through the thick and thin like family did. When life got too hard, it was easier to drift away from an outgrown relationship than to ride the ebbs and flows of familial dynamics. And all of those friends had proper families of their own.

She thought back to Mariah and Peter, so sad and heavy with the burden of losing their child and three grandchildren. The guilt threaded deep into their marriage and lives.

There's nothing I can do to bring Mya, Maureen, Millie, or Mandy back.

I nosed around where I shouldn't have and caused more hurt.

Before she realized it, she'd parked in her driveway, safe from the black hole of tragedy in the Walton house. Her skin still coated with a film of grief, she wanted a shower, but there wasn't enough time. She walked in the door to wait for Greg to return.

Her FaceTime chimed. It was Jillian.

"Hi, Jilly," Kat said, answering.

"Happy birthday, Mom. You look nice. I've never seen that necklace. Whatcha doin'?" Her red hair was tied in a bun perched high on her head.

Kat's hand fluttered to her necklace, and she looked down at her floral blouse. Again, she'd forgotten it was her birthday. "Oh, I figured when Dad gets home, he'll take me to dinner. I didn't want him to wait for me to get ready."

"Nice. Where are you going?"

"We haven't gotten that far yet."

"Maybe check out that new sushi place that opened

in town? Wait, are you wearing my glasses?" Jillian asked. Her freckled nose scrunched in a question.

Kat had forgotten, and pulled them from her face. "Oh, yeah, I was on the computer and my eyes were strained. I thought I'd try them."

"Did they help? I left them there because I'm pretty sure the blue light thing is a scam..."

"Not really, no. I probably need a prescription." Kat chuckled. "How are you doing?"

"I'm great. We're going out to dinner tonight, too. So, I'm going to have to get going in a few to shower, but I wanted to make sure I called to say happy birthday. I love you, Mama."

"I love you, too. Can't wait to see you soon," Kat said. Though there were no immediate plans for Jillian to come home.

Jillian made a kissing face and hung up.

Kat's eyes swept through the living room. It was so quiet without Jillian. She sighed, and went up the stairs to delete the pictures, and shred the notes to put the entire affair to bed. She opened the budget file, and before she stopped herself, took one last look at the girls at the murder scene. Kat studied the little Jillian looka-like, while she fished the light pink fabric out of her pocket and rubbed it between her fingers, almost nursing it to answer. "What happened to you, poor little Mandy?"

She flipped the photo to Millie and saw something, and gasped. To confirm her suspicions, she flipped to Maureen's floating body in the bathtub. Kat hissed through her teeth. *Oh my God, she didn't kill her children. And if Mya didn't kill her children, then what are the odds that Beatrice didn't kill Amelia, either? Only the murderer would have seen the note and been able to copy it. And there is only one person who has both families in common...*

Kat watched enough crime shows to know that murderers attended funerals. She researched when the funeral for Beatrice and Amelia was. *Tomorrow.* And it was at a place she was more than familiar with. One which she owed a visit to, anyway. She hadn't visited her mother and brother's gravesites since she was eighteen. Greg and Jillian didn't know they existed.

Duncan should have been ashes. Kat would have sprinkled him in the places he loved, and her mother was in two places at once. Her family thought she sat on the mantel when she really rested with Kat's big brother who never got the chance to grow up.

Kat's empty week was suddenly filling with tasks. One last internet search verified that Mya and her girls were also at the same cemetery. The singular link between the two families strengthened. Closing the file on her computer, she removed her laptop from Greg's desk and went to her closet to figure out what she'd wear to a family reunion.

NINETEEN

HER BIRTHDAY DINNER was like every other date night, marked by Greg's stoic silence. Kat typically filled the empty spaces with idle chitchat, but with Jillian grown and the recent cases on her mind, she'd run out of things to say. They stopped exchanging gifts years ago, and they spent the bulk of the evening with their noses in their pasta dishes, pushing around salty over-priced noodles, and listening to the hum of the other diners' conversations.

Greg said, "I'm working tomorrow."

"On a Saturday?" Kat asked as she took a long sip of her cabernet.

He took a large bite of pasta and mulled it around in his mouth. A small splotch of sauce dripped on his lip and into his beard. "Yeah, but just for a few hours. I'll be home by four-ish."

Mirroring him, she pointed to her face where his sauce was. "You've got something…"

"Thanks," he said, wiping his face with the cloth napkin and setting it back in his lap.

"Okay," Kat said in a voice she hoped conveyed disappointment. Now she wouldn't need to make an excuse about going to the funeral.

The next morning, after Greg left for work, she put on the one black dress she owned. As she combed her hair into a French twist, a text chimed.

Camila: Coffee?

Kat: Sorry, I've got a doc appointment. Raincheck?

Kat hit her head with her hand. A doctor's appointment on a Saturday? But Camila didn't notice.

Camila: Sure, same time tomorrow?

Kat: Perfect.

The lies built as she fed her friend another one. Their morning coffee routine was a highlight of her day, and Kat would have liked company at the funeral. But Camila had already warned her to stop, and there would be no talking her into going to the funeral to feed her morbid curiosity. Especially now that Kat didn't think Beatrice or Mya killed their children. Which meant the killer was still walking among them, and perhaps would be at the funeral watching.

She gazed at herself in the mirror. *I'm a stranger, inviting myself to someone's funeral.* Instead of turning back, she swiped on a shade of red lipstick and applied waterproof mascara. She would pay her respects to Beatrice and Amelia Richards; two people she'd encountered through their deaths. For them, she'd help her husband figure out who killed them, and maybe Mya's children, too. She put on her sunglasses, took the piece of fabric from her pajama pants and stashed it in her purse, grabbed her keys, and went to her car. She knew the funeral home well.

After the funeral, she would pay a visit to her brother and mother. Before Beatrice and Amelia, she'd thought the next time she'd see the inside of the funeral home was when they buried her father, and even then, she may not have returned.

The case was active, and Kat assumed the police officers would be in attendance for the same reason as she was. Greg worked cold cases, but since this was linked, could this have been his work event? She didn't know and forgot to ask anything during the doldrums birthday dinner.

Her wide-brimmed black hat and sunglasses would obscure her face and help her blend in with the other mourners. In case anyone asked, she searched the internet to build a fictional relationship with Beatrice. She sifted through the crime stories and social media to get an idea of who she was. Beatrice married Evan Richards three years ago, and she was a project manager at a small business firm that designed shirts. The firm employed about fifty people. *I'm a chameleon. Yesterday I was a journalist, and today I'll be a co-worker for a shirt company.*

She arrived at the funeral home, and as expected, among the mourners were media and photographers at a less than respectable distance. Kat exited her car, parked in the parking lot, and looked at her shoes while her wide-brimmed hat and large black glasses concealed her identity as she heard the shutters click and questions lobbed toward the attendees entering the funeral home.

Reporters asked, "How did you know Beatrice?" And "Did you suspect she'd hurt her baby?" She pushed her oversized sunglasses higher on the bridge of her nose. As she approached, the thought of the tiny coffin froze her in place. She considered retracing her steps back to the car, her stomach clenched, but she pressed on. While her brother was a child when he'd died, he had been sixteen. So at least he was an adult-sized child and laid in a coffin made for adults. Though the large box looked too big and too sophisticated for him. Like he was playing dress up in his father's suit for eternity.

A frail woman with a salt-and-pepper bob and red-rimmed eyes greeted Kat at the door. The woman clamped her hand on Kat's shoulder and she tried hard not to pull back.

"Hi, dear, I'm Viola. How did you know my daughter and granddaughter?"

Kat's stomach twisted into a pretzel. "I worked with your daughter. I'm so sorry for your loss."

Viola nodded an acknowledgment, dropped her arm,

and put her hand on the next person's shoulder behind her. "Hi, dear, I'm Viola. How did you know my daughter and granddaughter?" Her tone was even, and her robotic movements suggested she existed on auto-pilot.

When she walked into the chapel, it bore the same smell of must and stale flowers. Inhaling the decay brought her back to her twelve-year-old self, picking a casket for her big brother, and a few days later, another one for her mother.

There was an organ in the corner, but no one was playing it. Instead, there was the hum of soft hymns piped in through the speakers in the ceiling. Kat looked toward the front of the aisle and found she needn't have been afraid to see a tiny coffin. It was worse. There was a single coffin holding both mother and baby together. To lay in each other's arms for eternity.

A tear pricked her eye for people she'd never meet. She scanned the room for an out-of-the-way place to sit. The back may be too obvious or catch a police officer's attention. Kat assumed investigators roamed the funeral to eye suspicious people. She opted for the second to the back row of seats.

People walked to the casket and looked at their bodies to pay respects. Occasionally, the soft hum of the instrumentals was punctuated by a gasp or a sniffle. Kat kept her seat and did not approach the casket. It felt like a gruesome violation to be a part of something so private, and her legs simply would not take her there. Her sunglasses allowed her to watch.

A man younger than Evan, but with golden locks like

him, trudged up to the casket. He leaned down quickly and stood again. When he turned, his lips trembled and his features were clouded with sadness. The man avoided everyone and walked past her. He spotted Evan approaching the door, and he weaved out a side exit. Kat assumed he was an ex-boyfriend, and she decided Beatrice certainly had a type.

In person, Evan's striking blue eyes caught her breath. They were stunning, and no amount of photography caught their brilliance. He appeared to be about her age, perhaps a smidge older, and had white strands woven through his blondish locks, styled in a boyish haircut. If she didn't know better from the files, he could have been younger, but the math wouldn't add up for him to be both Millie and Amelia's father. He wore a thin black tie and a tailored suit, looking every part a distinguished FBI agent, though he wasn't.

Viola turned away from him. He put his hand out to touch her shoulder, but she shirked away and addressed the woman behind him. Evan pressed his lips together, looked at the ground, and walked down the center row to the white coffin at the front of the room splayed with lilies.

He stopped short and held on to the front pew for support. He crossed his forehead, lips, and heart. Then, he began again, like he was walking through mud, toward the coffin. Sensing the tension, the room fell silent, and all eyes turned to him as he ascended the last step. Evan bent over the casket, his shoulders shaking. Wiping his eyes, he turned around and headed to the last set of chairs behind Kat. Someone coughed out the word, "killer" as he passed, but Evan ignored the heckler.

Her stomach tied into a knot. It was her opportunity to provide comfort if he didn't do it and assess if he was lying if he had. Kat turned around and said, "I'm sorry for your loss."

He looked at her, his eyes glassy. "Thank you. How did you know my wife?"

"I worked with her. She talked of you often," she lied.

He nodded almost imperceptibly, his chin wrinkled, and his eyebrows furled as he wiped his eye with a tissue. Kat looked away, allowing him to compose himself. In the aisle across the walkway sat a man in a dark black suit. He seemed to observe all the mourners, and his eyes briefly met Kat's. She felt exposed despite the sunglasses obscuring her fear.

Evan followed her gaze. "Damn, they're everywhere." He sighed.

"Who's everywhere?" Kat asked.

"Oh, I'm sorry. I was talking to myself. The police. I guess they're trying to figure out if there's more to what happened to my family, but she did this to herself and took my baby girl with her."

The hint of anger in his voice caught Kat off-guard.

Evan said, "I waited so many years after... everything. And now, this. I can't believe it's happened. Why?"

"After what?" Kat asked.

His mouth turned into a straight line. "Nothing."

"Again, I'm so sorry for your loss. Beatrice told me so much about you."

His back straightened, and he looked directly at her. His intense gaze pierced through the sunglasses. "Bea never mentioned you. And no one called her Beatrice. You one of them?" He gestured his head over to the police, and his tone grew cold.

Kat turned, straightened her shoulders, and gathered her purse. "I-I'm sorry, I shouldn't have come."

"You with the press? Who are you?" His voice got louder and people were gesturing and looking at them both.

"I'm no one, really, nobody. I'm so sorry for your loss." Kat stood and ran out of the funeral home and toward her car.

She thought, *I'm not nobody, and you're not innocent.* But she had absolutely nothing to prove it. As she drove away, she thought she saw Chase's patrol car on the side of the road. *Great, how do I explain this to my husband?*

TWENTY

THE PATROL CAR in the parking lot had the "To Protect and Serve" with the last *e* peeling off. The car belonged to Chase. If they saw her at the funeral, why didn't they speak to her? She pirouetted through excuses during her drive home.

I wasn't there. No, that's too hard a lie to wriggle free from.

I went to visit a friend's site. I was compelled to visit a friend Greg didn't know on the same day as the funeral? Greg wasn't born yesterday.

Then it came to her. And it felt dirty.

Do I tell him, or wait for him to ask? I'll stay on the offense and tell him.

She pulled into her drive and rushed inside to shirk the shades of black off of her body. Kat donned a spring dress with more floral patterns than she typically wore and sat at his desk to text him.

Kat: I stopped by Parson Funeral Home today. I don't want my parents on the mantel anymore.

Greg: Oh, I didn't know you were planning on doing that. It's been a long time.

Kat: I know, I've been meaning to do it.

Greg: I could have gone with you?

Kat: It's okay. I checked to see if it was something I wanted and what the process was. While I was there, the funeral for the mother and daughter was happening.

Greg: I know. Chase is coming for dinner tonight. We've got some work. We'll be there at about six.

Kat: Small world. Anyway, I can make pasta and salad?

Greg: That's fine. See you at six.

She blew out a sigh of relief, though interring barbecue ashes at the cemetery would be a boundary she couldn't cross. Later she'd change her mind, but today her presence was semi-plausible. Pasta and salad were easy enough to throw together, and she'd add some wine. Chase hadn't drunk wine with them since the night years ago when he confessed his love, but the wine loosened Greg's tongue.

She settled into the hard, oversized desk chair and

googled Evan Richards again to scan the latest news. The media had not yet connected Evan as both Amelia and Millie's father.

She had the pasta, salad, and bread waiting in the kitchen when Chase and Greg arrived. There were three wine glasses on the table, with an open bottle of Merlot beside them. Chase walked through the door and looked at the wine. An unspoken message between them, he smiled.

"Hi, Kat. Hope it wasn't too much trouble for me to stop in for dinner."

She walked to him and kissed his cheek. "Never too much trouble." A singular butterfly flipped in her stomach, and she pulled away.

Greg was behind him. "Hi, Katie. Thanks for putting dinner together."

"Of course, anytime." She smiled and walked toward the kitchen to get the plates served.

Greg poured three glasses of wine, and Chase followed Kat into the kitchen. He placed his hand on the small of her back and whispered, "You okay? Greg told me you were looking at interring your parents, and that you were at the funeral home today."

"I'm fine, thank you," she said as breezily as she could muster. Anxiety clutched her stomach in a fist over the lie she'd told Greg, and shame for enjoying Chase's hand at the small of her back and his whisper in her ear. She brought out two plates, and Chase followed with the bread, salad, and third plate and placed them on the table.

As they sat, Greg asked Kat, "Hey Katie, what did you do today?"

"Oh, nothing much. I mean, I told you I stopped by the funeral home." She shifted uncomfortably in her seat and took a long sip of the red wine. The tannins nipped her tongue.

"You did mention that," Greg said. The silence settled at the table.

Quick on her feet, she blended a truth and a lie. "After I met with the funeral director, I stopped in the ceremony's doorway. I looked inside the room, it's probably too big for my parents. They've been gone twenty years, and I don't know who would come." The lies thickened and dried out on her tongue. She sipped the wine again and glanced behind Greg's head at the thrift store jugs full of barbecue ashes posing as her parents.

Greg leaned back and crossed his legs, Kat's stomach pinched, as if they'd begun an interrogation.

"I was ushered inside by the mother at the door. She was so sad, and I didn't want to be rude, so I sat in the back for a few minutes before leaving." She twirled the noodles around her fork and took a small bite of the al dente noodles. Kat liked them soft, but her husband preferred them with a small crunch at the center.

"Mmm," Greg said. Chase busied himself with dinner.

Kat took another small sip of her wine. "Anyway, I ran into the husband there. He sat right behind me. I think his name was Evan..." She waited for a reaction to his name. He was the link between the Three M Girls and this fresh case, but the news hadn't run the story yet.

Greg cleared his throat and patted her hand. "Katie, you know going to a funeral with an unsolved case is dangerous. I told you this case may be linked to the other one. You could have been hurt. We knew you were inside."

Kat sat straighter and smoothed the napkin on her lap. "I had no intention of going to the funeral. I already told you why I was there. When I got home, I sent you a text. How did you know I was inside? Are you tracking me?" She was right to be on the offense and text him earlier in the day.

He laid his palms flat on the table on either side of his dish. "No, I was there Katie, in my car. Watching people go in and out. Imagine my surprise when I saw our car, and one of our guys was in there, too. When I gave him your description, he told me you were near the husband."

Kat bristled. *It's always the husband.* Her stomach dropped. Greg was right, it was a naïve and selfish thing to put herself in the middle of it, jeopardizing her safety and his investigation. Yet, upon recognizing their car, he didn't come to her in the parking lot. "Why didn't you speak to me? You said it may be dangerous, yet you didn't come inside to see why I was there?"

Chase cleared his throat. "I'm sorry you had to deal with your parents' business today. Especially when there was so much activity at the funeral home."

She looked at her pasta, but no longer wanted to eat

any of it. She drained her glass of wine instead. "I'm sorry I went to the funeral home. I honestly didn't know," she lied.

"Don't do it again," Greg said louder, emboldened by his wine.

She didn't answer. He was speaking to her the same way he did when Jillian disobeyed him. When he used his gruff voice, Jillian shut down. She'd learned that from Kat. She could count on one hand the number of times Greg had spoken to her like that when Chase was around.

"Did you hear me? Katie?" Greg repeated.

Chase looked at his plate, and Kat's face felt hot with embarrassment.

"Yes, I heard you. I already apologized. What else can I say? It was a simple mistake." Kat's mostly empty stomach wound tight and the large glass of wine fogged her head.

"Say you won't do it again," Greg repeated.

She flashed her eyes at him. "Yes, okay. I won't accidentally visit a place on personal business, where you are also working on a case, ever again." The lie was laced with acidic sarcasm and felt sharp on her tongue.

Chase said, "Since you were inside, did you notice anything?"

Greg rolled his eyes. "Don't encourage her. She isn't a detective."

Kat straightened her shoulders and narrowed her eyes at Greg, then turned to Chase. "Actually, yes, I did. The mother, I think Viola was her name, wouldn't talk to the husband when he came in. He said he waited years after and now he can't believe it happened again." He didn't say again, but Kat knew what he meant.

"Hmmm, he said that?" Greg asked.

"Yes, yes, he did. Then he accused me of being a police officer or a member of the media. He acted paranoid, so I got up and left. The woman at the door who introduced herself as Beatrice's mother didn't stop me." *Less is more*, she thought. *Stop talking.*

Chase's eyes grew wide with concern.

Greg said, "You should have told me."

"I'm telling you now. On a different day, I will handle my parents' affairs. I left because of the funeral activity and the media. Should I clear all of my errands with you beforehand?" Her chest felt a smidge of relief dishing his snideness back.

"Okay, okay, I got it, Katie. You didn't know. I was worried." He waved his hands and twirled the pasta around his fork before taking another large bite.

She crossed her arms and leaned back, narrowing her eyes at him. "You knew I was there at the funeral home. If you were worried, you would have got out of the car, or out from behind the bush, or wherever you were and checked on me." A surge of power rushed through her as she turned the tables of the interrogation.

Chase interrupted her. "That's not fair."

"Really? I was asked to make dinner to stage an intervention. I think *that's* not fair. This seems less like you care about me, and more like you wanted to punish and humiliate me. I'm not hungry anymore." She pushed the plate toward the center of the table and stood, marching up the stairs and slamming her bedroom door. *That'll teach them both*, she thought. Greg and Kat were married long enough for both to know following her to their room wouldn't help anyone.

Greg talked louder with wine, and their room was next to the office where they'd be working. She sat on her bed and leaned back into the soft orange throw pillows. Her heartbeat slowed to normal as the anger, that had felt so acute she nearly believed the lie herself, dissipated.

Thirty minutes after her huffed exit, dishes clanged in the kitchen. Then, footsteps fell past her door, and she crouched close to the shared wall to listen.

Their muffled voices were still discernible. Greg said, "Look at this apartment." The disgust in his tone sifted through the walls. "There is an undeniable link with the father."

"What motive would he have to kill his family?" Chase asked.

"The normal ones, money, child support, or strung out on drugs. The father put his life together, but there were some drug charges on him around that time. Maybe she never asked him to kill the kids, but she thought she did it when she was high?" Greg said.

"What was his alibi with the first case?"

There was a pause and Kat assumed they shuffled through the case file. Greg said, "Looks like his mother said he was at her place."

"Let's see where she lives now," Chase replied. A clanking of keys on the computer. "Hm, nowhere. She's dead."

Greg snorted. "Guess he can't use her as an excuse again."

Kat opened her phone and typed the new information in.

Drug arrests.

Mother is dead.

Chase said, "Something still isn't right about this. Those three children suffered awful neglect. Why would he kill a second family and leave the same note?"

Kat caught herself nodding her head with her palms pressed to the wall.

Greg's voice. "Unless he killed his first family. Mya thought she did it and killed herself. The guilt got to him and he snapped, did it again and wanted to be caught?"

Kat considered Greg's explanation. Certainly plausible.

Chase said, "And now he wants us to figure it out. The note, connection, motive, they're all there." Kat heard the papers rustling. *Our walls are thin.*

"We're on the right track. Let's get a warrant drafted to the judge," Greg said.

There was quiet. "But is it enough for the warrant? Paternity and a similar note from an already closed case?"

"That's on the judge," Greg said, and Kat recognized the finality in his tone. When Greg meandered through a topic and settled on a direction, there was no changing course.

She scratched her chin. They created quite a wine-infused narrative to fit Evan in a killer-sized hole. Though every aspect of their story was plausible. *That's why they're the detectives and I'm not.* The theory wasn't a bad one. And it aligned with what she'd spotted in the photograph with Mya's children, though she hadn't heard them mention it. And it explained the note. If the person who wrote the note still lived, they'd know what it said. But why wouldn't Evan have killed himself?

Then it came to her.

He's Catholic. He crossed himself before saying goodbye to his family. Killing his family was more forgivable than killing himself. But if the police caught him, and sentenced him to death, then the law took care of him, and he'd die forgiven and would reunite with them in heaven.

The backward methodology of it baffled her.

Everything fit, except a nagging gut feeling from when Kat had spotted him at the funeral. Grief had marred his face and permeated his being. And if he didn't kill Beatrice or Amelia, then he didn't kill Mya and her girls. The parent in her screamed Evan didn't do it.

TWENTY-ONE

THE NEXT MORNING, Kat awoke and her first thought was of Evan. Everything fit neatly into place. Maybe too neatly? Or were crimes simpler than the podcasts, movies, and books portrayed? Not everything was an elaborate mystery. She lay in bed and stared at the ceiling until the smell of coffee beckoned her downstairs.

Greg was a pressure cooker, sloughing off the anger and annoyances of the day as he slept, while Kat was a slow cooker. She envied his fresh start each morning. Her rage built and simmered over time, and the only thing that tamed her anger was productive actions of her own, by herself.

Today if she wriggled out of errands with Greg, she planned to repay a visit to Parson Funeral Home to see her mother, brother, the Three M Girls, and Beatrice and Amelia. She wondered briefly if she'd find an unexpected inhabitant at the Grant gravesite. Her father had not reached out to her since she ran away at eighteen. Had he died? Surely it would have made some small splash in the news, but she never searched the obituaries, too scared to know.

Kat was sure he was alive, but she planned to use the opportunity to see Mr. Parson again. Ask him about Beatrice and Amelia while checking on her family's gravesite. She'd meant to visit the Grant gravesite after the funeral, but when Evan had raised his voice, and she'd spotted Chase's car, she got spooked and hurried home. Seeing her brother and mother was one of those errands she'd put off for years that became decades. And she'd let it wait another day.

She came down the stairs to spot Greg, with his nose in his phone in a freshly pressed shirt with his hair neat. His hazel eyes met hers and she looked at the table, her coffee already in front of her seat, waiting for her.

"Thank you for the coffee," she said. She sat and took a long sip and rubbed her temples. A mild headache seeped in and she teetered between aspirin and coffee to fix it. "Why do you look like you're going somewhere?"

"Chase is picking me up in fifteen minutes or so."

"You're working today too? It's Sunday."

"I know. It won't be a long day. We're combing through some details of this case. But I'll take a long weekend and then we'll do something fun?"

"Yeah, fine." Her tone signaled that her fiery anger from the previous night burned brightly.

"What are your plans today?" He spoke to her in a gentler tone. Tip-toeing around the edges to sense the mood of the room. The long-understood waltz of a functional marriage.

"Well, I wasn't able to meet with the funeral director yesterday, for obvious reasons. So, I'll be going back today. Should I clear that with you? May I go to the funeral home today and take care of my personal business? Pretty please?" The edge of her voice had only sharpened after a solid night's sleep.

Greg sighed and shook his head. "Look, I'm sorry. I shouldn't have overreacted. Can we forget about it?"

Kat crossed her pajama-clad legs. "That's fine. But as a reminder, I am an adult, and from time to time I may do adult things without clearing them with you first. I know that's hard to fathom. And one of those adult things is taking care of my parents." She gestured to the barbecue ashes sitting on the mantel. The ten-year span between them sometimes nipped at their dynamic. But Kat was nearing forty now and as she rose into her power, the shift threatened their decades-old peace and pecking order.

Greg nodded. "I know. I'm sorry. As an only child, I understand how hard it is to bury them. So, are we good?" His eyebrows turned up in question as he leaned back and finished his cup of coffee.

"Yeah, we're good. Just don't do that to me again." Kat sighed. "Why did you bring Chase over for that?"

He offered her a small smile as a peace offering and reached a hand out to her on the table, but she moved her hand to her lap.

"Okay, I see. We're not okay yet. Chase and I saw

you, and we were both worried. We had to work late, so he was coming anyway. It wasn't an intervention. It's just because we care about you, Katie."

She bristled at being called Katie, so insistent to call her a name she didn't care for. The older she got, the more sure of herself she became, and she did not like the name Katie. It punched her ego every time it slid out of his lips, but she remained quiet on the subject.

"Let's drop it and start again," she said. "Good morning, and thanks for the coffee." She smiled with her lips closed, and it didn't reach her eyes.

The tension unraveled in his brow. "You're welcome. Good morning." A text chimed, and Greg glanced at his phone. "He's here." Her husband stood and kissed her head. "I'll see you later."

"See you tonight," she said to his back as he grabbed his keys and left.

Kat refilled her coffee cup and went upstairs and combed through her closet. She didn't want to wear the black dress, but nothing cheery either. She was going back to the funeral home, after all. Kat put on dark slacks, ballet flats, and a crimson blouse. She tied her hair in a low ponytail and got her purse and notebook, just in case there was anything of interest at the Three M Girls' or Beatrice and Amelia's gravesites. She searched their site numbers and scribbled their forever locations in her folder.

Kat stopped by the store and bought pink roses speckled with baby's breath for her mother, but couldn't decide what to get her brother. A forever sixteen-year-old boy wouldn't appreciate flowers the way her mother would. At the checkout for the flowers, Kat spotted M&M's. The yellow ones were Duncan's favorite. She picked them up and headed to the car.

At the funeral home, the parking lot that had been bustling with mourners yesterday was eerily quiet. She pulled into the same spot her father had when they came to pick out her brother's casket, and a week later, when they picked her mother's casket. Kat wondered if she was supposed to call first to make an appointment with death and if it was even open on a Sunday. There was a crack in the sidewalk that led to the door, and she didn't remember that detail from years past. *Even funeral homes show their age, eventually.*

The Parson Funeral Home looked partially like a Victorian home, but had a portico, balcony, and a cheery white exterior. The shutters and steps leading to the door were green, but the door was red, and that was new since her mother and brother had been buried there.

It looks like Christmas, she thought. Kat placed the M&M's in her purse, grabbed the roses, and walked up the stairs to the door, for the second time in a week. It was shut. *Do I knock? Walk in? What is the protocol here?*

Before she decided, a man opened the door. It was Mr. Parson. He looked familiar, but decades had passed since she'd last seen him. Now she was nearly forty. The hair he had on his head was gone, but his white Santa Claus beard made her think of Christmas again. The whites of his eyes were yellowed a little, and he swam in the suit he wore. She wondered if he may be sick. He looked at her flowers.

"Can I help you, dear? You don't have to check in here to visit the cemetery around back," Mr. Parson said. His kind voice with a slight Caribbean accent was laced with empathy. Well-versed in grief, he conducted his business with eloquence.

Her tongue grew thick in her mouth. "Oh, no, I mean yes. Thank you. I wanted to ask about the Grant gravesite before heading out back. Frankly, I wasn't sure you'd be here today."

His eyes softened around the edges, and he scratched his white beard. He opened the door wider. "Come in, my dear. There will be a viewing later, so I'm here." He shuffled down the hall, and she walked in and shut the door behind her. "Let's go to my office."

She followed and put her hand in her slacks pocket to touch the shred of fabric, reassuring herself it was still there. As they strolled down the long hallway, she mentioned, "I stopped by yesterday, but there was so much going on."

"Yes, it was quite a large gathering yesterday," Mr. Parson replied. "Some ceremonies are more eventful than others."

He circled his large oak desk and sat facing her. He offered no more information on the funeral. Kat appreciated his protection over his dead charges, as it meant her brother Duncan was looked after, too. She would have to visit the sites on her own to see if there was anything interesting at the Three M Girls' and Beatrice and Amelia's sites.

He gestured for her to sit at one of the two chairs in front of his desk. She eyed the small green couch behind the chairs. It was where she'd sat when her father and mother brought her to witness them arranging Duncan's funeral. Then, shortly after, when her father and she arranged her mother's funeral, she sat in the chair opposite the one she sat in now. The one she sat in now had belonged to her father.

"Now, Ms..."

"Eland. But please, call me Kat."

"Okay, Kat, how can I help you?"

"Well, I'm not sure about the procedure for this. But I'm the next of kin to my father, Caldwell Grant. We... um... we are estranged. I wanted to make sure, before I went out there, that my name isn't on any of the stones and I'm not registered to be buried here. Your cemetery is lovely, but I have my own family now. I know when I was twelve he wanted to make... room for me. I don't want to be buried here, no offense. It was a lifetime ago." Kat let the silence fall between them.

Mr. Parson leaned back in his chair. "Hmm, I see, yes. Let me pull up the file. Caldwell, Grant."

"Yes, the grave would be for Evelyn Grant, his wife, and Duncan Grant, his son. My brother." Her throat caught at the mention of her brother. She hadn't spoken his name out loud in years, and it surprised her how much it still hurt. Her sole regret at running from the life she'd had was that Greg and Jillian would never know about Duncan and his legacy.

"Alright, let me see if I can find anything." He put on his wire-rimmed spectacles, but instead of opening his computer, he stood and shuffled to the large metal file cabinet in the back corner of the room labeled D-G. His fingers ran along the tabs of the multiple names of the dead or near-dead. "Ah, here it is. His plot is 1256, which is next to Evelyn Grant. And it is vacant. The standing order for daily flowers is still there. He also hired a gardener. Though we provide that service here." He thumbed through the paperwork. "It looks like there are four plots together."

She puffed out a breath of relief. He wasn't dead yet. Maybe one day they would reconcile. "Yes, thank you. Wait, did you say four plots?"

"Let me see here." He pulled the brown folder out of the cabinet and shuffled back to his desk with an uneven gait. "Yes. That's interesting. Yes, I remember this now. Many years ago. You said your name is Kat Eland."

Kat's stomach dropped. "Yes, but Eland is my married name. My maiden name is Grant."

He scratched his beard again. "Yes, that makes sense. Well, let's see here. There is a fully paid invoice for his arrangements. You have a reserved plot, too." He slid the paperwork over to Kat.

"He has a spot for me, too?" She swallowed hard.

"It appears he made the purchase of all four at the same time."

"I don't want it," Kat said flatly.

Mr. Parson's eyebrows drew together. "Okay, these are all changeable, not to worry. I'll need to contact him to get your name removed."

She put her hands up. "Please, not yet. I need some time." Her father didn't know where she was, and she'd slipped up and given the funeral director her real name. But if he wanted to, he'd find her. So far he'd honored her veiled threat. Once she buried him she'd take herself off the plot. She stood.

"Hmm, wait, that's interesting, hang on. Please." He gestured to the chair.

"There's a note in here, to you. This was over twenty years ago, so I'd nearly forgotten. It struck me as sad, and it was definitely unique. My mind must be slipping, too." He slid the note across the desk to her.

> Mr. Parson,
> If Katherine Grant visits, please provide her with this letter. Let her know I have handled all of my arrangements.
> Thank you,
> Caldwell Grant

Kat's throat caught. She recognized his handwriting and the stationery immediately. Like a song it brought her hurtling back to the past and a life she thought she'd outrun. She was eighteen again. Alone in their mansion. The embossed stationery was his, and she remembered her mother had bought it for him, a birthday gift, the last year she was alive. He was passionate about writing letters, and her mother had laughed and said, "What do you get the man who has everything? Personalized and embossed stationery." That was before her brother died, and their life tumbled to rubble.

Kat smiled with her lips closed and folded the letter and held it to her chest before tucking it safely in her purse. "Thank you, Mr. Parson."

"Oh, that wasn't the letter, Ms. Eland. The letter is here." And he handed her an envelope; written across the top, *For my daughter, Katherine.*

She held the letter in her hand. The soft creamy linen in the paper had withstood the test of time. Kat turned it over in her hands and saw that it still was secured with a wax seal after twenty years. She wanted to tear it open and read it right there. Instead, she tucked it away in her purse.

Mr. Parson looked at her, disappointed. Perhaps he, too, sought closure to the mysterious letter. Kat cleared the emotion from her throat. "Thank you, Mr. Parson. I am going to visit a few people now."

"Can I help you find anyone?" he asked.

"No, thank you. I'll make my way." She stepped out of the building and stared at the innumerable stones peeking out of the ground. It was time for a family reunion.

TWENTY-TWO

HER MEMORIES BLURRED, but her feet navigated themselves toward her mother and brother. She stepped around old cracked stones peppered with new ones marked with fresh sod. Her nose ran in the cold, and she stopped and rummaged in her purse for a tissue to stop it. Wiping her nose, she glanced up and saw a woman sitting beside a stone, a picnic in front of her. Kat turned away and tried to keep walking toward her brother, but not before the woman smiled sadly at her. She glanced again at the marker. It looked old and small. A tiny lamb sat on top of it. *Her child,* she thought. Kat thought of Jillian, her mother, Beatrice, and Mya and knew she too would be eager to join her daughter. Outliving a child was the sharpest of life's tragedies.

She spotted their graves from several rows off and her heart beat hard against her chest wall. Her mother's stone was hard to miss. It was an enormous pink and gray granite marker etched with flowers and flecked with gold. It was larger than Duncan's because her father opted for the most expensive one available. Kat hated that Duncan's was smaller considering more of his life was stolen from him, but she had to admit, it fit him better.

It was so quiet the crunch of the leaves beneath her feet shattered the silence as she walked to their site. Fresh pink roses peppered with pops of baby's breath sat on her mother's grave. Her supermarket flowers looked puny and insufficient by comparison.

Kat read the stone. Evelyn Grant, Wife and Mother. Forever in our Hearts.

"Hello, Mother," she said. There was a cool breeze, and the clouds obscured the sun, chilling her skin. "I've been thinking of family a lot." She stared at the bundles of flowers sitting at her mother's grave. "Hmm, Father's flowers are still right on time. I'll just leave these here." She laid her smaller bouquet on top of the stone. They were wilted compared to her father's extravagant daily delivery. The personal gardener her father hired would clear both her mother's and brother's stones within days. There were a couple of pine needles on top of her mother's stone that Kat cleared off, so the gardener was probably due any day now. "Are you still angry with me?" she asked as she traced the word *Mother* in the cold stone.

Kat's eyes drifted to the gravestone that hurt to see. Her mother had insisted on having Duncan's face etched in the black marble. After it was installed, Kat never visited. Duncan hated the picture, and Kat hated seeing any likeness of him etched in the cold stone.

"Duncan Grant. The Heart of our Family. Gone too Soon," she whispered the words. Her stomach pinched. He had always been the golden child, but it still hurt seeing her inferiority immortalized in stone. This visit was a grim reminder that Kat had never been good enough. She wasn't good enough to keep her mother alive when she'd been all her mother had left.

She sat cross-legged in front of his large gray stone. "Hi, Dunc." She dug in her purse and fished out her bag of M&M's. "If anyone could understand, it's you, but I'm sorry I haven't been out here. I really am. I miss you so much. God, you would have loved Jillian. She's so much like you. She loves M&M's like you, and her favorite color is yellow."

Kat popped the first brown M&M in her mouth and the sweet chocolaty flavor reminded her of childhood. The next one was yellow, and she sat it on top of his stone. She ate the bag, leaving the yellow ones for him. There were seven yellow candies lined up on his stone when she was done.

"I miss you, Dunc. I'm sorry I killed you. Your death changed everything." She patted the top of his stone and walked away to find the Three M Girls.

Kat retraced her steps away from her mother and brother's gravestones and pulled out the paper with the other locations and headed in the Three M Girls' direction. The small headstone where the woman had dined, now sat alone in the cemetery amongst the other outcroppings. Curiosity nearly pulled her toward the marker, but fear of being spotted by the woman continued her on. The Grants, the Three M Girls, and Beatrice and Amelia were enough people to visit in a day.

When she spotted Mya and her girls' marker across the stone soldier battlefield, she tucked the notepad back into her purse. It was a single large slate marker for the three girls and their mother. Mya's last resting place was with her daughters, even if she'd killed them. Mariah and Peter would have one place to visit their entire world.

The etching at the top of the stone was of what appeared to be Mary and Joseph with a childlike Jesus and they all wore halos. On the headstone was a large print of their last name, Walton. Beneath Walton was etched: Mya, Mother, and Daughters Maureen, Mildred "Millie," and Amanda "Mandy." Forever Together. Both the cemetery and headstone were lavish expenses, likely paid in part by Mya's life insurance policy. The girls' last names were absent, but Kat knew Maureen had the last name Short, Millie was Richards, and Mandy was Walton.

There was no sign on the stone that the police had found Mya responsible for killing her girls, of course. The gravestone was clean, and there were artificial flowers and a teddy bear at its base, so she wasn't sure how often anyone visited. She picked up the bear, and it was moist in her hands. It had been there at least a couple days, absorbing the dew from the early morning fog that covered death's front yard.

Kat wondered which girl had been left the teddy bear. If it had been Mariah or Peter, there would have been three. Art Short, Maureen's father, was dead, Millie's father was Evan, and Mandy's father likely didn't know she existed.

Kat rubbed the tiny cloth in her pocket and placed the bear back against the stone. Leaning on the cold headstone to stand an immediate sorrow shot through her. Then she felt a regret at not bringing a small token for the family. But a token of what? She didn't know them. It would simply have been a token of her curiosity. Kat opened her purse and pulled out her investigative pad of paper. Her hand brushed against her father's letter and she tingled with curiosity, but this was not the place to read it. She fished out her pen and wrote: t*eddy bear, fake flowers, and extravagant gravesite. Who brought the teddy bear? Evan?*

Then she flipped the page back to where Beatrice and Amelia's location was and made her way across the cemetery. Kat spotted the fresh sod and recognized the bouquets. Before approaching the burial site, she looked around furtively to ensure no one was there. After yesterday's unpleasant run-in with Evan, she wasn't keen on doing it again.

A plot of another child laid immediately to the right of Beatrice and Amelia's placement. Kat wandered over to the small stone and read it. The stone belonged to a girl named Charity who was born and died on the same day in 2012. There was no last name, just the first name and an etching that read: *To our Fairy Princess, Born Asleep.*

On the stone perched a cross-legged fairy, holding a bouquet of daisies with a small chip off of her left wing and a crack that ran along the seam of the right hand. There were no flowers, fake or otherwise, adorning it. Charity's family either moved on, or like Duncan's, the site was too painful to visit.

Two plastic markers flanked Beatrice and Amelia's fresh plot of sod, marked with heaps of flowers. Headstones took longer to install than the burial process. There was also a teddy bear. It looked similar to the one on the Walton grave, but fresher.

Did Evan leave the teddy bear for Millie? She scribbled on her pad *similar teddy bears on both graves.* Kat pulled out her phone to snap a photo, but thought better of it and tucked it back in her purse. She wouldn't want anyone taking a photograph of Duncan's grave even all these years later.

She was careful not to stand on top of the fresh sod, knowing that beneath was the coffin of Beatrice still holding Amelia for the beginning of their eternity. Footsteps crunching leaves fell behind her and she froze.

"Hello?" Evan asked. The edge in his voice rooted her in place as she turned. His eyes were still stunning blue and red-rimmed, his blond hair had a widow's peak and he was balding a little in the back. She hadn't noticed his thinning hair yesterday. He wore jeans and a button-down white collared shirt. He hadn't brought flowers, but there were still plenty on the site.

She turned fully toward him. His eyes grew wider. "Wait, you're that lady who ran out yesterday after I caught you lying about being Bea's co-worker. What are you doing here?" His voice lowered to a growl. "Why can't you all leave me alone?"

"I'm sorry. My mother and brother are buried here, and I was visiting them. This was my last stop on the way out. I went to another site and visited another family..." She let the reality of what she said settle between them. Kat looked around. It was broad daylight, but they were alone, and she took a small step back.

"Fine. What do you want?" he asked.

"The truth."

TWENTY-THREE

HIS SHOULDERS SUNK as his voice leaned into its grief. "If you're the cops or media, it doesn't matter anymore." He gestured at the plastic markers bearing their names. "Amelia was the light of both Bea and my life." His voice cracked on their names.

She blurted. "What about Millie? Was she also the light of your life?"

His eyes narrowed as he shot a glare at her. "That's a nasty thing to say."

Kat stepped back again, creating more space between them. *Too far*, she thought. *Can I run fast enough?* Her ballet flats weren't a good choice, not against his sneakers. She cast a glance at the funeral home. Without realizing it, Kat had wandered several acres away in her curiosity-driven adventure. *Will anyone hear me scream?* A cool panic inched up her neck.

He leaned toward her, but didn't move his feet to close the gap between them. "How do you know about

Millie? You're a cop, right?" His tone wasn't hostile, but curious. A vein twitched at the side of his neck.

"No, I'm not a police officer." *Just the wife of one.* "I'm nobody."

"I don't believe that. No one has mentioned Millie. But I suppose they will soon enough. Are you a journalist? Private investigator? Did Mariah and Peter hire you? Viola? If I ask, and you're a cop, you have to tell me. I'm pretty sure that's a rule somewhere," Evan babbled on. He took a step toward her and puffed up his chest like a prey animal making himself look larger to camouflage himself as a predator.

Kat answered with calmness in her voice. "Viola is Beatrice's mother and Mariah and Peter are the parents of Mya, right? Why would they hire anyone?"

"Screw it. I have nothing to hide. Whoever you are, and whoever hired you, can know the truth. Nobody will listen to me, maybe you'll have better luck," Evan said. "I don't want to talk about it here. Let's go someplace more private."

Kat's stomach clenched. "Like where?"

"How about my car?"

"No, I'm not comfortable with that." Millie's grave was closer to safety. "How about Mya Walton's gravesite?"

His chin scrunched, but he nodded. "Okay."

Evan led the way to his first daughter's grave. Kat scanned the cemetery for any witnesses within earshot and kept him in front of her. When his steps slowed to a near-glacial pace, so did hers. As they wandered through the stones, the sides of her ballet flats wetted her feet with dew.

Kat scanned the parking lot and cemetery, and they were still the only ones outside. Perhaps Mr. Parson could see her from his windowed office. Biting the inside of her lip, she tucked her hand in her pocket and let her fingers run along the edge of the worn fabric square. The mace her husband gave her six birthdays ago sat idly in her nightstand drawer at home. She wished for it now.

Nearing Mya's gravesite, Evan's shoulders rounded as he shoved his hands in his front pockets. "I'm sorry that I've been hostile. I know what it looks like." He kept talking as they walked.

His shoulders hunched. "Viola is Bea's mother. If she didn't hire you, then you met her yesterday. She's a widow, her life was Bea. I never made it a secret with them about what happened to Millie. Initially, Viola hated me, but I thought she'd come around. Now, she blames me for everything. She's right, I guess. Because how could it happen twice? None of this would have happened if not for me." Then his shoulders tensed again and he stood straighter. He pulled his hands out of his pockets and balled them in tight fists.

Kat's chest squeezed, listening to the hurt in his voice. He didn't turn to her as they neared his first daughter's grave.

"I see," she said. Someone who was not an impostor may know what to say, but words failed her. As they walked, she sat with her thoughts:

I'm not a real investigator, journalist, or police officer.

But I'm an excellent liar.

His grief seems real, but so does his anger.

Evan broke the silence. "Bea and I had our problems, but we were working through them. Viola tried to get her to move on, but after Amelia came along, we were trying to make it work. Viola fell in love with Amelia, and I grew on her. Well, I thought I grew on her. Bea didn't drink, and she never did drugs. Do you know what kind of drug she had in her system?" he asked, but didn't wait for a response. "Morphine."

Kat said nothing.

He sighed. "She had back surgery a while back. Maybe she had some pain medications left over from that. But she wasn't suicidal, and she'd never hurt Amelia. She didn't do this. They are blaming postpartum depression. But I would have noticed, right? She didn't do this," he repeated.

She stood beside him, but still outside of arm's reach as they stood before the Walton grave with the Jesus peering down at all the names and the teddy bear sitting on the stone. It was Millie's teddy bear from her father, Kat knew that now.

"Then who did?" Kat asked. She kept her face turned toward the stones.

"That's the real question, isn't it? I hired a private investigator when the cops wouldn't do their jobs and the media turned a blind eye. I know who sold her the drugs that killed her, and I reported it to the police. They wouldn't do anything. Said 'not enough evidence,' and 'we'll look into it,' and brushed me off. Nothing ever happened. They decided Mya and her children weren't worth the effort. My child wasn't worth the effort to justify her murder." He punched his fist in the air and looked at Kat. His nostrils flared. "Mya fell on hard times after her family lost everything. I didn't realize how hard of times. I met up with TJ—the person who sold her drugs—pretended I wanted some. She wasn't what I expected."

Kat said, "She?"

"Yeah, and she looked nothing like what I thought a drug dealer would. Blonde, pretty, and above any level of suspicion. That's probably why the cops didn't bother. TJ was actually nice," Evan said. His chin trembled, but his tone was stone. But not the cracked heartbreak reserved for Amelia. Time had healed his grief and Mya and Millie were old scabs. When picked, they revealed new skin beneath. "I was a grieving, absent father who was trying to seek justice for a daughter I barely knew."

"So, Mya didn't have a drug problem until you left?"

"No, never touched the stuff, but she had a lot of money and wasn't afraid to flaunt and spend it."

"What happened between you and Mya?"

He looked away from the stone. "We were young. Too young, I was going to college, and I had a long-time girlfriend. I came home for summer and met Mya. She got pregnant and told me after I was already gone. Mya wanted us to get married and move in together. God, we were kids. I was only nineteen, she was twenty-one. Christ, I wasn't even old enough to drink. And I was going to be a father? She was already a mother to

Maureen. I didn't know it because she lived with Mya's parents. She never told me. I think she set me up to build an instant family. I wasn't ready." He shook his head.

"So, were you a father? A father to Millie?" Kat asked.

His brow furrowed and he looked away from her. "No. After I got back to campus, I got back with my girlfriend. I told Mya we were done. I paid child support. She was so angry. I never missed a child support payment, not one. Look it up. I had little, but I got a job and paid for my responsibilities. Before her family went bankrupt and she was able to pay for everything, she made me pay child support. I was angry about it and told people as much. Which is what landed me as a suspect for the first time. She insisted I pay for diapers." He sighed. "In hindsight, she was right."

Kat stood in silence. He wasn't a loving father to Millie, but trying to pay for her care was something. And admitting his failures as a father was growth.

Evan continued, "Mya was heartbroken and immediately met that Jesse guy. My girlfriend and I didn't work out, and I went to get back together with her, because I wanted to give being a family a chance, but by then she was already over me. I didn't know she was on drugs, or I would have taken Millie."

"Would you have, though?"

At Kat's brazen question, he turned to her.

His eyes flared in anger, then quickly cooled to the tame, sad blue sea again. "You're right, probably not. But I would have called child protective services or something. I would have done something."

"Was Jesse still around when she was pregnant with his baby?" Kat asked.

"I don't know..." Evan said, considering Kat's question. "After her parents went bankrupt, she went MIA. She was heartbroken and pregnant and alone. I paid my child support, but now I see that it only funded her drug habit. It was an awful mess."

They were close enough to the funeral home now, and if she needed to run, she had a better chance.

"Do you think Mya killed her children?" Kat asked.

"Mya was a lot of things. She had problems and issues, but she loved her girls. Hell, she was running through men trying to find a father for them." He blew out a sigh. "I'm sorry, that wasn't kind. Anyway, she was either high on something awful, or someone else did it. Of course, now that this has happened all over again, I can't help but think someone is after me, punishing me for something. I've not been an angel, but why hurt innocent children?" He rubbed his hands over his forehead.

"Drugs make you do a lot of things. The conditions they found the children in weren't good," Kat said.

He bristled and looked away. "It was a long time ago. I was a different man. A less responsible father. I waited twenty years to try again. I thought that was enough." He kicked an imaginary stone with his foot. "This time I was better. I didn't know the extent of it until they took me in for questioning and showed me the pictures. I never missed a child support payment."

"Yeah, you said that. And child support is expensive, isn't it?" Kat asked.

"Yes, it was. Wait, are you saying that was my motive?" Evan asked and took a step closer to her.

She stepped toward him. *I will not let him intimidate me.* She didn't answer his question, but posed one of her own. "You know the sole link between these two cases, right?" Kat asked.

"Me."

"Exactly," Kat said flatly. Her jaw clenched.

"Listen. Tell whoever you're working for the truth. I didn't do it. Bea and I, we had our troubles like any other couple, and maybe we wouldn't have made it for the long haul, but neither of us would have hurt Amelia." His nostrils flared as his voice grew louder.

Kat took a step back, her hand overplayed. He grabbed her by the arms and the whites of his eyes gleamed.

"Let me go!" Kat yelled.

He squeezed harder. "Please, who did this to my babies? Who killed my Amelia? Please tell whoever you're working for the truth. I didn't do this. Find out who did. Stop wasting time on me! Find who did this to my baby." Evan was yelling now, and a man with salt-and-pepper hair cast a glance at them from across the cemetery. The stranger started a slow jog in their direction.

His grip loosened, and she yanked her arm back and the blood rushed back to her tingling fingers. She turned and ran toward the safety of the parking lot.

Her feet hit the ground at the same cadence that the blood pounded in her ears. If he was behind her, she wouldn't know, and she didn't dare crane her neck to look over her shoulder. Her breath billowed out in tiny cloud puffs, and her chest ached for more air as her nose paid no mind to the chaos and dripped away. She opened her mouth wider, but no more air would come.

Get to the car. A stitch in her side pinched. Without missing a beat, she fished her car clicker out of her purse and the sedan beeped in response. If Evan saw which car she ran toward, she didn't care. Sliding inside, Kat tucked her feet in and slammed the door hard, securing her safely inside. Her fingers fumbled to lock the doors and after the satisfying click of the lock she breathed.

She bobbed her head over the steering wheel to see where he had gone. Craning her head back and forth, her only company in the cemetery were the sentries of stones standing watch over their charges. The man who spotted Evan squeezing her arms was no longer in view. The only other cars in the lot were the hearse with purple drapes and another older but well-cared-for Cadillac.

"Where did he go?" she whispered. Her hands shook as the adrenaline seeped out of her body, and her head grew dizzy. "What am I doing?" she asked the air. Kat put her head on the steering wheel and breathed deep. Then a knock on her window startled her.

She jolted and looked at the passenger side window. Mr. Parson was tapping on the glass.

"Mrs. Eland?"

Kat lowered the window and plastered a pleasant smile on her face. "Hi, yes. And it's Kat, please."

"Are you okay? I saw you running from a man." His eyebrows drew together with concern.

"Thanks, I'm okay. I appreciate you checking on me." Kat started the car and gave Mr. Parson a final, reassured smile.

He tapped on her door as she put the car in reverse. "Okay, you take care. I hope to see you again, but not too soon. I mean... You know what I mean."

"I do, and same," Kat said, and waved at him as he removed his hands from the window. She pulled out of the driveway and headed home to read the letter.

TWENTY-FOUR

KAT PULLED into the driveway with a few hours to spare before Greg returned. What would her father have to say? She went to Greg's office and rummaged in his desk drawer for a letter opener. Sliding the silver blade under the linen fold of the envelope it resisted, and then finally gave and revealed its contents.

Settling into the oversized chair she laid the sliced envelope on the desk and stared at it. The paper had a sheen to it, and she thought, *this paper probably isn't recyclable*. Her mind didn't want to read what was inside, but her curiosity could stand it no longer.

After all this time, what does he want?

She took the folded stationery from the envelope and laid it flat on the desk. His rough cursive strokes were somehow both professional and familiar. She knew herself as Kat, her husband called her Katie, and her father called her Katherine. A name she no longer recognized as herself at all. Three separate people—Katherine, Kat, and Katie—stood in the wreckage of her fractured identity.

August 23, 2001

She sucked her breath in at the date. He wrote her this message shortly after she climbed into Greg's car and ran away. When this was written, Mya, Maureen, Millie, and Mandy still walked among them, but not for much longer.

> *Dearest Katherine,*
> *If you get this letter before I pass, please, I'd like to see you again. There are things that need to be said and apologized for.*

She paused, her stomach twisting into a hard knot. *An apology to me, or from me, Father?* She read on.

> *My greatest wish is to see you at least once more. Forgive those things we never forgave, and move on in peace. You are all I have left of my dear Evelyn, and our Duncan. You're the perfect blend of them. The determination of your mother and the kindness of your brother.*

The familiar pang of anger pricked her heart. *You never knew me to be determined or kind. To you, I was an inconvenience, and the last and least favorite person left of your family. Just someone who reminded you of others you loved,* she thought, then read on.

> I've given you your space as you wished, but I want nothing more than to see you once again. Though I will respect your wishes and will never try to find you. In your last letter to me, you said you would leave this life if I were to enter it again. That is something I could not bear. I would rather have you a stranger to me, and still existing under the same set of stars.

A grieving young adult had written the letter he'd received when she was eighteen, fumbling into a cruel world she didn't understand. Today, she was a full-grown woman. Did she still mean the things she'd said? She didn't know.

> I should have shown you what you meant to me and been a better father. I have done deceitful things, unethical things, but not all the things you've blamed me for. If you get this after I've passed, then the things

I've wanted to share and tell you... they'll be here. At the house. You know where they are.

She gasped. *Dad knew about mine and Duncan's hidey hole? Of course he did. This was his childhood home, too. He'd known her secrets from the beginning.* She read his last words.

I'm at peace with your decisions. But there are things you didn't know and I want you to. I would like one last embrace. Perhaps it would be our first and last hug. I know I wasn't the father you needed, and of all my life's regrets (and there are many) it is chief among them.
Love,
Father

P.S. I watch over your daughter. She is beautiful, and I promise I'll watch over her from afar for as long as I shall live.

Anger rose like a tide in her chest. *Stay away from Jillian,* she thought. She glanced at the date on the letter again. He wasn't talking about Jillian. *Not that daughter.* He was talking about the other baby. The one she'd birthed at eighteen and sent away. The one Greg, Jillian, and everyone in her new life knew nothing about. A hot shame rushed into her face as her hand shot to her pocket, where she rubbed her first daughter's blanket hard between her fingers. The nubbly piece of cloth dulling the ache.

Kat glanced around the room. There was no one to call to share this information and figure out the next right step. She was alone. The note was written many years ago. *Did he still feel the same? If he wanted to see me so badly, why didn't he respond to the letter I sent years later? Maybe he changed his mind about everything, but never retrieved this letter from Mr. Parson.*

One last hug, that wasn't a tall ask. She could visit him and not tell him about Greg or Jillian. Her daughter grew up without grandparents. Telling Jillian she kept a grandfather from her wasn't something she looked forward to. After his death, she'd share the information, and a sizable inheritance would cushion the blow. A windfall minus the grief.

Perhaps even then she could weave in a lottery lie and avoid bringing Caldwell back into her life. It was too late for Jillian to love a grandfather she didn't know, anyway. Kat would bear the weight of the grief for them all. But first, her heart ached to see him one last time. She didn't know that she wanted to before she'd laid eyes on his familiar handwriting in Mr. Parson's office. *After this is done, I'll see my father,* she vowed. What did he know of her first daughter? She rubbed the piece of cloth once more.

To see her once.

And know that she is okay.

She's a missing piece of me wandering in a world I don't know.

I'm not that unlike my father...

Her father knew how to bring her home. Through her child. The tethered connection between parent and child pulled her back into her father's orbit.

Kat ran her fingers over his words, touching the soft stationery and carefully folded the letter back into the envelope. She gathered the papers from her journalistic detective adventure and stacked them, along with her father's letter, in her shoebox in the closet of the third bedroom that had become an office. It wasn't the hidey hole, but it would have to do. Suddenly, her monotonous life was filling with tasks.

TWENTY-FIVE

KAT'S PHONE RANG, it was Camila. They texted and never called. Worried, she picked up.

"Hello?"

"Hey, I need to talk to you. I got a call from Peter and Mariah Walton about me doing a newspaper article on that case we were talking about at your house the other day. Do you know anything about this?"

Kat's stomach dropped. Giving Camila's name was a seismic error. Why didn't she think of any other name, or at least do a mashup of names she already knew? She gave them her number. Why would they call Camila? She glanced at her phone. Kat forgot to allow unknown numbers. So, they were going straight to voice mail and conducted some investigative work of their own. *Damn*, she thought.

"Let me explain. It's a misunderstanding, really. Can we talk in person?" She was met with silence. "Camila?" There were children with chaotic voices in the distance.

"Yeah, I'm trying to figure out how much time I have. Horace is at soccer. I have a few minutes."

"That's plenty of time. See you soon." And the line went dead.

Kat had crossed a boundary and owed Camila an apology. It wasn't fair to get her involved, especially because she explicitly told Kat to drop the case, and Kat promised she would.

Camila arrived a few minutes later, and Kat opened the door before she knocked. Her friend's arms were crossed, and her mouth was a straight line. Before Kat could eke out an apology, Camila said, "I know that look. You're still looking into that case. After you said you'd let it go." She tapped her foot and jutted her chin out.

Kat forced out a laugh. "Come in, come in."

Camila eyed her suspiciously. "Promise me you aren't looking into that case. It's dangerous. I don't want anything to happen to you. Or, frankly, to me either."

Kat opened the door wider, and Camila walked through. She didn't answer or promise that she wasn't looking into the case. They both knew the answer to the question. They sat on the couch and Camila glanced at her watch and kicked her foot nervously. Horace's soccer practice, which was several small children chasing one another up and down the field with a ball sometimes in between them, would be over soon.

"Why did they call me, Kat?"

Kat crossed her legs and rubbed her forehead. "Because... I said I was you."

"I gathered that. Why would you do that? Why *me*, of all people?" Camila's voice tensed.

"I... I didn't mean to. Mr. Walton, Peter, asked for my name when we were on the phone. You and I had just talked. Yours was the first one to pop into my head. It was a stupid mistake. I'm sorry." Kat's shoulders rounded as she made herself small.

"Why wouldn't your name pop into your own head, Kat?" Camila countered.

"I don't know. I'm sorry, I shouldn't have done that," Kat said. She turned away from Camila's penetrating glare.

"Or, you thought it wasn't safe, so you didn't give your name, but you gave mine." Camila crossed her arms tight.

"No, not that at all. They are older, mourning parents. I was trying to find out if there was more to the story. It was stupid." As Kat said the words aloud, she realized how quickly her ad hoc investigation had spun out of her control. "I'm so sorry."

Camila's shoulders softened. "Well, she seemed as confused as I was."

"What did she say?" Kat asked.

"Well, she called and before I knew who she was, she said, 'I've got more information for you. Something I think you should know that may help you solve my girls' murder.'"

Kat leaned forward in her chair. "She said that? What did you say?"

Camila glared at her friend.

"I'm sorry. I know you have every right to still be upset with me, but please tell me." The anticipation shot through Kat's toes. She wished she had her notebook handy.

Camila blew out a sigh and shrugged. "It was nothing, really. Well, nothing that will help your husband. Let's be clear here, Greg is the police officer, Kat. You are not. Anyway, I told her I didn't know what she was talking about. Then I asked who she was. She said 'Mariah Walton from our visit earlier,' and then a man's voice said 'and Peter.' I told them I didn't know what they were talking about, and they hung up. We were both confused." Camila shrugged. "Then I sat there for a little while and realized that this had something to do with you."

Kat tapped her finger on her chin.

Camila's eyes flashed, and she snapped her fingers in front of Kat's face. "What are you doing? I know that look."

She leaned forward and let the words spill out quickly. "You can't tell me you aren't a little curious. What she knows? What she wants to share?"

"I didn't say that, but I'm not as curious as I am scared that you're using my name. I have a family, Kat. A family I want to keep safe. I'm married to a computer programmer, not a police officer. You have... protections that I don't." Her hands absently tapped the gaudy necklace of birthstones.

Kat turned away from Camila. She hadn't thought about the privilege of protection she had at being the wife of a police officer. Her only thoughts were of affecting his investigation and getting caught. Poor Edward, who wore socks and Birkenstocks while he mowed, did not provide the same level of safety Kat enjoyed every day.

"You're right. I'm sorry, I'll straighten this out."

"Thank you. I don't have time today, but maybe tomorrow we can talk a little about it?" Camila asked.

"Ahhh, so you *are* curious? I thought so," Kat said, smiling. "It's not like I gave your name to a drug dealer or suspect. These people are parents like you and me. Still mourning their loss. They've been so sad for over twenty years..." She swallowed the lump that was forming at the thought of it, and added, "But I still owe you an apology."

"It's sad. I don't know what I'd do in the same spot." Camila looked at her watch. "Ugh, I've got to go. Horace is going to be the only kid out there waiting with Coach Simmons, who already doesn't like me because I brought the wrong snacks for the last game. I forgot the team was 'peanut free'. Why do kids need so many snacks for literally an hour of running around?" She stood, gathered her purse, and headed for the door. She looked over her shoulder before she left. "I might be a teensy bit curious."

Kat smiled as the door closed behind Camila. What started as a mistake may have gotten her an ally. Things were lining up perfectly.

TWENTY-SIX

KAT WENT UPSTAIRS for her notebook and settled back on the couch.

How do I contact them without suspicion?

My cover is blown.

Since when do I say 'my cover'?

Then it came to her. The simplicity of it shone bright, and she wondered why she hadn't thought of it before. Before talking herself out of it and putting the case out of her head, she dialed Peter.

"Hi, this is Camila O'Brien. I'm following up with you on the article from a couple of days ago. I see a missed a couple of calls from you," she said in a professional tone.

There was a muffled sound, followed by a click. "Yes, you are on speaker."

"Hi to you both. I wanted to update you. I went to Beatrice and Amelia's funeral and visited the cemetery.

They are in the same cemetery as your daughter and her girls."

Mariah's answer was tight. "I know they are. They shouldn't be. Evan should be nowhere near Mya and the girls, but you can't get a restraining order on a grave." The pain was palpable through the line, and Peter's soothing voice comforted his wife, though Kat couldn't make out what he said.

"I understand this is difficult," Kat pressed on. "At Mya's site, there's a teddy bear. Do you know who brought that?"

Peter answered, "No, it's been there for a while now. We didn't move it because we weren't sure if it was Maureen or Millie's old classmates or someone else. Sometimes there are trinkets, and the caretakers clean them up every few weeks."

"There was also a teddy bear at Amelia's site," Kat said. "It wasn't the same kind, and teddy bears themselves aren't unusual. But I saw one. And I ran into Evan Richards." The silence charged through the phone line.

"Be careful with him," Mariah warned. "He's dangerous." The alarm in her voice shocked Kat. She thought about how fast he'd gripped her arm and how intense the squeeze was, the tingling in her fingers as the blood was cut off in her arm.

Kat nodded into the phone and said, "Yes, I believe he is, too."

"Do you want to get coffee tomorrow?" Mariah asked. "To talk about the case?"

"Sure," Kat said.

Peter said, "I have a doctor's appointment. How about later this week?"

"It's okay," Mariah said. "I'll touch base with Camila, and maybe we can all meet again if there's anything we don't cover."

They made plans to meet and hung up. *There's something she doesn't want to talk about with him,* Kat thought. And she needed her alone to find out.

The next morning, after Greg left for work, Kat got ready for coffee with Mariah. She received a text.

> Camila: Want to meet for coffee?

> Kat: I have plans. Lunch?

> Camila: Sure, want to go out?

> Kat: Let's meet at my place. I'll bring food in.

> Camila: Sounds good.

Once Kat learned what Mariah wanted to share, she'd circle back to Camila. She couldn't do that in a restaurant.

Once dressed in jeans and a blouse, Kat went into the office to retrieve the notepad from the shoebox. The last picture of the girls alive slipped to the floor as she put the box away. She took that as a sign that she was doing the right thing for these girls and tucked their picture away and slipped the notebook in her purse. She would find out who killed them and somehow get Greg to figure it out, too. It was ridiculous that the police officers couldn't see what was clear to her in the photographs.

Kat pulled into the coffee shop a few minutes later, and Mariah was already outside the door waiting. Mariah's slight frame shifted nervously from one foot to the other. Kat approached her.

"I wasn't sure you'd come," Mariah said.

"Why?" Kat asked.

She shrugged almost imperceptibly. "I don't know. No one has listened to me about what happened to Mya and her girls before."

"I'm here to listen," Kat said.

Mariah's shoulders loosened, and Kat followed her inside the shop. As they waited in line to place their order, Mariah said, "Peter worries about me. Neither of us are over what happened, but he's been able to find joy in life again. But as a mother, I can't."

Kat nodded, and they placed their orders and she paid for them both. "That must be so hard," she said as they waited for their coffees.

"I've tried to trust the authorities for decades—Mya and the girls have been gone for more than twenty years —but that didn't work out well, did it? Now, there's another baby who's dead. And there he is, walking around freely while our children are gone."

The barista set their coffees on the pickup counter and called out, "Camila." Kat's gut pinched once more for using her friend's name as they picked them up and found a quiet corner in the back of the café. No one was there at ten on a random weekday morning.

"I understand," Kat said, pulling her notepad out of her purse and setting it on the table between them. "A mother's role is different. Something in us is wired to care deeper, more viscerally." She thought of Jillian, and also Jillian's older half-sister. The one she carried with her via a scrap of fabric every day.

"Are you a mother, Ms. O'Brien?" Her emphasis on O'Brien startled Kat. It was shocking to hear her being addressed by Camila's name.

"Camila, please. And, yes, I am." She crossed her legs and fished her notepad out of her purse.

"How many children do you have?"

Kat paused. She wasn't sure how much information to give up on herself. "I have a daughter," she finally answered. Her hand unwittingly went to where the shred of fabric in her pants was. She added an *s* under her breath, for *daughters*.

Mariah leaned back in her chair. "So, you understand. The bond, it's unbreakable and fierce. And if something happened to your daughter, would you leave it to the authorities? Trust the process?"

Kat thought about the briefcase full of pictures, the cold cases, and how few they resolved after the trail went cold. She took a sip of her coffee and then answered, "No, I guess I wouldn't."

Mariah sighed and blew on her coffee. "Exactly, and that's why I'll never give up. Ever. I visit them every week. Even after all this time. And I've seen *him* there."

Kat looked at her coffee. "Who?"

"Evan Richards." She lobbed it like an accusation.

Kat sighed. "As a father, he may want to visit his daughter's grave."

"Maybe, but he was never involved. And Mariah feared him. Sometimes he hurt her. That's why they broke up, you know," Mariah said.

Kat thought about what he said about getting back together with a girlfriend in college. But she remembered how he'd squeezed her arms and rooted her in place in an instant. He mentioned he was not a good man, nor a good father. Her daughter's account was plausible.

Mariah said, "He goes to her grave sometimes. I wait until he leaves. But one time I was there, and he was on his way back to his car and I saw someone else familiar. They were having an argument."

Kat leaned forward in her chair. "Who?"

"A woman who associated briefly with my daughter. A pretty blonde woman. TJ," Mariah said. "They were acquaintances while Mya was going through a rough time."

A rough time. Evan told Kat that TJ dealt her drugs, a fact she had seen in the file.

"I never told Peter I saw her there. He'd tell me not to go back to the graveyard, and I couldn't survive that. Their presence is there—my daughter, the girls—and I feel closer to them there. Anyway, they looked like they were arguing. Evan's face was red, and she was jabbing her finger in his face. I couldn't hear what they said from where I was, but it's something I thought you should know."

Kat scribbled on the notepad - *Evan and TJ associates?* "Do you know anything else about TJ?"

Mariah peeked at Kat's scribbles and seemed satisfied with her conclusion, too. "Not much. Everyone thinks I'm crazy for believing in my daughter. Yes, she had a drug problem, but it was a relatively recent one. Just after Mandy's father left. But she didn't do it. She couldn't have. She wouldn't have."

Kat met Mariah's eyes and said, "I don't think she did it either." And she meant it.

Mariah blinked away tears. "I've felt like I've been shouting in the wind for so long. No one listened." She took Kat's hands in hers, her small-boned fingers squeezing Kat so hard her wedding ring bit into her skin. "Thank you for being someone who would finally listen to me."

"Of course." Kat gently withdrew her hands and put both of them on her coffee cup. Finishing it quickly. "If you think of anything else, reach out."

"Thank you so much, Camila. I appreciate it. Evan had something to do with the murder of my babies, I know it, and I will not stop until someone holds him accountable."

"I understand," Kat said. "One more question, Mariah."

"Yes?"

"Were there any credible threats in the letters and visits from your husband's failed business?"

Mariah jerked her head back and thought. "No. After Mya and our girls died, everyone forgot about the business. The letters and visits stopped. Maybe they figured our justice was served."

Kat tapped her chin and thought better of scribbling anything in her notepad right then. "Thank you. Let's stay in touch."

Mariah took both of Kat's hands I hers again and squeezed. "Thank you so much, dear. It means everything that someone somewhere cares about my girls."

Kat's stomach sank with guilt, but she plastered a sympathetic smile on her face. "Of course."

TWENTY-SEVEN

KAT LEFT the coffee shop with two distinct but opposing questions. What happened to the death threats the Waltons had received? And why did Evan leave out his ongoing contact with TJ? To get close to Evan again would be tricky. He bristled at her presence.

For her scheduled lunch date, she stopped at her favorite café and got two strawberry chicken salads. While she waited, she received a text.

> Camila: I'm at your place.

> Kat: Okay, let yourself in. I'll be there soon. Getting our salads.

Most of the neighborhood women had keys to each other's homes. Except Janet.

> Camila: Yum. I'll get some drinks ready. See you in a few.

Camila was early. *She must be really curious*, Kat thought. When she arrived at the house, Camila had set out two tall glasses of ice water, forks, and napkins on the table. Kat fished out the takeout containers from the bag and handed them to Camila.

Kat said, "Let me get the information I've got." She went to the office and grabbed the documents, and placed her notepad on top. She came down the stairs and found Camila had plated the salads. Kat would have eaten them out of their takeout containers.

As Kat sat down, Camila took a small bite. "Mmm, I was starving."

Kat's excitement and the coffee she'd had suppressed her appetite. She set the stack of papers in the center of the table.

Camila eyed the papers, but didn't pick them up. She slid her chair closer and leaned forward. Kat pretended not to notice and took a sip of her water. If she teased out Camila's curiosity, perhaps she'd find an ally in her quest for justice of the Three M Girls. She took a bite of her salad.

"The thriller group seemed interested in this case. I wonder if we should chat together. I mean, except Janet."

Camila shrugged. "Ramona had another chemo-therapy session a couple of days ago."

Kat wrapped her energy so tightly with the tragedy of strangers, she'd forgotten to check on Ramona. "I need to call her," Kat said. "What about Krista and Ann?"

"Ann is out of town until tomorrow. Maybe when she's back. Krista, meh, she's always so busy I'm surprised we even get her for thriller night. We must be a reoccurring appointment in that chaotic calendar of hers," Camila said. Her eyes lingered on the papers at the center of the table. Kat continued to ignore it.

"Well, I'm not inviting just Janet. She acted like I needed to ask my husband's permission," Kat scoffed.

"Look, I'm not her biggest fan either, but in fairness, you are going through your husband's work files."

Kat couldn't meet Camila's eyes and her chest tightened. *I'm out of my depth, but I've got something here.* She changed the subject. "Where was Ann going again? I can't remember."

"An amusement park for a few days. She took her kids out of school for that." Camila rolled her eyes.

"Oy vey. Jilly's grades would've never survived it."

Camila took another bite of her salad. She finished chewing and said, "That's quite a stack of paperwork."

"It is. There's a lot of information. I think I've made some progress too. Do you want to have a look?"

"You want to see if I agree? Like a different conclusion than what the police officers came up with?" Camila asked.

"Exactly."

She wet her lips and touched the corner of the paper with her French-manicured finger. "There's no harm in looking at what you have, right?"

"Right," Kat said. That's how she'd started, too. What's the harm? Then she was knee-deep in a web of lies she was trying to untangle and a growing affection toward the dead girls.

Camila set her salad aside and reached for the papers. "May I?"

Kat nodded and masked her excitement with another bite. "I'll get us some more water," she said and brought both of the glasses to the counter.

Kat turned to see Camila reading a letter. One she hadn't meant to include among the stack. Kat forgot her father's letter was among the items. Her stomach dropped.

"What's this?" Camila asked as she read the final part of the letter. "Who's Caldwell Grant?"

Kat unfroze herself from the shock and snatched away the envelope harder than she needed, and Camila flinched.

Camila held her fingers up and examined them. "You almost gave me a paper cut."

"Sorry," Kat said. A flush of heat ran through her entire body.

Camila put her hands in her lap. "You didn't answer my question. Who's Caldwell Grant, and how is he related to the case."

"It isn't related to the case. Caldwell Grant is my father," she said, the truth spilling out before she could stop it. *What have I done?*

"I didn't know your dad was alive." She eyed the thrift store urns on the mantel.

Kat's shoulders drew up like a marionette yanked by a child. "He is, but we're estranged. Let's keep this between us, please. I plan to tell Greg, I just haven't yet." Reaching across the table, she touched Camila's hand to convey the importance of what she asked.

Camila looked at Kat, clearly confused. She and Edward had no secrets, but all marriages weren't like Camila and Edward's.

"Of course," Camila said, and swallowed hard.

"Thank you." She blew out a sigh of relief and the knots in her shoulders unraveled. Kat tucked the envelope in her purse and pushed the other papers across the table at Camila.

Camila glanced at Kat before gingerly sifting through the papers. Her slender fingers hovered over the pictures of the dead children, as she picked the one up of Maureen in the bathtub and examined it.

"It's so sad, isn't it?" Camila asked Kat, changing the subject to dead children, safer ground for their friendship.

"It really is. But when you look at that picture, do you notice anything odd about it?"

Camila turned the picture around in her hands. "Before all this, I'd never seen a picture of a dead child before. Actually, I'd never seen a picture of a dead anyone before." She grimaced, but kept her eyes trained on the picture.

"After you get over the shock, pay attention to the details. I wonder if you'll see the same thing I noticed," Kat said.

Camila held the photo close, then farther and her eyes widened.

Kat prodded, "What do you see?"

"The bruising. The finger marks, they look... big."

"See, I thought so too. I went to Mya's parents' house and shook her mother's hand and it was just so small. Uncommonly small. Based on the pictures on the mantel, the two women were about the same size..."

"Those weren't her hands!" Camila exclaimed, completing Kat's sentence.

"Exactly, I don't think they were," Kat said. She handed the picture of Millie to Camila.

"Does bruising get bigger?" Camila asked.

"That's something I wondered about too. Here..." Kat said, handing her the picture of Amelia.

"The handprints on her neck are small," Camila said. "So maybe they were right about Beatrice, but wrong about Mya? Even though Mya seems like the more obvious one to do something like this? Or they found Amelia sooner after it happened?"

"I thought that too. But they each were found within a half an hour of death."

Camila's chin scrunched in understanding.

Kat said, "Mariah told me Evan argued with Mya's drug dealer, TJ, at the cemetery. Recently. And she's a woman. Maybe she killed his second family?"

Camila tapped her chin and looked up at the ceiling. "Maybe Beatrice suffered from postpartum depression and knew about the first crime. Did she?" She took another bite of salad and looked at Kat thoughtfully.

"Hmmm, I haven't considered the postpartum depression angle. But the Waltons met with Beatrice and her family, and they knew about the crime. Evan was questioned, so he likely knew what the suicide note said. This is a possibility... but it still doesn't answer who killed Mya's girls."

"It could have been Evan, and Beatrice knew and ended everything instead of being linked to a killer?" Camila's theory fit.

Kat stayed silent. But she considered Camila's theory with dark, unreasonable thoughts swirling as she filled the silence with her salad. *When I was in the thick of postpartum depression, if I found out Greg was a killer, would I want to continue on? Would I look at the baby we made together the same way?*

Camila asked, "Do you think Mya was there when it happened?"

Kat shook her thoughts loose and answered, "I don't think even high a mother would watch someone killing three of her kids and do nothing." She pushed the crime scene photo of Mya across the table. "This was only days after her children died. Look at her... Besides the track marks, there are no wounds showing any kind of struggle. Not a scratch, not a bruise."

Camila nodded grimly.

"There's something else, too," Kat said. She fanned the pictures of the crime scene photos in front of Camila. Their salads long forgotten.

"Hmm, what is it?"

"Well, Mya's daughters, Maureen, Millie, and Mandy, all have their eyes open. As a mother, you wouldn't look into the eyes of your children as you choked the life out of them. Or at a minimum, you would shut them once they were gone. But Amelia's eyes are closed."

"That could be a coincidence..." Camila said, her eyes big with curiosity.

"You're right, it certainly could be." Kat looked at the gruesome photos again. Maureen staring back. She was a tween, barely in the awkward bridge between childhood and adulthood.

"How are the police not able to see all of these things that you and I do?" Camila asked.

A surge of pride for the detectives ran through Kat. "The police have only so many resources. If the answer is simple and the public is no longer in danger... There are so many cases, and their priority is keeping the public safe. After their deaths," she tapped the photos, "the killing stopped."

"Until Amelia," Camila said quietly.

"Yes, until Amelia," Kat admitted. "Evan was forthright with me about a lot, but he protected TJ. He no longer trusts me, so I can't talk to him again. He doesn't think I'm a friendly, and our last interaction wasn't great."

"What do you mean by 'wasn't great'?" Camila asked.

"He's a suspect, and he is convinced I am working for the police or the press," Kat said. "If he was arguing with TJ... Well, dealers have bosses. Maybe he owed them money? I think Evan or TJ are tied up in all of these deaths. Mya may have killed herself, but what would you do if your children were murdered?"

Camila's face paled, and Kat nodded a silent agreement.

Kat said, "Evan is the only link between the two women. It's more than a coincidence. It has to be. He only mentioned TJ in passing. Did she threaten to kill his family? Is he a victim or a criminal? I don't know."

Camila waved her arms. "Whoa, whoa, whoa. It sounds to me like Evan and TJ are dangerous. How are you going to get this information to the authorities for them to do something with it?"

"Well, Evan knows me, so I can't approach him again..." Kat looked at Camila.

"What? Why are you looking at me like that? What would I even say to him?" Camila asked. "How would I even get close?"

Kat laid out her request. "Next to the grave marker for Beatrice and Amelia is a different girl. A stillborn infant. Her name was Charity, and it didn't have a last name on it. Perhaps, in the next few days, you can visit that stone?" Kat asked.

"Pretend I'm the grieving mother of a stillborn child?" Camila asked pointedly.

"When you say it that way, it sounds worse than what I'm asking you to do. I'm saying, visit a grave of one child for the sake of the other children who were killed."

"What if the real mother comes while I'm pretending I'm her?" Camila asked.

"It looks neglected. No one has visited it in a long time," Kat said. She let the silence rest between them as Camila considered it.

After a moment, Camila straightened her back. "You're asking a lot. I need to think about it."

"I know I am, but I'm asking for these girls. All six of them."

Camila dipped her chin to her chest in thought. "Let me get back to you. I've got to pick up Horace."

Kat hitched her hopes on Camila's curiosity. Her gut pinched at the omission of her last interaction with Evan. The light of day would ensure Camila's safety, she reasoned.

Except, I ran to my car in the light of day.

I'll watch her. And bring my mace.

She believed in Evan's innocence. But she'd been wrong about people before.

TWENTY-EIGHT

THE NEXT MORNING, Greg made her coffee, and they sat at the table.

Greg was in his uniform, and he looked more barrel-chested and boxy than normal.

Kat's eyes widened. "Are you wearing your bullet-proof vest?"

He puffed his chest out. "I am."

"I haven't seen you in that in a while. What do you have going on today?" Her voice hitched up in concern.

"We're closer to an arrest on a case we're working on. Maybe today, not sure. It's good to be prepared, just in case. I'm glad the uniform still fits..." Greg said as he rubbed his lower stomach. And it did, mostly.

Kat's stomach clenched into a fist. "Oh? What case?"

"We're looking at the one in the news, with the girl and the mother," Greg said. "There've been some developments."

"Interesting." She blew on her coffee and tried to appear as uninterested as possible.

"Mm-hmm, it certainly is," Greg said. The conversation ended as his attention returned to his phone.

"Stay safe, sweetie," Kat said, and rose to get ready. She patted his shoulder and took her cup of coffee toward the stairs.

There was a knock at the door and Chase walked in with his uniform on. They both still looked good in their blues. "Hi, Kat."

"Oh, you're both getting all police officery today. What is this? Halloween?" Kat teased.

"I mean... the waist is a little tighter, but it still fits, kinda," he said. He smoothed over the slightest pudge forming over his belt buckle. "Where's the big guy?"

She gestured with her thumb to the kitchen. "Finishing his cup of coffee."

As he strolled past, she caught the whiff of Irish Spring. He winked at her, and her stomach flipped against her desires. His arm rested innocuously on his service weapon and he craned his neck into the kitchen. "Are you ready to go, princess? We've got a big day."

Kat went upstairs, but stayed on the landing to listen.

"You ready to get this guy?" There was a husky growl to Chase's voice.

"Oh, yeah. Dumb move with the insurance. Today?" Greg asked.

"Don't know. Still waiting on the judge. But it doesn't hurt to be ready," Chase replied.

Kat came back down the stairs to see them off. Greg's chest puffed and there was a ruddiness in his cheeks. He glanced at Kat. "I may be home late. We'll see."

"I understand. I'll cancel our reservations," Kat said.

He hit his head with the palm of his hand. "Sorry about that, I completely forgot."

"It's okay. We'll reschedule, love. Please be careful. Both of you."

Chase said, "Yes, ma'am." He saluted her with his left hand.

Greg leaned in and kissed Kat on the lips. "I love you, Katie."

An electric pulse shot between them, and her stomach tingled with pleasure and surprise. Then worry. He never kissed her when they had company.

As they walked out the door, she put her fingers on her lips, still warm from his kiss. *He's scared.*

The detectives headed out to plan an arrest on a man who didn't kill Amelia. Of that, she was sure. Though, if they brought him in, he would probably never give up TJ or whoever was responsible, either.

She needed Camila's help now.

TWENTY-NINE

SHE WATCHED their car leave the drive and texted Camila.

> Kat: Can you come by?

> Camila: See you in ten.

Kat made a second pot of coffee and collected the paperwork from the shoebox. This time, careful to leave her father's letter behind. Mentally, she filed her father away until this was settled.

She pulled a cup from the washer that was embossed with a golden cat they didn't have. It was a Mother's Day gift from Jillian a decade ago. A play on her name and a subtle hint of her daughter's desire for a cat they never got. Steam billowed from Camila's coffee. Kat cooled it with the creamer she kept in the fridge just for her.

There was a knock at the front door, and it opened.

"I'm in the kitchen," Kat called.

Camila came into the kitchen. She wore jeans and a blouse with white Keds sneakers that stripped a decade from her age. "I see you already have the coffee ready." Sipping her coffee, she gathered the papers from the middle of the table and thumbed through them.

Kat crossed her legs and leaned back in her chair. "So," Kat said, "Do you think Evan did it?"

"I've been turning it over in my mind. I don't know that he's completely innocent... It happened to two of his children and two women he was involved with."

"Right, but?"

"The bruising on Amelia's neck is small," Camila admitted.

"They're similar, but not quite right," Kat said. "And I have some news."

Camila set the paperwork aside and looked at her. "What is it?"

"About Evan. I overheard Greg. There was insurance money. They're planning an arrest soon," Kat said.

Camila sipped her coffee. "How soon?"

"Today? Tomorrow? Not sure. Money changes things... Gives motive. They're waiting on the magistrate," Kat said.

"Fine."

Kat jerked her head back. "Fine, what?"

"I'll do it," Camila said quietly. "Just today, I'll stand at Charity's grave and wait. If he comes, he comes. If he doesn't, and he gets arrested, well, that's the end. After today, promise to drop it. Deal?" Camila held out her hand to shake.

Kat's face broke into a smile, and she shook her friend's hand. "Thank you so much." Her mind replayed running from him and dashing to the car for safety. The lie nibbled at her more.

"One condition," Camila said, looking at Kat.

"What's that?" Kat asked.

"I keep you on FaceTime in my purse. I don't want to forget, or mistake, anything," Camila said. "What do you want me to find out?"

Kat wetted her lips. "Does he mention TJ, insurance money, anything new? Maybe it's absolutely nothing, and Greg and Chase take him in, and that's the end. The police were convinced of his guilt before it began. Because it's always the husband." She finished her coffee.

"We need to finish this before school ends. I have to take Horace to soccer."

Kat rubbed her hands together and spoke quickly before Camila turned the idea over in her mind and backed off. "Okay, we can sit at the grave for thirty minutes. If he doesn't come, then we weren't meant to ask. If you go to the cemetery at ten, I'll park across the street. We should have a code word or something. Something that shows you need help."

Camila tightened her shoulders. "You said he wasn't dangerous. Why would we need a code word?"

"You're right, never mind. I guess I've watched too many cops shows," Kat said. She made a mental note to pack her mace. In her excitement, a memory came to her and Kat paused. "Camila, are you going to be okay doing this?"

She waved her hands like she was pushing away the grief. "Yes. That was a long time ago, but thank you for asking. You said Charity's death year was 2012, same as my stillborn angel. I'll take that as a sign I should help." Her voice grew soft, and she looked down.

"I'm so sorry."

Camila's stillborn shook the neighborhood. Everyone mourned, and it was the first time Kat had laid eyes on a tiny casket, and she had never wanted to see one again.

Camila finished her coffee and put the cat mug in the sink. "It's okay. I never want Hope to be forgotten, either. I'll go home and get ready and meet you there at ten."

Hope was her name. Kat had forgotten it and pressed it back into her mind to never forget it again. *Charity* and *Hope*—two of the three theological virtues. Only *Faith* was left, and perhaps Faith was Kat having the faith in herself that something wasn't right. She thought of the scrap of fabric in her pocket and related heartily with the loss of a daughter. Loss took many shapes and forms.

THIRTY

JUST BEFORE TEN, Kat parked across the street from the cemetery. She spotted Evan; he was already at Beatrice and Amelia's grave, knelt over the area where his family's gravestone would eventually be. Camila was not there, Kat texted.

Kat: *He's at the grave. The one to the right of the man crouched down. It has a fairy on it... that's Charity.*

Kat saw Camila's white SUV park in the lot, and the three dots of her texting back. Then she turned her head toward Kat and nodded. Camila opened the car door, and when she got out of the car, she was in a plain navy dress with a 1950s cut. She'd pulled her hair back in a low ponytail and wore a pearl necklace. She set her mouth in a straight line, FaceTimed Kat, and put the phone in her brown leather purse. The purse's short strap kept her phone close without suspicion. Camila said, "Can you hear me?"

Kat gave her a thumbs up through her front windshield.

Camila nodded. She went around to the passenger side and gathered a bouquet of Black-Eyed Susans. Kat remembered those were the flowers that had been splayed on Hope's tiny casket, and she looked away from her friend. The memory of Hope's procession still hurt in a place in her heart that she rarely visited.

Kat turned back toward her friend, who was nearly to the crouching man now. Camila stopped when she spotted the fairy tombstone. "I didn't know how hard this would be," she said into her purse. Her voice cracked. Taking a few steps forward, she stood in front of it. "Charity... I'm sorry sweet Hope. I'm so sorry." She laid the flowers down.

She stepped back and kept her face trained on the angel with a chipped wing.

The man stood and approached her, and Camila inched her foot forward and said, "I'm sorry for your loss."

He wiped his eyes. "Thank you, and I'm sorry for yours."

Camila sighed, and said, "I wish I could tell you it gets better, and that it doesn't hurt anymore with time. Some days are more bearable, but here I am so many years later and it still hurts."

The man nodded, and Camila took a step closer, facing the markers awaiting their stones. "Beatrice and Amelia... lovely names."

He smiled ruefully. "Unique names and they were

quite lovely, you're right. It's still so hard to use the past tense." He straightened his shoulders.

"I understand. Unfortunately, all too well. Time will help, but you'll never be the same."

"I know," Evan said, and he shoved his hands in his pockets and gazed at the sky. "There was no reason for this. None."

Camila took a step toward him. *Keep out of his reach*, Kat thought. *I should have warned her.*

"Do you mind if I ask what happened?" Camila asked in a small voice.

He cleared his throat and turned to her. "Tell me about yours first..."

Her hands fell loosely at her sides. "That is a hard question, isn't it?"

He took his hand out of his pocket and closed their distance with a small step, and touched her elbow. "You don't have to."

"It's okay. I asked it of you, it's the least I can do. I was a couple of weeks over nine months pregnant. When I tell you I was round as a beach ball, it's no exaggeration." She chuckled sadly.

"I'm sure you looked perfect," he mumbled, and shifted on his feet.

"Ha, I did not. But everything was so normal, almost a boring pregnancy. However, when it was time to have her, they diagnosed me with oligohydramnios. Isn't that a mouthful?"

"It is. What is it?" Evan clasped his hands together and lowered them as he continued to listen.

"Before my little girl, I hadn't heard of it either. It's having too little amniotic fluid. Everything was absolutely fine until it wasn't. The birth was traumatic, and they did everything to save her, but it was too late. She was born asleep, and she never took a breath." Camila's voice caught. This was her real birth story. Kat had never heard it before because she was too scared to ask. And it was awful.

In that moment, she saw Evan's shoulders relax, and his defenses tumble. Unimaginable loss tethered them and created an instant bond.

"I'm so sorry," Evan said.

"Thank you. Now, tell me about Beatrice and Amelia. If you can," Camila said.

Evan sat on the ground next to the fresh sod placed over his family. Camila sat beside him, with her knees tucked under her.

He cleared his throat full of phlegm. "Tragedy follows me. I'm cursed. I lost another child some time ago. And I tried to outrun it. You're right, though, it never goes away. I didn't think I'd ever try again, but then I met Beatrice." He pulled a couple of blades of grass from the ground and rolled them between his fingers.

Camila's hands fluttered to her mouth in mock surprise. "Oh my, I'm so sorry." Camila's lie was weak. Not like Kat. But Evan didn't notice and kept talking.

"Beatrice would never do this. She knew about Millie, my first daughter. Amelia was her life. Our life." He let the blades of grass he plucked sift through his fingers. "They'll come for me soon, but I don't care anymore."

Camila's back straightened, and her head swiveled, checking the cemetery as if to find someone watching them. Kat looked around, too. "Who is coming for you?"

"The police. It doesn't matter anymore," Evan said, and he stood and dusted off his jeans.

"Why would they be after you?"

"There was this woman at the funeral and here at my child's grave asking me questions and prying. Someone hired her or she's a police officer. Regardless, I got scared and put my hands on her, grabbed her arms. She ran, and I ran in the other direction. I don't want any trouble," Evan said. "I'm working on it, but I have a temper."

Camila's eyes glanced quickly over to the parked car and Kat shrank in her seat, away from her withering stare. She turned back to Evan. "I'm sorry to hear that. I'm not a police officer. But why would the police officers think you were responsible?"

"I'm an insurance agent, and I had insurance on my family, just like I do on myself. It isn't an uncommon practice," he said. "I never told the police, but in fairness, they never asked." His shoulders sank, he paused and then added quietly, "But I should have told them."

Camila smoothed out her dark blue dress and put her arm on his elbow. "Stay strong. I'm so sorry this happened to you. No one wants to meet under these conditions. But I'm glad I met you."

"You too. What was your name? I never caught it?"

"It's Kat. Kat Eland." Camila responded and looked across the street at where Kat's car was. A furious fire shot into Kat's cheeks and an immediate sweat drenched her.

"Well, Kat, it's good to meet you, and I hope to see you around," Evan said. "A life without them doesn't seem like it's a life worth living..."

Camila didn't respond to that, but walked back to her car.

After Camila got back to her car, she put the Face-Time up to her face. Her mouth wore a grimace. "Let's talk at your house," she said, and disconnected.

Kat started her car on her way back to their white picket paradise dotted with minivans and SUVs as she heard sirens in the background.

She pulled into her driveway, and Camila pulled in behind her. Kat walked to her door, and Camila closely followed and walked through the door without a word.

Once inside, she turned on Kat, fury sweeping across her face. Kat had never seen her that way before.

"You didn't tell me the whole truth. He said he put his hands on someone. That was you, wasn't it? You lied."

Kat shuffled on her heels. "I was right there the whole time, and you were in a public place. I had mace," she added weakly.

"Well, since he's so safe now, he has your name. Just like you gave mine out. I don't appreciate you roping me into this," Camila said. Her cheeks were flushed, and her hands were on her hips in tight balls.

"You're right, I'm so sorry." There was nothing more to say, and Camila was right. Despite Evan's frightening episode, she believed in his innocence. The dichotomy was impossible to reconcile.

Camila's shoulders relaxed at her apology. "For what it's worth, I'm with you. I don't think he did it. Sitting at their grave, I felt the weight of his grief. It's something that if you haven't lost a child, it's impossible to describe. We sense each other."

Kat went to the kitchen to get water, and Camila followed. All mostly forgiven. "So, if he didn't do it, then who?" She poured two glasses and handed one to her friend.

She took it and sipped. "He can't go to jail for killing Beatrice and Amelia. I looked into his eyes. He didn't do this. There was genuine pain there, so much hurt. He is broken."

Kat tapped her lip. "The insurance money gives motive. I'm sure his DNA was all over the house and Viola will probably testify that they fought, and he confessed to a temper with you."

"So, what do we do?" Camila asked.

"We've done what we can. When Greg comes home tonight, I'm going to tell him I ran into Evan at the cemetery. You gave Evan my name, so that'll check out."

"I'm sorry I did that. I was angry," Camila said. "It was a childish and dumb thing to do."

"It's okay, it works, actually. Because if he asks Evan about it, he met me there," Kat said.

"Right, but you were there for Charity..."

"Hmm, that's right. But I'll tell Greg I was there to finish out some of my father's affairs..." Kat's voice trailed off.

"About your father..."

Kat quickly changed the subject. "If they arrest him today, there isn't much I can do. But when Greg comes home, I'll say I ran into him."

"And tell him what? What would change the course of his investigation? Why would he believe you?" Camila asked, her eyes watery. "They're going to arrest him for a crime he didn't commit."

Kat's shoulders sank. "I don't know that we have anything, aside from a mother's intuition that he's innocent. Or at least not fully guilty. Maybe I can hint to Greg to re-look at the photos."

Camila shook her head. "No, because you weren't supposed to see the photos in that case."

"I'll mention the photographs I saw. The ones he knows about, and mention the large bruises. Say it bothered me. Maybe that will spark a comparison..." Kat didn't think he'd listen to anything she said. "And TJ is a woman. Maybe her hands were small enough to match the bruising on Amelia's neck? I'm still unsure of their connection."

Camila opened her mouth to answer, but Kat's cell phone rang. The screen said *Chase*. He never called her directly. She put the phone on speaker. "Hello?"

THIRTY-ONE

"KAT," Chase's voice was desperate as sirens in the background whined. "There's been an incident. I'm on my way to your house. I'll escort you to the hospital. It'll be faster than if you drove yourself. Greg has been shot."

Chase was still talking, but she didn't hear him anymore. The phone slipped from her hand and landed face down, clanking on the wood floor. Camila turned it over and held the screen to her ear. "This is Camila. I'll stay with her until you arrive."

Kat's hands were slick with cool sweat as she wrapped them around her waist, hugging herself. Feeling faint, she squeezed her eyes shut and let Camila guide her by the elbow to the couch. Her stomach twisted in knots, and she wanted to throw up.

Camila said, "You look pale. Are you going to be okay?"

"Yes, I'm fine. Dizzy from shock. Do you think he'll live?" Kat asked Camila, staring straight ahead. She thought of all the things she never told him. In twenty-plus years, he barely knew her.

"I do," Camila said, patting her arm. "I'm sure of it." Her voice cracked when she told the lie.

Less than five minutes later, Chase was on her doorstep and walked through the door. Kat stood and nearly collapsed into his arms. He wore his black bullet-proof vest on the outside, his shirt was missing. His vest felt wet; so much sweat. *If sweat got through, bullets did too*, she thought. He hugged her and whispered, "It's going to be okay."

She pulled back from Chase and looked down at her floral blouse. Blood. He was covered in it.

"Oh my God, what happened?" Her mind latched onto anything she could control. "Will this stain?" she asked staring at her blood-splotched top.

Chase answered her real question. "We went to arrest a suspect at the cemetery today, the one who killed his wife and daughter. He shot at us. A bullet nicked Greg's femoral artery," Chase said and shook his head. "We should go. If we hurry, we may get a moment before he goes into surgery."

The color drained from Camila's face, and she stood. "I should go."

Kat held Camila by the arm and said, "Can you call Jillian and tell her to call me? I want her to hear it from me first, and not on the news."

She nodded. "Of course. Take care, and let me know how he is, okay?"

Kat followed Chase to his car. He flipped switches

and a button, and the lights and sirens blared and he drove impossibly fast by the 'drive like your kids live' here signs.

Chase said, "This was supposed to be an easy arrest." He banged on the steering wheel. Kat flinched, and he looked at her. "I'm sorry. I'm frustrated."

Anger built in the back of her throat. "An easy arrest for someone you think is a killer?"

His jawline twitched. "That isn't fair, Kat. Domestics rarely turn into a suicide-by-cop situation. There were no indicators. I don't even know where he got the gun. There was no gun registered to him. I neutralized the threat."

"We were almost there," Kat whispered and looked at her shirt. Tracing the splotches of blood shaped like Chase's bulletproof vest.

Chase turned in his seat. "What was that?" His knuckles were white on the steering wheel.

"Nothing," Kat mumbled. "I meant, are we almost there?"

"Oh, yeah, we're close. Another five minutes. We'll go in through the back entrance and they'll take us right to him. I've already radioed it in," Chase said.

"What does neutralize the threat mean?" Kat asked.

He didn't meet her eye, but answered. "It means exactly what you think it does." His Adam's apple bobbed. They pulled around back where the paramedics brought ambulances and the staff snuck away for smoke and lunch breaks.

A buxom blonde nurse eyed Chase from the doorway. "Officer Weber," she said and bumped out her hip and smiled.

"Hi, Lydia. Do you know what room Greg Eland is in?" he asked.

Her face fell. "Oh, I'm sorry. Greg's here? Let me check. I just came in for my shift."

Kat came out from behind Chase and looked at the nurse. Chase said, "This is Kat, his wife."

Lydia's eyes slid to Kat's shirt and back at Chase. Her eyes grew wide. "Mrs. Eland," she nodded at her, "let me go check and get right back to you both."

Lydia hurried away, and they followed her into the building through the large automatic sliding doors. As soon as they crossed the threshold of the hospital, the bitter smell of antiseptics and hospital-grade cleansers accosted her senses. Kat's exposure to hospitals, apart from Jillian's birth, was always traumatic. She wanted to turn around and walk out.

Kat rolled her eyes. "You really have *friends* everywhere, don't you?"

He shrugged and pushed forward toward the front desk.

Lydia met them before they got to the reception area. She held a flip chart. "I'll take you to him. He's in the ICU."

"What's his condition?" Chase asked flatly.

She opened the chart and read through it as she walked. "He's serious, but we're stabilizing him. He lost a lot of blood. The field dressing is holding, but he's going in for surgery to make the repairs. He won't have a lot of time to talk to you. Maybe fifteen minutes before we need to prep him."

Chase put his hand on the small of Kat's back as he nudged her toward Greg's room. She tried not to meet the eyes of the patients languishing in beds plugged into IVs, and the doctors and nurses clad in different-colored scrubs racing around the building like mice in a maze. Her vision tunneled, focusing on his room.

She peered inside and her breath caught. The bed swallowed him, and his red beard was more prominent against the paleness of his face and the white sheets. Kat had an image of fragility flow through her mind, and what he'd look like when he was old. It wasn't attractive.

She went to his side without the injury and hugged his arm, careful she didn't break him. He was clammy to her touch, but there were no beeps or alarms. "I love you, honey."

He smiled at her. "I love you, too." Greg turned to Chase and extended his fist for a bump. "Thank you for what you did, brother."

Chase demurred. "It was nothing. You would have done the same for me. Just a little pressure until the paramedics came to do the rest..."

Greg laughed, and it ended with a hoarse cough. "Is that what he told you, Katie?"

She crossed her arms and rubbed her elbows comforting herself. "He didn't really say anything yet. We were focused on getting to you," Kat said. The beeps of the heart monitor were steady, and she focused on them.

"He stripped his utility shirt off and wrapped it hard around my leg. Which saved my life." He pointed at Chase. "Because of him, I'm still here."

Chase looked away. "All a part of our training." He turned back to Greg. "You're tough. You never lost consciousness. Maybe a little green in the gills. There will be a lot of interviews, and I guess I'll be getting a paid vacation." He chuckled dryly.

Greg smiled wanly and pointed at his leg. "Looks like we both will be. Desk duty is my favorite." He rolled his eyes.

Their gallows humor upset Kat, but she listened and plastered a passable smile on her face. This was a grim reminder of the danger his job entailed, and how quickly a widow was created. His leg was wrapped tightly and raised on a few pillows. It still had the dark blue police officer shirt wrapped around it and the top of the knot featured *Weber* with *To protect and Serve* stitched beneath. Her phone rang. It was a FaceTime from Jillian. She answered and put her on the screen.

"Hi sweetie, I'm at the hospital with Dad now. He's okay, but he needs a minor surgery," Kat said.

Jillian's chin scrunched. Kat turned the camera to Greg. "Dad, oh my God, are you okay?" Her brow gathered in worry and her eyes were glassy and red-rimmed.

His face was paler through the phone camera. The fluorescent lights in the room were kind to no one. Kat knew why Jillian was worried. She was worried too.

"You should see the other guy," he joked, but the look on Jillian's face stopped him. "I'll be on my feet in a couple of weeks. It's not a big deal, Firecracker."

Jillian rolled her eyes. "Of course it's a big deal, Dad. Someone shot you."

"Mom, I'm booking my train to get home tomorrow, okay?"

"Yes, that'll be perfect..."

Greg interrupted, "Isn't it finals?"

"It doesn't matter," Jillian said.

"Of course it matters. You stay and get your school done. Really, I'm fine," Greg said and smiled wanly.

"Are you sure?" Jillian asked, though her shoulders relaxed.

"I'm sure. Firecracker, I'm a bit tired and they're taking me in soon to get me a couple of stitches, so I'm going to hang up and scoot Mom and Chase out of here, too. I need to rest up so I can get back home."

"Okay. I love you, Dad." She tucked a loose ginger strand of hair behind her ear.

"Love you too," he said and ended the call.

Lydia returned to the room and met eyes first with Chase, then Greg. "I'm sorry, but we really need to get Officer Eland prepped for surgery." She turned to Kat. "Would you like to sit in the waiting room? We aren't sure how long it'll be until they get in there and take a look."

The white coats swarmed in and jostled Kat out of the way as if she wasn't there at all. The medical staff focused on the IVs and tubes and syringes.

Greg looked over Lydia's shoulder at Chase. "Can you take Katie home? She doesn't need to stay around for this. Babe, I'll call you." Kat lost sight of him in the sea of white coats and scrubs. They wheeled him away in front of her, and the words caught in her throat. She didn't say I love you, and if he didn't survive the surgery...

THIRTY-TWO

THEY DRIFTED BACK through the neighborhood, with the lights and sirens off. The silence lay heavy between them. For years, she worried what the neighbors thought of a police car in the driveway. But many of the neighbors felt safer knowing there was an officer in the neighborhood, and her apprehension had melted into pride.

When they passed Krista's house the curtains moved, and moments later texts flooded her phone in a flurry of beeps. She fished the phone from her purse and glanced at the notifications on her lock screen. The neighborhood telephone tree had been activated. The thriller group flooded in simultaneously.

> Krista: Is Greg okay?

> Ann: How are you? Do you need some brownies to help you sleep?

> Camila: Call me if you need anything. I'm here.

Janet didn't text. Kat assumed they omitted her from call tree. She sighed and slipped the phone back into her purse. There'd be time enough to respond.

As bone-tired as Kat was, she didn't want to be alone. "Can you come in for a while?"

"Sure, of course. But I need to get cleaned up. You do too." He pointed to her shirt and looked at his vest.

Her shirt's red splotches faded to a mud brown. She touched the bits of brown. *Greg. This is Greg.* She remembered the last time blood covered her. It had been her brother's. And he died. Bile crept up her throat.

Not this time. Greg will live. That isn't the same. She shook her thought loose. "Jilly's shower has everything you'll need, there's a towel in her cupboard, and I'll give you some stuff to wear."

He looked out the window. Then turned to her and nodded. "Okay."

Kat went into her bedroom, and Chase waited at her door, with his eyes turned toward the hall. The clothes on the bed were clean, and she rummaged in them and fished out a plain white t-shirt that Greg wouldn't miss, and a pair of shorts that he probably would if Chase didn't return them. Kat hoped he could re-wear his underwear, and she didn't offer any of Greg's.

"Here," she said. "After you're out of the shower, I'll wash your uniform."

His Adam's apple bobbed as he took the clothing from her and went to Jillian's bathroom without a word.

She returned to her bathroom. As she pulled the shirt over her head, she smelled the faint metallic scent of blood and looked at her chest in the mirror. There were rust-colored splotches on her chest too. She tossed the clothes in a pile in the middle of the floor. She'd wash them immediately, and if there was even a speck of blood left on them, she would toss them. She cranked the water to as hot as her body could stand and climbed in. The near-boiling water pelted at her back. The hot steam was thick against her lungs and she covered her face and cried quietly.

Sometime later, Kat emerged from the shower and wiped the steam from the mirror with a hand towel. The blood spots were gone, she noticed, but she was red from the onslaught of scalding water. She went to her room, put on her favorite sweatpants and an oversized sweatshirt, and automatically transferred the small piece of fabric into her pocket. She peeked out of her room and saw the back of Chase's head sitting on the couch downstairs. Her stomach grumbled, a reminder that she'd forgotten to eat lunch and it was quickly approaching dinner.

She called down, "Hey, are you hungry?"

He craned his neck around and looked up at her. "I already ordered pizza. It'll be here in about fifteen minutes."

Kat nodded. "Alright, I'll be down in a minute." His clothes were in Jillian's bathroom in a neat pile. The vest was emptied of its body armor innards and stacked neatly with his uniform pants. He must have removed the Kevlar shields and cleaned and stowed them. She gathered his bloodied clothes and hers from the bathroom and tossed them in the wash with double the amount of soap and put it on hot, hoping there was enough hot water to wash away the blood after two showers.

Kat walked down the stairs and headed to the kitchen, passing him without a word. She returned with two full glasses of wine and the half-bottle in the crook of her arm. When she offered him a glass, Chase looked at it, and then back at Kat, his gaze unsteady. He smiled nervously, showing off his crooked incisor. His flaws were so few, making that crooked tooth a stunning betrayal and reminder of his humanness. He had enough money and insurance to fix it, yet hadn't. He took the glass from her outstretched hand.

She placed the bottle on the table and held her glass up. "Thank you for saving my husband."

He clanked his glass to hers. They both took sips of the velvety cabernet in silence.

Without the food, the wine traveled to her head quickly. She could either sleep or eat, and she wasn't sure which was her preference. There was a knock at the door, and Chase got up, returning with the pizza a few moments later. As he set the box on the coffee table, Kat's stomach grumbled at the doughy smell of it.

Chase looked at her and laughed. "Someone's hungry."

Heat blossomed on her cheeks and she reached for a slice. She took a big bite of the deep-dish pizza and burned the roof of her mouth.

"It was a long day," she said with a full mouth. Kat crossed her legs like a child and took a long sip of wine. "What happened out there?"

"It was supposed to be simple. Greg approached the suspect at the cemetery. I stayed behind," Chase said. He bit the end of his pizza and chewed it slowly. "They had a heated conversation. Then, the suspect reached into his pocket and pulled out a gun. It was so fast, I barely had time to react. He yelled something..." Chase shook his head and took another sip of his wine.

"What did he yell?" Kat asked leaning closer.

"Find TJ," he said and took a large sip of wine.

"Who's TJ? Did he hurt someone?" Kat asked. Her lie felt thin, and she swallowed the doughy pizza and washed it down with too much wine.

"TJ is a woman. I don't know what her link is to this case," Chase said.

She put her hand on Chase's knee. It felt too intimate, and she pulled it back like she had touched a hot oven. "There's nothing you could have done. I know it. Do you think he's guilty?"

"Honestly, yeah, I do. You don't kill yourself for no reason. Especially by cop." He set his barely-eaten pizza back in the pizza box and opted to pour more wine into both of their glasses instead.

Kat knew he was replaying the moments in his mind. His lips were looser than they should have been, so the full glass of wine on his empty stomach was working its magic.

"Hmm, do you think?" Kat asked.

"What do you mean?"

"I mean, it's clear he may have shot at a police officer. But perhaps a life without his family was no life at all? Does that make him guilty of killing Beatrice and Amelia? I'm not sure how I'd go on without Greg or Jilly..."

Chase shifted in his seat. "How do you remember their names? The victims. Beatrice and Amelia."

A tightness climbed in her chest and she tried to wave off his question. "Oh, I don't know. This case fascinated me. Ever since I accidentally ran into the mother at the funeral, I've been following it in the news," Kat said, hoping her white lie was believable.

He shrugged.

Kat asked, "Will they pull what happened from Greg's body cam?"

"Greg's wasn't working. Didn't find that out until it was too late. Thank goodness they had mine. They'll interview Greg, though. I guess it doesn't matter much anymore." He swirled the wine in his glass and inhaled the tannins.

Kat wondered if there would be evidence she and Camila had been at the cemetery in the moments before Evan's death. "What about the cemetery? Are there video cameras?"

"No, unfortunately, there isn't anything like that. Mr. Parson is pretty old school."

Kat exhaled a small sigh of relief. She wouldn't have to tell them she and Camila were operating as their own small investigative team. She felt silly now for even trying. Evan had brought a gun to the cemetery and hadn't been afraid to use it. Kat could've had Camila's blood on her hands, and for that, she'd never forgive herself.

Chase leaned back and looked at her. He said earnestly, "I wish it was me in the hospital."

Kat's eyes welled up. "Don't say that."

"He's got so much to live for. Jilly and you. What do I have? Whatever lady I find at a bar for the night?" He shook his head and looked away from her.

"Maybe Lydia from the hospital?" She felt a pinch of envy and a flash of anger.

He blushed.

"Or whatever woman you run into in my neighborhood..." Kat said.

Chase blushed. "Yeah, sorry about that."

"Please stop shitting in my backyard," Kat said. She surprised herself with her wine-emboldened bluntness.

He flinched and sat straighter. "What does it matter to you, anyway?" He took another sip of wine, but held her gaze.

"It just does. The whole neighborhood will turn on one another. We'll have the 'slept with Chase' camp, the 'haven't slept with Chase but wants to' camp, and the 'judgy woman' camp, and I'll get no peace. Besides, these women cannot keep their mouths shut." She withdrew from his gaze and took another sip of wine.

"Oh?" He smirked. "Did they say anything... interesting?"

Her mind flitted back to the things Ann and Krista had said—they were very interesting. Things she wanted to do, things she imagined when she slept with Greg. Chase leaned forward waiting for an answer.

"Pretty unimpressive, really," she finally replied.

His shoulders sank. Then he grabbed another piece of pizza and considered her for a moment before he nudged her with his foot. "Liar."

"I know, but you're getting arrogant." She rolled her eyes. Her phone buzzed, and she glanced at the screen.

> Krista: How's Greg?

It was Krista's second text. "Shoot, I forgot to text everyone back. If I don't, they'll be an entourage at my door soon." She typed out a response.

> Kat: He's in surgery. Will be there for a couple of days. But doing okay.

> Krista: Thank God.

Then she texted Ann.

> Kat: Thanks for the offer of brownies, but I'm okay. Greg's stable.

She scrolled up to Ramona's text. She felt bad that she'd forgotten to check on her after her last chemotherapy. Yet, when she needed a friend, Ramona was always there. Surely her husband being shot would allow her a pass at her oversight.

> Kat: Thank you so much. He's stable. In surgery. I meant to ask, how was your latest chemo? Do you need anything?

> Ramona: Oh it was the same old same old. Don't worry about me. I'll be keeping you in my thoughts for Greg.

Finally, she followed up with Camila.

> Kat: Thank you, let's meet tomorrow.

Tomorrow she'd connect with Camila. Tonight, she wanted to be with Chase. Kat went to set the phone aside and received another text.

> Camila: Coffee?

> Kat: Sure, sounds good.

She wondered if Camila told the book group that they'd been at the cemetery, too. It wasn't a secret exactly, but they needed to get their stories aligned. *Was it still a crime scene in the moments before a shooting?* A response beeped in.

> Krista: Do you want to reschedule our dinner tomorrow? We can.

She hit her head with her hand.
Chase looked at her with concern. "What is it?"

"I'm supposed to have company tomorrow. I'm hosting a birthday thing for me and Ann." She typed a response to Krista.

> Kat: Of course we'll still have it.

> Krista: Are you sure?

> Kat: Yes, please let everyone else know. It'll be good to focus on something else.

> Krista: Okay, let me know if you need anything.

She flicked her phone to silent and set it on the table. If Greg called, he would call Chase, too. "Looks like I'm still hosting my and Ann's birthday dinner tomorrow."

"You don't have to do that." His hand squeezed her shoulder. An electric pulse shot through her as she suppressed her urge to lean into him. His charming eyes grazed her collarbone and pulled away. "I'm sorry."

She waved her hand to both recognize and dismiss his apology. "The dinner will take my mind off of Greg being in the hospital. I'm here all alone most of the time." She drained the rest of her wine from the over-sized glass. *What am I doing?*

"Look, I know this isn't the best time, but a long time ago, I tried to kiss you. Can we talk about that?" Chase was flush with either shame or the wine.

Her stomach flipped against her desires. "I... I... don't know that we should. Weren't we going to pretend it never happened? I'm sorry for slapping you that night. I should have handled it differently."

He put his hand up to dismiss her apology, then rested it on the back of the couch. "I deserved it. But let me spit this out before I can't. Greg met you first. I'm happy for him. For you and Jilly too. I shouldn't have come on to you that night. And every day I regret it and... I'm happy for him."

"You already said that," Kat said.

"I know. Sometimes I have to remind myself over and over. I'm happy for him." He smiled at her.

"Sometimes... I wish I'd met you first." She put her hands over her mouth after the confession tumbled out. "Oh my God, let's never talk about this again. Deal?"

"Deal." Chase smiled and drained his wine. "I should go."

"You can't drive with half a bottle of wine," Kat said.

"You're right. I'll make a bed on the couch."

As she went upstairs to go to sleep for the night, she wondered about Evan and where his body was. Who would claim the body of a killer? She put the clothes in the dryer and went to bed. One thing was clear. With his dying breath, he'd yelled, *Find TJ.* The second thing that was clear to her was her love for Chase.

THIRTY-THREE

SHE WOKE the next morning and looked at Greg's side of the bed, half expecting to see him there. Then she remembered, and she wished she hadn't. He was lying in the hospital after Evan had shot him. And moments before he'd tried to kill her husband, at her urging Camila had met him over an unknown baby's grave.

She brought her hands to her temples and rubbed, trying to erase the mild wine-induced headache. Had she really told Chase that sometimes she wished she'd met him first? She wished the wine would have wiped away the conversation. Bringing her uncomfortable feelings to light provided no relief, it only gave them substance and weight.

A selfish thought slipped in. *Did he sleep with half of the neighborhood to get my attention?* Chastened by the twinge of lust, she breathed in and blew out hard and went to the laundry room to get his things. But the laundry was neatly folded, including the shirt and shorts of Greg's he'd borrowed. It had been years since someone had done anything around the house for her. *Maybe he's downstairs.* Her stomach tingled in both delight and guilt for wanting him there.

She entered the kitchen, but it was empty, and he was gone. He left a brewed pot of coffee and a note.

Kat,

Stopping by the hospital on the way to work. Thanks for lending me the couch, and for the chat. I hope you have a good day and enjoy the birthday dinner.

Chase

The hospital. Where her husband was. Lying in bed recovering from a near-fatal gunshot wound. Her heart ached when she realized visiting Greg hadn't been her first thought when she awoke. It should have been. Kat texted Greg.

> Kat: Hi honey, how are you feeling?

No answer.

He's probably asleep, she thought.

She laced her fingers around her coffee mug, closed her eyes, and inhaled the aroma.

They'll close the case, she thought. There were too many other cases with fresh leads to track. The suspect was dead, and the case would be closed, leaving a killer on the loose. The prints around Amelia's neck were too small, just as the prints on Mya's children's necks were too large for her. They were the Goldilocks fairytale—too big, too small, so who was just right?

She drew a thick line on her notepad and asked her questions to the paper, hoping an answer would make itself clear.

Why did Evan yell, "Find TJ!" before he died?

Mya and Beatrice were linked by Evan.

Maureen's father (dead), Millie's father (dead now), Mandy's father (unknown)

Death threats had stopped after Mya's children were killed.

She examined her questions. The only two links were Evan and TJ, and one of them was already dead. Kat took a deep breath. She would find TJ just like Evan had demanded with his dying breath. But why had the death threats to the Waltons stopped after Mya's children were killed? She googled the car part failure again. There were seventeen deaths related to its failure and dozens of injuries. One story caught her eye. Three children and a mother had died, leaving a grieving husband and father alone. Her phone dinged, startling her.

Camila: Coffee?

Kat: Sorry, can't today. I'm going to visit Greg.

Camila: Want to meet before the birthday dinner? Help set up.

Kat: That would be great.

Camila's text piqued her curiosity. *What did she want to touch base on?* Camila had done enough for her, and she would ask no more of her regarding this case.

Kat got ready for the day, dressing in a pair of fitted jeans and a dark green top.

With the threat "neutralized" Kat planned to visit Viola to ask about Evan's burial arrangements and if she knew TJ. Her address was easy to find; it was a few streets over from where her daughter and grand-daughter were buried. Kat slipped her notebook into her purse and headed in that direction.

As she rounded the corner into Viola's neighbor-hood, it looked as if she had stumbled into Germany without a passport. The housing community was a rotation of five different models of Tudor-style homes reminding her of Hansel and Gretel. She'd never been to this neighborhood before, as it was tucked neatly behind a dying strip mall.

She parked along the street, took out her notebook, and walked up the cobblestone driveway. Walking toward the door, Viola peeked through the front window holding a coffee cup. Kat couldn't find her phone number, so she hadn't called. As she watched Viola's eyes bore into her, she flipped through what cover she would use. *Maybe I'll be a reporter again,* she thought. *Will she remember me from the funeral? She'd been on auto-pilot and likely remembers nothing.* People spoke to reporters, families wanted to get the word out that their children and grandchildren didn't die for no reason, and everyone would remember them for who they were and not what happened to them.

The frail woman opened her large wooden door that was rounded at the top and tightened her eyes at Kat. "I remember you..." she said. "You were at my daughter and granddaughter's funeral, but then you left after he spoke to you." She spat out the word *he*.

"Are you talking about Evan?" Kat asked.

"I don't speak the murderer's name. Good riddance."

Kat swallowed hard. "I understand. I was wondering if you knew who his next of kin is?"

She crossed her arms over her body. "I assume me. He didn't have any family left. Killed them all. Let him rot in hell for all I care. It'll serve him right." She shrugged. "Not to be rude, but why are you here? I don't know who you are."

"Oh, I'm sorry. I'm a freelance reporter doing an exclusive story. I was looking into this case and how it may be linked to another, and I'm just asking some questions..." Kat said.

"I thought you were Bea's coworker?"

Her tongue tripped on the lie. *Damn, she remembered.* "I'm sorry I told you that. I didn't want to make a scene during the funeral."

Viola's gaze swept over Kat, and she clenched her jaw. "The other case? Are you talking about Mya and her girls?"

"Yes, Mya was blamed for those murders." She hugged the notebook to her chest.

Viola's guard slipped. "I know he was guilty now, but before... Bea and I believed him. We even met Peter and Mariah. They were such a sad couple, and I couldn't fathom it. But look where I am now."

"I knew Mariah and Peter met Beatrice, but you all knew each other?"

"Yes, when Evan told Bea she insisted she meet the other family, and she wanted me with her. Bea and I were very close, talked every day on the phone, visited several times a week. He took everything from me." An edge clipped her voice.

"Would you mind telling me what he told you about Mya and her girls?" Kat asked.

She shrugged again. "Why not? Come in." She opened the door and retreated to stand in front of a plain brown couch while Kat surveyed the living room.

There were family pictures on every horizontal surface and on the walls, much like Peter and Mariah's home. Pictures of Viola in her younger days with a handsome man, her smile impossibly big on her small face, then the handsome man was no longer in them, and Viola's smile lessened but was still there in the pictures of her and Beatrice. Then Beatrice and Amelia covered the walls and the table behind the couch. A few people Kat didn't recognize were sprinkled in amongst the images who shared common physical features: family. There were no pictures of Evan. Viola had erased him from existence, at least in her home. One photo was unevenly cut with a disembodied arm around Beatrice's waist. In place of the owner's arm, was a haphazard picture of Amelia in her bassinet. Viola perched on the brown cushion of the couch and a Calico cat hopped onto her lap and curled up. It turned lazily toward Kat and blinked. Kat sat across from Viola on a velvet chair and crossed her legs.

Viola reached across the table at the back of the couch and picked up a photo of Beatrice and Amelia and handed it to Kat.

She cleared her throat. "Those are my girls, Bea and Amelia. Look at how happy they are. So much joy they bring. So much joy they *brought*..." Her voice cracked at the correction.

Kat winced internally as she took the picture from her. "They really were lovely."

She handed the framed photo back and Viola took it and pressed it to her chest and squeezed her eyes tight. "They are. And he took them from me. And he took Mya and her girls from this world. It's so sad what happened to them, and I'll never forgive myself for believing him."

Kat leaned forward. "Believing him about what, exactly?"

"When he met Beatrice, he told us about Mya, Maureen, Millie, and Mandy. Or, as the media called them, the M girls. He told us he had a daughter and an ex-girlfriend. But that his ex-girlfriend hurt his daughter and ended her own life." She stroked the Calico between its ears and it purred out a response. "He said he hadn't known she suffered from postpartum depression. They weren't together any longer and he paid child support. Kept repeating 'I paid my child support,' like that makes him a father." Her lip curled in disgust. "The bastard said she wasn't capable of doing that. It makes sense now. Because he did it."

Kat clasped her hands in her lap on her notebook. "Why do you think he'd do it?"

Viola stared straight ahead. "Child support? He mentioned that a lot. I can't understand why anyone would hurt a child."

Kat crossed her legs and leaned forward. "This may be difficult, but were there troubles in his and Beatrice's relationship?"

"No more than the usual things. She met him right after hopping out of a relationship with a nice young man named Steven. I wish they would have stayed together..." She sighed. "Anyway, after Bea got pregnant, I knew he would be around for the long haul and I tried my best to accept him. He had a temper, though. There were a few holes in the drywall, but I never saw a mark on my Bea or Amelia. I would have done something if I had." Then she wrapped her arms around herself again and crossed her legs. The Calico hopped to the floor and gazed back at Viola's vanished lap before turning down the hall, clearly irritated.

Kat remembered a grief-stricken man at the funeral walking in, visiting the coffin, and quickly exiting. She assumed it was an old boyfriend. *That must have been Steven.* "The police closed the case with Mya. They determined she was responsible for her children's deaths."

"And you believe that? Bea never took drugs. Yes, she had back surgery and was taking some pain relief. She lived for Amelia. She would not have snapped. You cannot tell me that this would happen twice to the same father. He is the only commonality. It's him. They won't blame my daughter for this." Viola spat out the words. A droplet of spittle shone on her bottom lip.

"Speaking of commonalities, did he have any friends or people he associated with?" Kat asked.

Viola tapped a finger to her chin. Kat noted she wore a wedding ring, but the handsome man had disappeared from the photos long ago. "There was a woman who came by from time to time. Blonde, with pretty blue eyes. I think she had initials or something for a name. He said they were cousins, but I never really met her."

Kat leaned forward. "When was the last time you saw her?"

"Hmm, I was over at their last Sunday dinner. We used to do that together. Have dinner every Sunday evening..." She exhaled audibly, her eyes glistening. Her back straightened as she regained her composure. "Anyway, this woman knocked on the door and he went out to speak to her. When he came back, his face was flushed. Bea asked him if he was okay." She looked pointedly at Kat. "Did that woman have something to do with what happened to my family?" Her voice hitched up an octave.

"I don't know, but I plan to look into it." She jotted a

note: *TJ and Evan's conversation on last Sunday before B&A death.* She changed the subject. "Were you aware of an insurance policy for your daughter and granddaughter?"

"Yes, I am. I am the beneficiary now that everyone is... gone."

Kat nodded.

"But no amount of money is worth losing everything," she said. "I'm sorry about that police officer who got shot, but I'm glad *he* killed himself. Saved us all a lot of time and money. That bastard can burn in hell. Besides, if the police had done their jobs right the first time, my Bea would still be here and I wouldn't be living like this."

Kat didn't think Viola sounded too sorry or sympathetic about Evan shooting her husband.

"Well, thank you. I should get going. Can I get your number in case I have any more questions?" Kat asked.

"Of course." She rattled off her number while Kat fumbled through her phone to program it as they walked toward the door. "If that woman had anything to do with this, let her burn alongside him." She shut the door, and Kat heard it latch behind her.

Kat put the notebook in her purse and walked to her car. She felt Viola's eyes still on her. She thought of her mother, and how her brother's death had killed her, too. *Maybe it was better to die than survive the loss of a child*, she thought.

But Evan couldn't have done this. Or at least not alone. All roads were leading to the mysterious TJ.

THIRTY-FOUR

SHE STARTED her car and glanced at her phone as a text chimed in. It was Greg.

> Greg: Chase just left. Doing good. Looks like I'll be out tomorrow night.

> Kat: I can swing by and visit today before the birthday dinner.

> Greg: That bullet was nothing. The food here is killing me.

> Kat: Too soon. I'll get you a burger.

She chuckled and slipped the phone back into her pocket. Grumpy's Burgers was busy, so she swung through the drive-thru to order his favorite, The Works. She ordered a single burger for herself. The fries were big enough for them to split, or for her to at least steal a few off the top without his noticing. A brunette boy with greasy hair handed her the bag from the window, and the scent made her stomach grumble. She'd forgotten to eat breakfast. Kat ripped the receipt off the bag and stuffed it in her purse and shoved large bites of her burger into her mouth en route to the hospital.

When she walked into his room, Greg was propped on his pillows, smiling and talking to Lydia, the buttery blonde nurse shaped like a coke bottle from the previous day. A brief shot of envy pulsed through her, and she tucked her hair behind her ear, the fatty contraband scent emanating from her purse.

Lydia excused herself and smiled at Kat as she walked out the door, her floral perfume casting a lingering trail in her wake. Greg's cheeks had more color than the previous day, and he eyed her arm around her purse.

"Ah, there's my wife. I see you have a gift for me." He rubbed his palms together and his eyes flashed eagerly at her.

Kat laughed and took the bag out of her purse and placed it in his outstretched hand. "The Works and fries. Your favorite."

He made a gesture on his cheek and said, "I see someone already ate. You have a smidge of ketchup there, darling."

She wiped her face. "Sorry, sweetie. I was hungry. I ate mine on the way. I didn't have breakfast."

"No worries," he said through a full mouth. She watched the food visible between his molars and grimaced. "I was too. I can't survive on this Jell-O and whatever that is." He pointed to a silver tray of gray stuff, a biscuit of some sort, and apple juice which looked suspiciously like urine.

As he ate, she sat on the corner of his bed, careful not to rustle the mattress, and placed her purse with the notebook next to her. It peeked out at her and she moved her purse to the floor then pushed it under the bed with her foot. His leg was under the blue blanket, and an IV still protruded from his left arm as he ate with his right hand.

He smiled at her. "This may be the best burger I've eaten in my entire life."

"They are pretty good, but you're hungry. How are you doing?" She gazed at the IV sticking out of his arm and wondered what the doctors were pushing through his veins.

"I've been better. But I'll bounce back. You aren't getting rid of me that easily. At least we can close the case..."

How did they not see that there was more to this case? "Didn't you say the two cases were linked?" she asked, taking a fry from his bag and popping it into her mouth.

"Yes, they'll both be closed. All it cost me was a brief field trip to the hospital." His eyes gleamed. "I may even get an award for this. Closing a cold case, solving a fresh case, and getting shot. All in a day's work."

Kat smiled at him. "I'm so proud of you, honey."

"Yes, he's the only link to both. Motives for both, too. It all came down to money. Isn't that what it always comes down to?" He shrugged and took another bite.

"He killed his family for money. Dumbest insurance agent I ever met."

Kat raised her shoulders. "It isn't always money, is it?" She slid her hand into her pocket and rubbed her finger along the edge of the soft fabric.

"Aw, Katie. Those thriller books are getting to you."

The heat rushed to her cheeks, but she said nothing. If she'd been within arm's reach, he would have tousled her hair like a toddler.

Greg said, "Aw, c'mon now, honey, don't be mad. I'm playing. Look at me, I was shot. Don't make me be in trouble, too." He gestured toward the leg under the covers and pouted.

She looked at her feet. Squabbling about patronizing did feel petty. "Yeah, you're right. I can't wait to have you home."

He put The Works burger back in the bag and reached his arm out. His hand shone with a bit of the special sauce. "C'mere," he said.

She stood from the foot of his bed and went to him, knowing the special sauce would be wiped on her jeans. They were her favorite pair, flattering her in the right places. Hopefully, it would come out.

Leaning forward, she kissed his head. It was dry. "Are you getting enough water?"

"Yes, Lydia is taking good care of me, Katie."

She stiffened, but smiled. "That's nice." *Why is she so pretty?*

His hazel eyes held her gaze. "Are you jealous?" He playfully poked her arm.

She rubbed the spot where he poked in mock pain. "Of course not," she lied. Glancing down at her deflated chest that somehow grew flatter with age, she compared herself to Lydia's buxom curves and her envy blossomed.

"Haha, you are a little jealous. Darling, blondes aren't my type. I like brunettes," Greg said.

Somehow, his joking didn't ease the ache of jealousy. "Your only type is the brunette standing right in front of you," she corrected.

"I see I struck a nerve. Yes, of course, love," he said and puckered his lips. She leaned in to kiss him, and he kissed her and tousled her hair.

She stood and smoothed her hair back into place. "Well, I've got to get to the grocery store. Get a few things for the dinner tonight." Kat crouched and retrieved her purse, zipping the top shut before she stood. Then she backed away toward the door and a warm hand splayed between her shoulder blades.

An electricity zapped through her, followed by a heated flush. His familiar scent of Irish Spring tickled her nose. "Hey there, Kat, I'm behind you," Chase said. He stepped around her and approached Greg's bed. "How's my favorite princess?"

"Screw off," Greg said, and chuckled.

"I was just swinging by to see if you needed something to eat. Seems Kat already took care of that," Chase said, eyeing the bag on the bed.

"Katie takes good care of me. Don't you, darling?" He winked at her, and her stomach flipped.

Kat blushed crimson and backed herself out of the room. "Alright boys, I've got to go. I'll talk to you all later."

Greg waved absently, but returned to his hamburger. Chase looked at her, and half his mouth twisted up in a smile.

Kat sat in her car, her phone cold in her hand. There were calls to make. Mariah and Peter would be overjoyed to know the one responsible for their world's destruction was dead. And Viola would want to know both cases were being closed, that the police had their killer in Evan. And then there was Camila. Kat needed to call her to see what time she'd be over to help with the birthday dinner preparations, but she also owed Camila another apology...

THIRTY-FIVE

VIOLA FIRST, Kat thought. *Her wound is the freshest.* She found her name in the contacts and dialed.

A man's voice answered the phone. "Hello?"

She almost hung up. *Maybe I put the number in wrong... she rattled it off so quickly,* she thought. "Hi, my name is Camila O'Brien, and I was calling for Viola. Do I have the wrong number?"

"Hang on," he said. There was a rustling on the line, and Viola's voice whispered, "Thank you, Steven." Then her voice became clear to Kat. "Ms. O'Brien?"

"Yes, hello. I wanted to tell you our investigative journalist team met with law enforcement. It seems they are closing both cases based on the facts that Evan was responsible." *Investigative team? Is that even a thing?* She waited for a response. It didn't matter.

A sigh poured into the line. "Thank you. It means so much that you followed up with me. The police officers haven't given me much."

Why is Steven there? It's not my business, of course, but it seems odd he'd be there with Viola.

"Of course. I hope you find some peace."

Her voice shook. "I will never have peace. I meant to reach out to you, but I never got your phone number. You mentioned the woman the other day. TJ. I asked Steven if he knew anything about her, and he did."

Kat's ears perked. "Oh, what was that?" She rummaged in her purse for the notebook.

"Oh, it's probably nothing. I mean, the case is closed. Maybe we should just leave it alone?" Viola asked.

"Sometimes minor details help. It couldn't hurt," Kat lied. Truths did cut straight to the bone.

"Let me put you on speakerphone. I don't want to misstate anything."

The line rustled as Viola found the speaker button. A man said, "Hello, Ms. O'Brien. Bea and I remained close after our breakup. It may sound strange, but what we had was special. We stayed good friends. She and Evan were in a troubled marriage, but they tried to keep it together for Amelia."

Friends. Right. But Chase and she were just friends, too. "I understand how children complicate things."

"Yes, of course. And the woman, TJ, hung around a lot. Came by and talked to him. She wasn't friendly to Bea, but she wasn't unfriendly either. They said they were cousins. But I've never seen cousins make out," Steven said quickly.

"Wait, what? Make out? Where did you see this?"

"At the local hardware store, of all places. It was

winter and like six o'clock. So, even though it was early, it was already dark. They were in a parking lot, and I recognized Bea's car. She has these little stick people on it, with a Baby on Board decal, it's unmistakable. Two people in the car looked like they were fighting, and Bea had told me Evan had a temper. The car was moving, and I thought Bea was in trouble. I ran toward the car, there was steam on the windows..."

Kat gulped. "How do you know it was TJ and Evan?"

"I tried to open the door, but it was locked. They couldn't hear me, and I knocked on the window. I thought TJ was Bea, and I almost broke the window. But she wiped away the steam, and I saw her. He didn't see me. It wasn't Bea, and she wasn't there against her will, so I left."

"Did you tell Beatrice about it?"

"I did, and she was so angry. Not angry enough to leave him, but it inched her closer. She gave her family a last chance. For Amelia. It was a few months ago, so Amelia was still so tiny," Steven said, his voice cracking with emotion.

"I'm sorry for your loss," Kat said finally. "You know Beatrice well. May I ask a delicate question?"

He paused. "Of course, anything to help."

Kat kept her tone soft and neutral. "If something happened to Amelia, what would Beatrice have done?"

There was sniffling in the background from Viola, and he choked back his emotions and cleared his throat. "She lived for that little girl. She'd die for Amelia, and with her gone, I suppose she had nothing left to live for. Even me."

She scribbled on her notepad.

Amelia prevented Beatrice and Evan from separating.

Motive TJ.

Motive Steven.

"All I have about TJ is her name." That wasn't exactly true. There was a picture in the file and outdated contact information.

Viola was back on the line. "The hospital released Bea's phone to me. Bea texted TJ. She must have gotten her name from Evan's phone. I assume it's TJ, at least. She saved her contact as *Home Wrecker*. I'll text it to you. She can rot in prison if she had any involvement in this."

"Thank you for your time, Viola, and the information. I'll certainly pass this new lead over to law enforcement," Kat said.

"Thank you for caring," Viola said. Then she heard sobs and a man's voice offering comfort before the line went dead. A new text beeped with the contact, *Home Wrecker*.

Her mind quickly flitted through the possibilities. The similar note and the non-forced entry still led to Evan. Except for those hands on Amelia's neck. TJ likely knew about the note from Evan. TJ and Steven both deeply loved others with a mutual obstacle: Amelia.

Kat tapped her pen on her lip. No forced entry. But how often did her door remain unlocked when she was home? The police report said Beatrice's hair was wet, like she'd been in the shower. Anyone could have come in, hurt her baby, and disappeared. Especially someone who didn't look suspicious at all, like TJ. A wolf in sheep's clothing. Perhaps their plan backfired spectacularly when Beatrice found her daughter. She shook the thoughts loose for now to call Mya's parents. Their family deserved closure. One thing was clear: their daughter did not murder her girls, and that's what was important. Exonerating their daughter.

She dialed Peter and Mariah, and they picked up on the first ring. "Hi Camila, you're on speaker."

Kat cringed. *Damn, why didn't I pick any other name?* "Hi, I wanted to let you know they're closing Mya's case. I believe they'll be holding Evan responsible."

Relieved laughter poured through the line. "Oh, thank God," Mariah said.

"It must be a relief to put this to rest. I hope it'll give you some peace as you move forward."

Peter said, "There is no moving forward from something like this. But yes, it'll give us peace."

"There's something else," Kat said.

"Oh? What is it?" Mariah asked.

"Well, it seems a woman killed Amelia."

Mariah gasped.

"No, that's impossible," Peter said. His tone was gruff and raw.

"I haven't shared my findings with law enforcement yet, but do you have any information on Evan's contacts or maybe Mya's contacts during that time? I was hoping to gather it all at once and send it to them," Kat asked. "Maybe TJ, the drug dealer? She was having an affair with Evan."

Mariah said, "Oh my God. Were they working together? Wasn't there a life insurance policy? I heard that in the news."

"Yes, he had life insurance. Sometimes, though, these cases aren't what they seem and money isn't the motive," Kat said.

"Money is the root of all evil," Peter said. "When we ran out of it, Mya went down a dark path and never returned."

"I'm sorry. Well, thanks for the information. I will pass it to law enforcement once I get more information. I wish you all peace." Kat scribbled on her notepad.

"Thank you, it has," Peter said, and hung up the phone.

Her last call was to Camila. She owed her a hearty apology for putting her in the path of a killer.

"Hi," Camila answered. "How's Greg?"

"He's good. I'm in the hospital parking lot, finishing up. He'll be home in a couple of days."

"Ah, that's such a relief to hear. Are you sure you still want to have the birthday dinner tonight? I'm sure everyone will understand if we cancel," Camila asked. "You must have your hands full."

"Not really. I'm going to the grocery store to pick up a few snacks and the cake I ordered, and then we can have it. I want to keep things as normal as possible, you

know? Besides, with Greg out of the house, it's so quiet."
Kat abhorred boredom, it fueled her curiosity, and she
wanted to be done with all of it.

"Alright, let's do a late lunch then. I wanted to talk to
you about something."

Kat nearly forgot there was something Camila
wanted *to touch base on*. Offensively, Kat apologized
again. "Look, I'm so sorry I thought Evan was safe.
Please forgive me."

"Oh, it isn't about that. I'm not sure of his guilt after
all. If my kids were killed, I don't think I'd be itching to
stay around either," Camila said.

Then Kat told her everything. TJ, Steven, the rocky
marriage, and the affair.

Camila sighed. "When I talked to him at the grave, I
didn't think he did it. You may be on to something."

"If Evan didn't do it, then whoever did is still out
there. Or if TJ did it with him and he covered for her with
the note, then she's responsible."

Camila breathed into the phone. "Kat, this isn't your
problem anymore."

"I know," Kat said. "Wait, if that wasn't what you
were going to talk to me about? What is?"

"Let's chat when we meet at your place, but you
have to promise not to be mad," Camila said.

"Uh, that doesn't sound good." Her stomach knotted
into a tight ball.

"You owe me for this mess. Promise you won't be
mad?" Camila asked again.

"Okay, I promise," Kat said. *I bet she slept with Chase.* And, against her promise, she seethed as she hung up the phone.

THIRTY-SIX

CHASE AND CAMILA. She swallowed the sour taste of envy as her heart pounded in her ears. "Breathe, breathe, breathe," she said to the steering wheel. Saving her marriage with Greg was built on the idea that a real marriage like Edward and Camila's existed. If Chase had slept with Camila, then her hopes of anything salvageable were dashed by her best friend and her... Whatever Chase was to her. The puzzle pieces fell into place. Camila's active disdain for him and his avoidance of her. Both emboldened by her husband's badge, and fueled by her anger, she clicked *Home Wrecker*. And thought of Chase and Camila as the phone rang.

"Hello," said a cautious woman's voice.

"Hi, I'm an investigative journalist, and I have evidence of your drug deals. I will report you if you don't talk to me," Kat said. To the point. A little blackmaily. She smiled to herself. *I'm getting better at this.*

Silence on the line, then, "What do you want?" The voice was angry.

"How close are you to Ventura Hardware?" Kat asked. She was ten minutes from the hardware store. Seemed poetic to meet her in the same place she'd had sex with Evan in Beatrice's car. Maybe that's where the couple hatched the plan to kill his wife. And it was public, so she was safer.

"Fifteen minutes."

"I'll see you in twenty, TJ," Kat said, and disconnected the line. *What am I doing?* She peeked inside her purse and spotted the innocuous pink tube of mace mingling at the bottom with lipsticks, pens, and random change. She plucked it out and put it in her pocket.

As she navigated to the hardware store, her fiery anger clouded her judgment. A week ago, boring old Kat would be putting the finishing touches on another mundane neighborhood dinner where the women would gather and discuss the same dull things. *I'll go back to that life and be grateful for my boring, privileged existence. After I finish this,* she thought.

After this, I'll find a new purpose.

Witness advocate?

Go back to school for criminal justice?

Suddenly the possibilities spread out before her, and a small flame of hope fired up, which cooled the heat of the jealous anger burning inside her.

I have no right to be jealous about what two adults do with their time.

But I have a right to feel betrayed. By both of them.

Her jaw clenched, and her tongue pinned tight to the roof of her mouth. She pulled into the parking lot and there were a few cars toward the front door by the nursery. It was still before the dinner hour, and many people were locked away in their offices for another hour or two. A sign sat at the front of the nursery—bare root roses, buy one, get one—beckoning the local gardener in. Kat pulled up under the Ginkgo tree at the corner of the lot and parked. She let go of the steering wheel and studied her hands. There were small half-moons dug into her palms from her nails. She rubbed her hands together and texted Home Wrecker. *Park at the tree.*

Kat emerged from the car, leaving her purse behind, but kept her phone in her back pocket and the mace in her front pocket tucked away with her small square of fabric. A squish under her ballet flat caused her foot to slide. A fleshy fruit from the tree smeared on the bottom. It smelled like dog poop.

This will give us privacy. No one wants to park beneath the shit tree.

Scanning under the tree, it was full of the fleshy landmines. The awful berries plastered themselves against the soles of her feet. Kat decided she'd leave her shoes sitting right there in the parking lot. She considered getting back inside her car, but a carjacking would land her who knows where, and maybe even the back of her trunk.

No, we'll do this in the light of day. If it was a private enough place for her to have an affair, then it was private enough for a conversation. But within earshot of a scream.

An old Volkswagen Beetle pulled in beside her. Refinished and a deep orange, it didn't look like a drug dealer's car. Kat wondered if TJ was out of the drugs business. Maybe she'd become a hired assassin. A hired assassin in a VW Bug. Kat chuckled bitterly and touched the outline of mace in her pants, reassuring herself of its presence.

TJ rolled down her window. "You the one who called me?"

"Yes." She placed her hands on her hips.

TJ got out of her car and stood at least six inches above Kat. Her long blonde hair cascaded down her back past her bra strap. Oversized sunglasses shaded a good portion of her face. They were well-balanced by her oversized lips, augmented to plumper-than-normal proportions. Her lower lip looked like a water balloon ready to pop.

Each woman stood by their cars in a standoff. Not particularly close, but the mace would reach Kat's target if she needed it. "How did you know Evan?" Kat asked. No hello. No introductions.

"What's it to you? What the hell is that smell?" TJ asked and fanned her nose. "Did you step in shit?"

"It's the tree. Evan's dead," Kat said flatly.

TJ regarded her coldly. "I know. Is that why you brought me out here?"

"How did you know him?" Kat asked.

"Wait... he told me about you. You're Camila O'Brien, right? The lady pretending to work with his old lady?

What's it to you?" She crossed her arms over her middle and jutted out her puffy lip.

Kat's mouth fell open. *He talked to her about me.* "I'm a reporter, and I'm investigating the Mya and the Beatrice case. My investigation led me to you as Mya's drug dealer," Kat said. She clenched her jaw and hoped TJ didn't notice the bluff blossoming up her neck.

Silence for a beat. "What do you want to know?"

"Start from the beginning. How did you know Evan?"

TJ sighed. "It's complicated. When his first daughter died, he hired a private investigator after they closed the case. Didn't believe Mya did it. I didn't know who killed her girls, and he believed me. Anyway, we saw each other sometimes. It didn't mean anything, though. He was a good lay, and sometimes when he fought with his old lady, he called me. That's all it was. Maybe it meant more to him, but not me. I see a lot of people," TJ said. "I ended it anyway."

"You ended it?" Kat asked.

"Yeah, his old lady started sending me texts, threatening me, and calling me a home wrecker. I ain't no home wrecker. He was married, not me," TJ said. "But I'm not about some drama. There are enough other good lays out there to get stalked by someone's pissed-off wife. So I ended it."

"How did Evan react?"

She shrugged. "Our fling meant more to him than it did me. He started talking about leaving his family for me, and how his wife was a jealous witch. Man, I always try to go for the guys in a solid relationship. I knew this one had gone on too long. Missed the mark on him, I guess." TJ shrugged, kicked a Ginkgo berry, and wrinkled her nose.

Like Chase, Kat thought. Kat opened her phone and scrolled to the crime pictures of Amelia lying on the ground, a woman's handprint upon her tiny neck. Would Kat recognize remorse? Or would TJ look at it coldly? It was the only way to know for sure. "Look at this," Kat said. She turned the picture of the dead baby beside her mother toward TJ.

"Oh my God, get that out of my face!" TJ said, bending over and retching.

Kat slid the phone back into her front pocket. "You feel guilty for hurting her, don't you?" Kat pressed. "You killed that little girl."

She wiped her face with the back of her sleeve. A small wet patch on her blue shirt darkened to black. "I never laid a hand on that baby. Or anyone. All I did was sell Mya the stuff. I gave her what she bought. It was a sale. But I didn't kill nobody."

"Well, I wonder if it might be important for the police to know your involvement in both cases. You and Evan are the only connection between the two—"

"You better watch yourself," TJ said, cutting her off.

"Is that a threat?" Kat took a small step back and glanced at the hardware store doors. No one was outside.

"Not a threat, a promise." TJ curled her lip and growled. "You don't know who you're messing with. You

251

may have your own protection, but don't think I don't have someone watching over me, too. I ain't going to jail for nobody." Her eyes slid to Kat's pocket holding her phone. "Are you recording me?"

"So, what if I am?" Kat asked, bluffing. *Why didn't I think about recording her?*

TJ reached out, making a grab for Kat's phone, but Kat got there first. They tugged it back and forth until it slipped through their fingers and landed on the ground, cracking the screen.

Kat pulled her mace from her other pocket and sprayed it at her assailant's face. A gust of wind caught it and shifted it into Kat's eyes. The spicy hostility of the liquid blinded her as she covered her eyes and slipped on a Ginkgo berry and fell to the ground, her knees hitting hard and her keys falling from her hands.

Hurried footsteps faded away, and a car door opened and closed, then the engine turned and the tires squealed away from her. TJ was gone. She kneeled blindly on the pavement, running her hands over the parking lot for her phone and her keys. Then approaching footsteps hustled toward her. Her adrenaline tried to force her eyes to cooperate, but they would not open. They were slammed shut and her tears ran steady torrent streams down her cheeks. Mucus covered the spots of her face her tears missed.

"Ma'am, are you okay?" asked a man's voice.

"No, no, I'm not. Do you see a phone or my keys on the ground?"

"I don't," he said.

"I tried to protect myself and mace her, but the breeze... It... it made it worse for me." She coughed trying to clear the mace from her windpipe. "She got away," Kat cried. "Please, help me? Can you make a call?"

"Yeah, but let's get you cleaned up first," the kind voice said.

She nodded, and let the man lead her blindly toward what she hoped was the store. The pain came in waves as her eyes tried to defend themselves and blink open. Time was a flexible thing as a large hand with a kind voice escorted her to the hazmat station. She pried her eyes open with her fingers and stared into the cold water as her eyes tried to blink her sight back.

Through blurred vision, she excused herself and went to the restroom where she studied herself in the mirror. Her face bore the red mask of a raccoon, and her nose relentlessly dripped. She took two small pieces of toilet paper, rolled them, and stuck them up her nose. The stench of the berries permeated her nostrils, and she threw her shoes in the trash. She brushed the berries still clinging to her slacks and washed the violent stench from her hands.

Barefoot, she left the restroom to find someone to call Chase. A portly man with thick glasses and a green apron stood at a respectable distance. "Are you okay, ma'am? I called the police and they're on their way." The kind voice matched the one who'd escorted her blindly to the hazmat station.

"Thank you. I actually know a police officer. He's a friend." She recited Chase's number from memory.

. . .

SHE GLANCED AT HER WATCH. She was late to her own birthday dinner set up with Camila. Chase arrived forty-five minutes after she cleaned herself up and gathered her in his arms. His arms on her waist felt intimate, more so than when he'd barely looked at her at the hospital with Greg eyeing them both. He kissed the top of her head. "I was so worried. We got the call, and I took it from Officer Jenkins, who was en route. I'm on desk duty, but I'll make the report. Are you okay?"

"I am now," she said, relief rushing through her nestled in his arms. *Safety.*

Chase's face was clouded with worry as he peppered her with questions. "Your eyes are still really red. Can you see alright? Where are your shoes?"

She ignored his question about her shoes. "I don't have my keys. I was mugged."

"What did he take?"

"She. She took my keys and phone. I locked my purse in the car."

Chase escorted her to his police vehicle, and she got inside. He didn't start the car, but turned to her. "We'll deal with it later, but let's stop by your car. God, Kat, I'm so glad you're okay. What are you doing here? I can't imagine why you'd be at a hardware store."

"It's nothing." Kat looked at her hands.

Chase got out of his car and got on all fours in the berries, ruining his pants. He ducked his head beneath the car and leaned farther in. He stood and held up the keys and phone triumphantly.

"It's cracked, but it still works," he said. Chase unlocked her car, grabbed the purse, and put the phone inside. He locked the car and tucked the keys away as well.

Kat's vision was still blurred, but she was relieved to see nothing was stolen.

He returned to the car, handed her the purse, and climbed inside, the smell of the Ginkgo berries permeating the vehicle. He grimaced as he restarted the car. "God, those berries smell." He turned his hand over and flicked a small piece of berry out the window. "I'm going to have to get this car detailed."

She smiled and tried not to breathe, rolling down the window. Bile built up in her throat and she pointed her nose toward the open window.

"Look at me, Kat." She faced his piercing green eyes. "What happened?"

"It wasn't a random mugging. I've something to confess..."

THIRTY-SEVEN

HIS JAW TWITCHED as his police car grumbled to life. "What's going on, Kat?"

She ignored the question. Her curiosity nipped hard at her with the few moments she had with Chase. The last moments before something would change forever and he admitted to having sex with her best friend.

"Camila is probably trying to get a hold of me. We were supposed to meet. She wanted to tell me something. Asked me to promise I wouldn't be mad." She slid her eyes over to him. "Do you know what she'd want to talk to me about?" Kat asked. She felt a tightness in her chest. Even if things would never be the same, she had to know.

"What? Why would I know that? Camila can't stand me," Chase said. "I like to stay the hell out of her way."

Kat breathed an audible sigh of relief.

He stopped his car for a red light and turned to her. "Wait. Did you think we were having an affair?"

"I don't know. Maybe. It isn't necessarily out of character for you. I wonder what she wanted to talk to me about?" Kat crossed her arms over her chest and closed her mouth. Then it came to her. *The letter. From my father.* Her guarded protection over the letter had piqued Camila's interest. *Oh. My. God.* The life she'd built around her secrets for two decades was unraveling.

"So, what do you have to confess?" Chase said. He pulled his car into her driveway, but made no sign of getting out. "C'mon Kat, you've got to tell me so I can help."

She tipped her head back, looking at the roof of the cop car. He touched her knee, grounding her back into the present, and her amber eyes met his. "You know I saw the crime picture. Greg made a big deal about it."

He grew unnaturally quiet, unnerving her. "Yes... I remember," he said, finally.

"Anyway, he made it seem like I don't know anything. I was angry and curious, but mostly angry and... bored. I felt useless." Admitting her diminished sense of self made tears spring to her eyes, and the burning sensation returned from the mace. She blinked them back. "I looked at them. Snapped pictures of the case file."

"I'm sorry you had to see that," Chase said.

"Don't patronize me," she said curtly.

He flinched. "That's not what I meant—"

"I'm sorry, I'm on edge from this, and from being made to feel smaller all the damned time," Kat admitted. "Sometimes, I wish I was more like Krista and Ann, and could follow my heart. Or at least my passion." A flush crept into her cheeks and she looked out the window, away from his stare. "We've got this birthday thing tonight, and I didn't even go to the grocery store and pick up the cake. Camila's probably already inside. We can probably text one of the ladies to pick it up." The air was hot and tight. She reached for the handle and opened the door to escape the car. His stare. His cologne. His footsteps behind her a reminder that their conversation wasn't over.

"We've got to get the police report started, Kat," he said to her back.

"I know, I know, but Camila's here and the rest of the ladies will be here in like fifteen minutes. And you need to get cleaned up."

She opened the door of her house and set her purse on the stair landing. Camila wasn't on the couch tapping her crossed leg in annoyance, as she'd expected.

"Camila?"

The kitchen was empty, too. No sign that she had come by at all. *Do I have the dates wrong? No, she was definitely supposed to be here.*

A cool panic settled into her bones. The only name TJ had was Camila's.

Chase said, "What's wrong? You look like you've seen a ghost?"

"We need to get to Camila's house. Now. I'll explain later." She ran three houses down, knowing he would be quick on her heels.

Camila's dark red front door was ajar. Camila didn't

lock her house, but she never left the door open. Kat's vision tunneled as she lunged for the door, but was pulled back hard by her waist.

She turned and met Chase's wide eyes as he put a finger over his lips and whispered, "Go stand in front of the garage. Now." It wasn't a request. His fingers dug into her arm. She retreated and watched him pull a gun from his ankle holster.

"Police, I'm coming in," he said. There was nothing but silence in response.

Kat's heartbeat thundered in her ears. If something happened to Camila, then she was responsible. *I don't deserve to wait by the garage.* She stepped over the threshold and followed Chase inside.

Chase was bent over a body administering CPR. He yelled over his shoulder, "Call 9-1-1!"

Camila's brown hair cascaded around her like a halo. On the other side of Chase, her legs were splayed, still wearing her skinny jeans and white sneakers. *Why is he pounding on her chest like that? Is this life-saving?* The violence of it left her unable to move. A sickening crack popped like a tree limb in a storm. Camila's rib.

"Call 9-1-1!" Chase shouted again, snapping her back to reality. She looked around. She didn't have a phone.

His phone skittered across the ground, landing at her feet.

She picked it up and pushed the emergency button on the lock screen.

"9-1-1, what's your emergency?" a woman's voice asked.

She shook her head and crumpled to the floor. "It's my friend. Something's happened. Please hurry." Kat spouted the address and hung up. Picking herself up, her legs wobbled as she took another step forward toward Chase and his violent life-saving attempt.

He put up his hand behind him, his fingers trembled. "Stay back, Kat. Stay back. I've got this."

"I can't." Her lips trembled.

"I mean it, back up," he yelled.

Her pulse raced, and she walked toward her friend lying on the ground. The bruising on her neck, the bulging vacant eyes, the blue-tinged lips. The necklace full of her children's birthstones had sliced her skin, a trickle of blood smudging her neck. She was gone.

"Her kids," Kat choked out. She ran through the house and peeked into all of Camila's children's bedrooms, but no one was there. Her eldest were likely at jobs and sports. But Horace. He was due to be picked up. A voice answered her thought in the entryway.

"Camila, honey?" Edward's confused question sifted through the door.

Kat raced to the entryway and blocked his and Horace's view of Camila lying on the kitchen floor with Chase pounding on her chest.

"Mommy? Where's Mommy?" Horace asked, and he craned his neck around Kat, and she took a small step to block his line of sight again. "Who's that?"

His chubby finger pointed around Kat's back at Chase, toiling away, counting. "One, and two, and three, and four." She heard another crack and Chase's whispered, "I'm sorry."

Kat's jaw clenched, and she said, "Hi, buddy. You and I are going to my house for a bit, going to get a snack, okay?" Edward hadn't moved. He stared straight ahead with his feet rooted in place. She only dared observe him through her peripheral.

Horace nodded, but didn't move. Kat approached the boy, still using her body to shield his view. Putting her hands on his narrow shoulders, she spun him around back toward the door. Edward let go of his son's hand as he walked toward his wife.

"I've got some fun treats," Kat said. "Some that Jilly left behind."

Halfway down the driveway, an animal's cry came from the house, and Horace tried to turn around. "What was that?" he asked.

Edward expelled his grief in a mournful howl. "Hmm, maybe someone has a movie on?"

He put his hands over his ears. "It's too loud."

She took one of his hands from his ears and held it as they retraced her steps back to her home. As they walked over the threshold, the sirens blared down their street.

THIRTY-EIGHT

THE PAIR WALKED INSIDE, and she led Horace into the pantry. "Take whatever you want, kiddo."

His plump fingers pushed aside the Melba toast and found Rice Krispies Treats Jillian left from her last visit. Kat opened the treat and led him to the couch.

He stopped. "I'm not allowed to eat on the couch."

"Oh honey, it's fine." Knowing he'd never be fine again, she turned from his large blue eyes. He grinned and climbed up. She went to the front door and fished her phone out of her purse, assessing the screen. It would need to be replaced, but Chase was right, it still worked, so she plugged it in and hung her keys on the rack at the door.

A knock on the door jarred her. She cracked it open and Ramona, Ann, Krista, and Janet were huddled on her porch in a colorful display of dresses.

The birthday party.

"Do you know what's going on at Camila's?" Ramona asked. Her voice was, impossibly, louder than her new violet hair, which was shocking against her traffic cone-colored dress. All eyes turned to Kat.

"Come on in. Hey, Horace honey, why don't you say hi to everyone?" she said in a false sing-song voice. The women nodded in understanding. They weren't alone.

Janet walked over to Horace and ruffled his hair. "Hey, buddy. Look at that Rice Krispies Treat. I have some granola in my purse. Would you like some?" He nodded and grasped her Tupperware of homemade cereal. She sat with him as the others retreated to the kitchen.

Krista set her wine bottles on the counter. "What happened?" she asked. Her voice was barely above a whisper.

"It's Camila. I think she's dead," Kat said.

Ann gasped and covered her mouth. Ramona let out a yelp, and Krista looked away, shaking her head.

Kat said, "I'm sorry. I wish there was a way to say it better. We were supposed to meet here to help set up. But when I got home, she wasn't here. I went to her house with Chase to check on her."

"Where's Chase?" Ann asked, her eyebrows turned up in curiosity.

"He's still there. He was doing CPR when I left. Edward and Horace got home. The other kids must be at school, jobs, sports, whatever. She was there alone. When I saw Horace walk in, I grabbed him and left."

"How?" Ramona asked.

"Was it a natural cause?" Ann asked with hope hitched in her voice.

"No, she was strangled," Kat said, her hand absently rubbing the corresponding spot on her neck where the necklace had dug into her friend's skin.

"Someone strangled her?" Krista asked.

"Yes." Kat's lips trembled, as she thought about Camila's bulging, vacant eyes, the sound of her ribs cracking under Chase's chest compressions, and his whispered apologies.

Ramona's tongue clicked against her teeth. "Who would want to hurt her?"

Krista asked, "Maybe it was a robbery that went wrong?"

Or maybe I'm responsible. Kat stared at her feet, the macing incident long forgotten. She said nothing.

Horace's musical laughter wafted into the room, cementing the tragedy. When Kat's brother and mother died, it was her fault by accident. This was different. Kat was responsible for her best friend's death. She gave out Camila's name to anyone who would listen.

The ladies sat in silence with their shock, interrupted by Chase's footsteps into the kitchen. His black hair clumped in sweat. "Hey, we're keeping Horace tonight. Edward is going to be... tied up," he said simply and shook his head.

Ann let out a small cry.

Krista nudged Ann with her elbow and hissed, "Shh, Horace is in there."

Ann turned her head toward the floor and covered her mouth. Squeezing her eyes shut, she wept quietly.

Ramona took a bite of the brownie, her cancer debrief conversation long forgotten. "What's that smell? Is that you Chase?"

"Ginkgo berries, long story," he replied.

"Is Edward alone?" Kat asked Chase.

"No, his three older kids are with him, and his daughter, Chloe, is coming home from college to be there. He wanted you to keep Horace tonight. I'll stay here, too," Chase said. "Tomorrow I'll need to get to the office to make my reports. The detectives on the scene took my initial statement. They'll be more, though."

Ramona interrupted Chase. "Is she really gone?"

Kat watched as he assembled himself into the police officer's version of himself; she recognized the mental armor he erected as the same kind she'd watched Greg construct whenever he got a call. This was the Chase who wound up on doorsteps to tell the next of kin of their tragedy.

"Yes, I'm afraid she is." He plucked a notepad out of his pocket. "Did any of you see her today? Have any conversations with her?" His eyes would not meet Kat's. She'd be interviewed tonight.

Ramona opened her phone and tilted it to Chase. "She texted me a few hours ago. Asking if I was bringing red or white wine tonight. We were coordinating. Nothing out of the ordinary."

Krista said, "I haven't talked to her since last Thursday."

Chase scribbled notes. "Ann?"

She looked at Chase, her muddy eyes wet. "I can't believe she's really gone. Our friend was murdered right here in our neighborhood. This doesn't happen to us. It happens to other people. Why Camila?" she asked the room. He touched her elbow lightly, and she yanked her arm away. "Don't touch me."

Chase flinched. "Okay, it's important I know if you talked at all lately."

"We didn't," Ann said and walked out of the house.

The remaining neighbors looked at one another.

"It's shock," Chase said.

Kat cleared her throat. "No more petty neighborhood crap. Our friend is dead. We all know she and Chase slept together. She's in shock. Chase, you shouldn't have touched her." Her envy, tinted with grief and shock, reached a hostile breaking point.

"I'm sorry." He looked at his feet. "I'm just doing my job."

"A hazard of sleeping with half the neighborhood, I guess," Kat said. Snapping had released an ounce of pressure, and feeling bad for being mean felt better than the pain of losing Camila. Kat's bare feet slapped against the floor as she stomped out of the kitchen.

She went to the front room to find Horace. The bickering in the kitchen would not mar his last few hours of innocence. It was the least she could do for her friend. Krista and Ramona quietly let themselves out. Kat met Janet's eye over Horace's head and she shook her head sadly. Janet's breath hitched in her throat, but she kept her expression still. Janet looked at Horace. "I tell you what. Why don't you hang on to this granola to snack on it tomorrow, too?"

"Really? Thank you," his small voice eked out. Blissfully unaware of how his world had shifted on its axis. No hint of grief or sadness.

Janet collected her purse and looked at Kat. "Well, I better be going. Will you be alright?"

"I will. Thank you, Janet."

"Of course." And she walked out of the house as quickly as her legs could carry her.

The house grew quiet. Chase said, "I can't sit or do anything in these clothes. I'm going to have to get cleaned up."

"Of course. I'll get Horace into the bath, too. Can you keep an eye on him while I get some clothes for him? I'll be right back."

Horace looked at Kat, his eyes as big as saucers. "A bath? I love baths." And he ran up the stairs in front of both of them.

"I better catch that little guy," Chase said with a tired laugh.

Kat went to the garage to sort through the bags of children's clothes she'd never brought herself to take to Goodwill. As she walked in the stale air, she fell to her knees with sobs wracking her body. Everyone in the house was two floors up so she allowed herself this moment to ride a sea of grief.

There would be no more morning coffees, late night chats, or brunches with her best friend. The laughter, tears, secrets—life would forever be less. She stood, paced back and forth across the cluttered garage. Anger boiled inside, Camila had five children, a loving husband, and everything to live for.

Kat breathed in the scent of musty clothing sitting in bags and stale oil from mechanical things that run a house. An old onesie already stained with what looked like Jillian's favorite spaghetti became a handkerchief as she wiped her running mascara and blew her nose hard into the soft fabric.

"Compose yourself," she said aloud. "For Horace and Camila."

She fished out pajamas with rubber duckies with hats from all different jobs: police, fire, train conductors. Kat didn't remember Jillian wearing them, so they may have been hand-me-downs from someone else in the neighborhood.

On her way up the stairs Horace's laughter and splashing sounds wafted through the air. Kat met eyes with Chase in the hall and he nodded and went to Kat's bathroom to shower.

She leaned against the door frame as Horace took an empty shampoo bottle and filled and squirted it over his head with peals of laughter. Looking away she swiped another tear from her eye.

"You about ready buddy?" Kat asked.

"Ah," he whined, but he already pulled the plug as

he waited for her to wrap him in a giant bath sheet that could wrap him twice.

Kat lifted his slippery body out of the tub and wrapped him up. He smelled of the lilac in the shampoo. "There you go, snug as a bug in a rug."

She put Horace in Jillian's bed after his bath and went to tuck him in, she kissed his head and her heart leapt back more than a decade when it was Jilly's head getting a kiss, asking for water, sneaking snacks.

"G'night buddy," Kat said.

"G'night, Mommy," he replied. His thumb, wrinkled with a too-long bath, wandered lazily into his mouth.

Descending the stairs, Chase was dressed in the shorts from the previous night and there were two heavily poured red wines on the coffee table. She settled in beside him.

"I can't find the words," Kat said. Her eyes brimmed with the tears she'd kept at bay with Horace.

"I know," Chase said, his voice gruff with emotion. He opened his arm on the couch and, without a word, she nestled in with her glass of wine.

TJ threatened me as Camila. But she was close enough to me to know that Camila was not me. Then her eyes widened, and it came to her. She threatened TJ with the police, and it took over an hour to clean up and get back to her home. Her words tumbled out fast. "I need to know. Was she killed from behind?"

"What do you mean?"

"Like, did whoever did this face her?" Kat asked.

"I'm not sure. I was trying to save her. But there were no fingerprints suggesting she was facing the suspect. He may have turned her around, though."

"Are you sure it's a he?" she asked, her voice quaking.

He straightened. "Do you know who did this? Does this have something to do with earlier?"

"No, I don't know for sure. But Camila and I look similar from the back..." Her breath hissed through her teeth.

"But why would anyone be out to hurt either of you?"

"You aren't cop-Chase right now." Then she repeated the words Camila said to her. "Promise not to be mad?"

His brow furrowed.

She weaved a patchwork of half-truths, with enough information to tell him what he needed. TJ hurt Camila. It had to be TJ.

Chase's Adam's apple bobbed. "If anything ever happened to you..." He didn't finish his sentence.

She rubbed his back. His taut muscles beneath her fingers made her stomach jump. "I know, I'm sorry."

He leaned back into her hand slightly. "But TJ was with you, right until the mace, right?" he asked finally.

"Yes, but she wasn't hit as badly as I was. The wind put it all in my eyes. She was mobile almost immediately. Is there any way TJ would have figured out where Camila lived and got to the house that quickly and waited for me?"

The wine fizzled in her brain, and she pushed against the alcohol to get the pieces to sort into place.

He tapped his finger to his chin and took a sip of wine. "After your first call, she may have researched where you lived. Known exactly where to go if she felt endangered. How long between when you were maced and when I came to get you?"

"It took me a while to get cleaned up, and for you to get there. Maybe an hour and a half?"

"She would have had to go to your house after cleaning herself up. That's pretty tight," Chase said doubtfully.

"Agreed. Maybe this was a random attack," Kat said with relief. Though she didn't believe it.

"Maybe," Chase said, rubbing the back of his neck.

"Greg's coming home tomorrow," Kat said.

"I know. But tonight I'm going to stay with you and Horace and make sure you're safe."

She didn't want to go to bed alone, so instead she stayed in his arms, sitting on the couch in silence. Evening her breath, she let the silence sit between them and her mind drift. His head leaned against the back of the couch as he drifted to sleep.

TJ would know soon enough that she'd killed the wrong woman—a better woman—and a white fiery rage roiled in her. She'd make her pay for what she'd done. Then she thought of Jillian, and what it would mean for her to lose her mother. The devastation would be insurmountable. Or worse, if TJ exacted revenge on her family and killed everyone close to her. Her best friend was gone. Jillian. Chase. Her husband. Everyone could be in danger. Recovering from the loss of Camila would leave a hole in her heart forever. But Jillian... She couldn't survive that. She wasn't Viola or Mariah. If someone hurt Jillian, she'd jump into the grave, letting the earth cover them both.

THIRTY-NINE

THERE WAS a knock on the door the next morning. Kat opened her bleary eyes and rolled her tongue across her dried lips. Her mouth was open and her head lay in the nook of Chase's arm.

Chase said, "I was scared to move. You looked so peaceful."

"Oh, sorry," Kat said. She spotted the small dark spot of drool on his sleeve and blushed. She wiped the sides of her mouth with her hand and looked up the stairs to see Horace with his light hair spiked and dipped, rubbing the sleep from his eyes, as he padded out of Jillian's room and into the bathroom, closing the door behind him.

Kat got up, stretched her back, and opened the door. Edward stood on her stoop, staring at her through red-rimmed eyes. She hugged him, but his back straightened against her embrace. He coughed, camouflaging his grief.

"She had something for you." He wiped his nose with the sleeve of one arm, and under his other was a pile of letters tied together with a satin sash. Kat recognized the stationery immediately.

Her father's. *Damn*, she thought. *Please tell me she didn't go to him.* But she knew the answer.

His hands trembled as he showed her the stack of envelopes. "These say Katherine." Mercifully, her father did not add Grant, the last name no one knew. She reached out to take them, but he snatched them away. He fished a phone from his back pocket and his hands trembled as he handed it to her. "Please, open this first." He held out Camila's phone. "It may help find who did this. It'll take the police a long time. Then I'll give you these."

His quiet desperation shocked her, and Kat took the phone from him. The weight of his request was heavy in her hand. Camila and Kat had each other's passwords with the playful joke that if either one of them died, to delete all the private chats. The ones where they ranted about husbands, children, and general life inconveniences. They said so many things they didn't mean in rant-chats because there was no judgment. It helped them be more present and kind to those who depended on them. The 'delete our chats' promise was a joke, but would Camila want her husband and children to be privy to their private, and sometimes hurtful, banter?

She took the phone from him and said, "I wrote the password down, but it's upstairs. Let me see if I can find it. Come in and sit and I'll go get it."

He came inside and sat on the couch, his shoulders slouched. Chase said, "I'll put some coffee on."

On the way up the stairs to buy time, she opened Camila's phone, and it was on Google Maps. Kat knocked back on her feet. *My childhood home*. How? Why? Would the police investigate the device? And see her deletion? Maybe. She didn't care. She opened her texts with Camila, and her fingers ran quickly to delete their chat. And she removed the Google App, too. The pictures, the chats between her children and her, Edward, could have the rest.

Kat locked the phone and retreated down the stairs. "Her password is 0704," she said from memory and gave the phone back to him, locked.

His eyes teared. "I should have guessed. My birthday."

Thank God he didn't, Kat thought.

Kat looked away as he typed the code into the phone and it sprang to again to life.

He handed the stack of envelopes to Kat, and she took them gingerly. "Thank you. I'm so sorry for your loss."

"I don't know what we're going to do without her." He bent his head into his hands.

Horace ran into his father's arms, nearly knocking his mother's phone on the floor. Edward stood and tucked the phone into his back pocket and lifted his son into his arms, holding him tight to his chest.

Horace arched his tiny back to examine his father and blather on about his adventure. "Daddy. I got to eat treats on the couch and take a long bath. It was so fun. I love being at Aunt Kat's house."

Kat smiled and rubbed Horace's back gently. "I loved having you here too, buddy."

Horace stared at his dad, his head cocked to the side like a puppy. "Where's Mama? What's wrong with your eyes? They're so red. Do your eyes hurt?" His tiny hand rested on his father's right temple.

With his son in his arms, Edward turned on his heel without a goodbye to Kat, and said, "C'mon buddy, let's go home."

She closed the door quietly behind them and rested her hand against the hard wood of the door to steady herself. Horace, Edward, Chloe, and the others. Life irrevocably changed forever, torn asunder. She squeezed her eyes tight. A warm hand pressed against the small of her back, and she turned to Chase.

"Are you okay?" he asked, handing her a cup of coffee.

"No, I'm not. My best friend... She's dead." She slipped the stack of envelopes under her arm.

Why did Camila go to him?

I should have told her, and everyone, the truth.

Chase's eyes were trained on the paperwork. "What did Edward give you? It may be important to understand what happened." His police persona peeked through.

"It's nothing," Kat snapped. "This has nothing to do with what happened to her. It can't." But she wasn't sure.

"Kat..."

"No, this isn't your business, Chase."

He cleared his throat. "I'm sorry. I'll call Greg to see what time he's coming home today."

"Thank you." She retreated upstairs and closed the office door behind her.

She'd apologize to Chase later. The front door opened and closed as she steadied her breaths and laid all the letters on the table. They were dated throughout the years. The first one was fresh, dated the day Camila died and sent home with her.

She ran her finger along the seam of the fresh envelope and felt the satisfying rip as it tore. Her father's familiar scrawl now had jagged lines in the cursive, like his hand trembled. A tear smudged the ink of her name. Until then, she hadn't realized she was crying.

Dearest Katherine,

Do not be upset with your dear friend Camila. She is a lovely person whose only indiscretion is to care too much. I've escaped to my office for a few stolen moments to tell you exactly how it feels to be almost close to you again. When I saw her, I nearly thought she was you, and my breath caught. But when she opened her mouth and introduced herself, I knew she was not my Katherine. She came because of you, though, and for that I am grateful.

You had a different best friend once. Minerva. I hope one day you'll find it in your heart to forgive both her and me for what we did. If we could meet, once. All of us. To explain the reasons, perhaps we can all move forward, together.

I see you received the letter from Mr. Parson. That brought your friend to me. It took you a long time to find yourself there. You are resolute in your terms. I hope it was the universe that brought you back to me. I've waited over twenty years and hope to not wait much longer.

I badly wanted to ask Camila how you are, what you're doing, about your life. But these are conversations for you and I. She kept guarded about your well-being, but shared you have a daughter. Not the one you and I know about, but a different one. When I inquired further, she quieted. She is a good friend, but Minerva was a good friend, too.

I only wish you understood why, and did not run. I should have further explained my position instead of relying solely on my authority as a father. I understand that now.

I've run out of the luxury of time, so I implore you once. Come and see me. There are things left unsaid. Without tearing open old wounds, there are people who would love to see you again.

I am still at the house, waiting for you. I'm sending these letters home with your friend, but there are secrets still here. Ones I cannot send along with a courier. Read the letters I've sent, or better yet, come home and have the conversations in person.

I am ill, and not long for this Earth. Please come home.

Love,
Father

A tear smudged the word Father. As always, the two were bound by unspeakable pain. No matter how far she ran, she felt him once again so close. There he was in the curled T's, the smell of the stationary, the silky feel of it in her hands. She rubbed the tiny piece of fabric in her pocket. She raised one daughter, but had two. But he'd lost both of his children.

Kat tucked the rest of the notes away in her shoebox to read once she'd had time to bury her adult best friend.

Minerva, Minnie. She hadn't thought of her childhood best friend in ages. A fresh pang of jealousy pinched her side.

What will my family think of the ashes on the fireplace mantel and all of my lies? Greg and Jillian wouldn't believe Kat was capable of such deceit, but her desperation had bred ingenuity. A chameleon. She'd manufactured a new person, one she liked more. Or thought she did. But the sins of the past never retreated. They stood sentry from the mantel, watching her every move.

She would unravel the knot of her childhood and beg forgiveness from everyone she'd hurt after this was done.

FORTY

HER CELL PHONE RANG. *Peter Walton.*

"Hello?" Kat asked.

"Camila?" his tone was laced with worry.

How do I answer this?

"Yes." Her voice trembled. Yesterday's scene snuck back into the edges of her psyche.

"Oh, thank God. The news said Camila O'Brien was murdered. I was so worried something happened. But when I saw the picture on the news, she looked similar, but different," Peter said.

Kat choked back a cry. "She was my neighbor. Actually, my best friend."

"Oh," he said, his confusion clear. "I'm sorry for your loss."

"Thank you. She was a lovely person." The past tense sat thick on her tongue.

"She had the same name as you?"

She let some of the truth tumble out. "No. I used her

name. My husband is a police officer, so I tried to protect his identity. It was an accident."

"I see," Peter said. "Your husband is a police officer? So you aren't really a journalist?"

She bit the inside of her lip. "No, I'm afraid I'm not. My husband had your daughter's case, and I stuck my nose somewhere it didn't belong." Her cheeks burned.

"Will my daughter be vindicated?" The reason for his call.

Kat hedged. "Maybe." She corrected herself. "Probably." Then she added, "My husband was shot by Evan."

Peter gasped. "Oh, my God. He was your husband? I saw the story on the news. Is he alright?"

"He's okay. Though he almost wasn't. He didn't know I poked around the case. I'm sorry for lying. This afternoon, when he comes home, I'm going to tell him everything I've found and leave it to law enforcement. There are some conflicting facts he isn't aware of that I've found." The heat crawled up into her ears and she wanted to disappear.

Peter's throat cleared. "Do they think Evan killed our daughter?"

She hesitated. "I shouldn't be in the business of investigating anymore."

"Please, if you aren't sure, we found something to prove it. I want you to have all the facts before you talk to your husband. Before you, no one cared or listened. Please. We trusted you."

She sighed. He was right. They put their trust in her,

and she'd betrayed them. "Okay. Where do you want to meet?"

"Mya's grave. We found something there. Can you meet in an hour?"

She glanced at her watch. Greg wasn't to be home for three hours. "Okay, I'll be there. But I can't stay long."

Peter disconnected the call.

She thought of Camila again. Her body in the morgue waiting to be laid to rest with her daughter Hope. Her rage boiled over and she dialed *Home Wrecker*.

"I bet you thought I was dead," Kat hissed, her heart racing and pounding against her chest wall.

"What are you talking about? Was macing yourself not enough?" the familiar voice spat back. "You don't know what you're doing."

TJ was right, and it chipped her ego. "You're about to be arrested for the murder of Amelia and Beatrice." She took a breath, before adding, "And Camila."

"What are you talking about?"

"You're the living link between Mya and her children and Beatrice and her daughter."

"Evan was the one in common," she said. "And he's dead now."

An image of Camila's white sneakers shaking with each pound of CPR permeated her memory, and her vision blurred. "You're going to pay for all of it." A fiery rage burned in her chest.

"What? What do you want?" TJ asked, her confusion genuine.

"Meet me at Mya's gravesite in an hour and fifteen minutes. If you aren't there, I will call the police." Then she hung up.

Peter and Mariah deserved to face TJ and ask their questions and get to the bottom of the case. While a man killed their grandchildren, TJ supplied the tools for Mya's death.

Kat ran upstairs to get her notebook and tucked it in her purse. She pursed her lips. *I was just there. What did I miss?*

It was like a piece of lint on her tongue. Grasping with her mind, yet she couldn't, the facts wouldn't snap into place. She tapped her chin, grabbed her purse and her keys from the hanger at the front door, walked outside, and blinked back the sun. The car was gone. She hit her palm on her head. It was at the hardware store, where she was maced.

She called an Uber. While she waited for the car, she checked her phone's percentage: sixty-five. No time to charge it before she left, so she flicked it to power save and shut her extra applications. Her browser was open, reminding her of her unfinished research on the car part and the accidents. A woman and her three children killed, husband left behind.

The husband. A thought from her thriller group came floating back. *It's always the husband.* She scrolled through the story and her finger caught on the cracked screen. "Ouch," she said and shook her finger before putting it in her mouth and tasting copper. More carefully, she scrolled and searched his name. News stories about the failed car part, media interviews, and a civil lawsuit he'd won returned. Then she saw it, his obituary the day after Mya's children's deaths. She jerked her head back.

"My God," she said to the air. *He killed himself.* This father took Mya's children to exact his revenge. Then took his own life. Her mouth fell open. After Mya's death, the letters had stopped coming. This was why. She rubbed her head and thought, *How did this fit with TJ's role as the drug dealer, her affair, and the small hands on Amelia's neck?*

The time ticked by, as she bit the inside of her lip and glanced between her watch and the window for the Uber, pacing the floor. Finally, fifteen minutes later a white sedan pulled into the drive. Kat rounded the rear to confirm the license plate and climbed in. As they navigated to the cemetery, she called Chase.

"Hi," Chase said, his voice shy.

"Hi. I'm sorry I snipped at you this morning," she said. She shifted in her seat.

"You're under a lot of stress. And grief. I get it."

Kat shivered and brushed aside the things left said and unsaid between them. "I wanted to talk to you before Greg comes back. There are things that need to be said."

After a moment of silence, he cleared his throat. "Okay, how about now?" His voice was gruff with a rawness.

"Actually, I'm on my way to the cemetery to finish up my parents' arrangements. I had to catch an Uber because my car is still at the hardware store. Can you pick me up from the cemetery in about thirty minutes, and we'll talk on the way to my car?"

"Great, I'll be there."

"Thanks, we're pulling up now, so I've got to go." Her gut twisted with another lie. *This is my last lie about my parents.* And she disconnected the line.

FORTY-ONE

THE CAR DROPPED her at the side entrance and the canopy of willows guided her toward the other end of the cemetery. She quickened her pace to beat TJ to the site. As she dodged stone markers of those long and newly dead, she approached Beatrice's plot on the way to Mya's. The frail frame of Viola was there, hunched over the green temporary plastic placeholders. She met eyes with Kat as she tried to hurry away.

Viola stood. "What are you doing here? Are you here to see my Beatrice?"

She turned to the grief-stricken mother. Maybe it was better Viola came too. Get it all done at once. Like a Band-Aid. "No, I'm here to see Mya's parents," Kat said.

Viola rubbed her chest and her eyes watered, deep in her own grief. "Did you know her last word was mama? My daughter called for me in her last moments of life. That's what the police report said. Something I think about every day. It breaks my heart."

"I'm deeply sorry for your loss," Kat said. "My best friend recently died. And I think what happened to her is related to all of this."

Viola's breath caught. "How? Why?"

"Well, Steven was right about TJ. She'd been having an affair with Evan for many years. Which gives her a motive. She's on her way to meet me. Somehow I know it's all related, and I intend to figure out how."

Viola's mouth fell open. "He's dead and paid for what he did. And now you think maybe he didn't do it?" Her tone dripped with exasperation and grief. Kat wished she was as sure as the Waltons and Viola of Evan's guilt.

"I'm not saying he's completely innocent. But I think the police were too hasty," Kat said slowly.

"You don't think Evan did it? What makes you so sure?" she asked as she closed the distance between them.

"The bruising on Amelia's neck. I saw the crime photos. The handprints were small. Like a woman's. TJ is the only one who knew about the other crime, the note, and had a motive."

"What about your friend?"

"I don't know who hurt her," Kat admitted. "I was using her name, and maybe TJ thought she was me. She is linked to all of this."

Viola asked, "So you've never met TJ?"

"No, I did. We had an altercation. Maybe she hired someone, I don't know. A week ago, before I got involved with any of this, my friend was safe." Her gut twisted at the thought it could still be her father, tethering her back to him. "The Waltons said they have something else to prove Evan's guilt. I have to know everything so I can hand it over to the police and let them unravel and close both cases. TJ will be here, too."

"Well, if TJ has anything to say about my daughter and granddaughter, I want to be there. I'm coming too." Viola walked beside Kat, and they fell in silent lockstep as they wandered through the stones.

"How well do you know Steven?" Kat asked.

"I feel like he's my son. They were engaged before Evan came. They were on a brief hiatus, and that devil slipped in," Viola growled.

Kat was about to ask another question about Steven, but she spotted Mariah and Peter with their hands on Mya's gravestone. Their heads bent in what looked like a prayer. Their shocking white hair in the sunlight aged them. Peter saw them first and put an arm on Mariah's shoulder. She turned as Viola and Kat made their way to them. Mariah's fingers wandered to her lips and confusion clouded her features.

As they neared the gravesite, Kat explained, "On my way, I saw Viola with Beatrice and Amelia."

Viola reached out and hugged Mariah. Tears Kat hadn't seen yet from Viola streamed down her face.

Viola said to Mariah, "I'm so sorry for the loss of your girls. No one can imagine or describe how awful it is."

Mariah returned her hug and said, "We meant to come to the funeral. But we couldn't bring ourselves to do it." Peter placed his hand at the small of Mariah's back in comfort.

Kat said, "We have little time. TJ is going to meet us here. I believe she has something to do with my friend's death. And somehow she's tangled in all of this."

"The drug dealer?" Peter asked.

"She's got more to do with this than the police know," Kat said. "I want to ask her questions about her relationship with Mya, why she supplied the drugs, and anything she may have known about the crime. But before she gets here, what was it you found?"

Mariah's arthritic finger pointed to the teddy bear. "It's been there for weeks, but in the week Evan died, someone moved it. I visit Mya and her girls twice a week. Someone touched this teddy bear. It had to be Evan saying his last goodbye."

Kat eyed the bear tipped on its side. Maybe a gardener, Evan, anyone, could have knocked it over. Even her. She bit her lip and drilled her brain, trying to recall if when she'd touched the bear it had fallen over. Had her investigation caused yet another hurt to Mariah and Peter?

Viola's eyes grew wide. "Beatrice and Amelia have a teddy bear, too. It looks nearly the same, but newer." Her eyes teared up.

Someone cleared their throat behind them, and Kat jumped.

Kat turned to the blonde woman who stood with her hands on her hips and her chin jutted out defiantly.

Kat said, "You're early."

TJ said, "Evan put both of the teddy bears on the graves. He loved both of his girls. Why is everyone here?"

FORTY-TWO

MARIAH'S EYES flashed at TJ. "You killed my daughter."

"I never put drugs in her. She took them herself," TJ said. "And Evan loved his girls. Anyone could have moved the stupid bear. That don't prove nothing." She pointed at the teddy bear.

Peter said, "It had to be Evan. A last goodbye because he knew the cops were closing in."

Kat turned to TJ. There wasn't much time to get what she could from her before she got spooked. "TJ, you said your affair was casual." She tapped her pen on her notepad and gazed at TJ.

TJ bit her over-plumped lip. "I may have told a white lie. We had a relationship. But I never killed nobody." She crossed her arms over herself. "I cared for him."

Kat asked, "In his dying breath he yelled 'find TJ'. Why do you think that is?"

She shifted uncomfortably and glanced at Viola,

then back at Kat. "Because I was his alibi. We were together that day."

Viola sucked in her breath.

TJ looked at her and said, "Oh, get off your high horse. Beatrice was still with her old boyfriend, too."

"No, my daughter would never," she said.

Kat's eyes narrowed at TJ. This was her chance. "If Steven was with Beatrice, and you were with Evan, it seems the only thing standing in anyone's way was baby Amelia..."

"I didn't kill that baby or his wife," TJ spat.

"I didn't ask if you did," Kat said.

TJ crossed her arms and spat away from the grave. "I ain't stupid, lady. I know what you're thinking."

Mariah interrupted Kat's amateur interrogation. "It was Evan. He's the only one linked to both. He did it, and thank God he's dead."

Peter nodded in agreement.

Kat patted Mariah's shoulder. The thin blouse did little to hide her thin clavicles. "I know you want closure. But he couldn't have done it all. Yes, I believe a man killed your family. But, not Viola's granddaughter."

Viola's jaw dropped open. "What?"

Kat turned to Viola, whose chin trembled. "The fingerprints left on Amelia's neck were smaller than Evan's. The hands of a woman. And once the coroner finishes Camila's autopsy, I wonder if they'll find the handprints match."

TJ's face reddened. "I told you I didn't kill nobody. Yes, I sold Mya drugs. It ain't my business what she did with them. I didn't kill her. And you can't prove I killed that baby neither." She wagged her finger at Viola.

"Her name was Amelia," Viola said, her eyes flashing.

"Evan killed all of them," Mariah said. Her face reddened in frustration and grief. "He's guilty of killing my grandchildren."

Peter rubbed her back, and she shook off his gesture.

Peter said to TJ, "Just admit it was Evan. Stop protecting your lover. He's gone."

"That wouldn't explain the small hands on Amelia's neck," Kat pressed.

TJ said, "Fine, say what you wanna say. No matter who done it, it won't bring anyone back."

She turned to the Waltons. It was time to provide them with closure. "I researched the car parts accident, Peter. And there was a family who died from a car accident."

His lips trembled. "What does that have to do with anything?"

"Well, a man's family was killed. The day after Mya's children were killed, he died by suicide..." Kat let the words soak in.

Peter gasped and turned to Mariah with wide eyes. "The letters stopped coming."

"No, no, no, no," Mariah said. "It was Evan. It had to be," she whispered.

Viola gazed at the sky and turned pale, then turned to Mariah. "Wait. Wait, a damned minute. My daughter called me mom, never, ever, mama."

Kat worried Viola would need to be transported again for shock. It was too soon. "Are you okay?" She took a step toward Viola, who seemed to see no one but Mariah.

"It wasn't *mama* my daughter said in her last breaths." Then with a sudden certainty she said, "It was *Mariah*. I was confused because she never called me mama. It was you." Her bony index finger jabbed at Mariah's collarbone so hard that Kat thought it might snap.

Mariah stumbled back, but her face turned white.

FORTY-THREE

KAT'S MOUTH fell open and her body tensed at the revelation. "What? How?"

Peter stood between Viola and Mariah. "Leave her alone, Viola."

Viola poked her crooked finger into Peter's chest so hard he stumbled back. "Why?"

"I don't know what you're talking about. Evan is responsible," Mariah choked out. Her eyes slid to her daughter's gravestone. "It was Evan. He caused this."

Kat rubbed her forehead. "How?" she asked Viola.

Viola's eyes flashed. "She's a hospice nurse, meaning she has access to anything my daughter would have taken. She made it look like an overdose. I don't know why. But I know my daughter said Mariah. Not mama. I know it now."

Peter cleared his throat. "Evan killed our girls."

Viola clenched her fists as they shook. "Who killed mine?"

Mariah backed up a step and shook her head. "No one cared about my Mya because she was an addict. Then Evan gets to start over and leave us with nothing? He gets to have a brand-new family? No, it wasn't fair." She wrapped her arms around herself.

Viola let out a strangled cry—its pitch hit a chord that would have harmonized with Edward's cry when he'd seen Camila on the floor—and she crumpled to the ground.

Kat placed her hand on her shoulder. Her tiny bird-like body trembled with grief. Rage would be next.

Viola leered up at Mariah, her fist beating her chest. "How could you do this?"

Any emotion on Mariah's face flicked off like a switch had been flipped, and she stared straight ahead.

Peter answered for her. "It was because of Evan."

"You strangled a baby," Kat said, her mouth falling open.

"Don't forget my daughter," Viola added, then turned on Peter and Mariah. "You knew how you'd suffered. You met Beatrice and Amelia. Why would you do this to me? To us? We welcomed you into our home."

Mariah answered in a voice devoid of emotion. Her eyes were dark and blank like a shark's. "Evan didn't deserve to have a new life. He killed my girls. He didn't suffer like he should have. Your daughter knew what he was accused of. What he'd done, yet she stayed with him. She sealed her fate."

Kat's skin tingled with discomfort as the cold realization sunk in. She turned to Mariah. "But it wasn't

Evan. It comes back to the letters you brushed off. The car part Peter made."

TJ smirked at Mariah. "What does that make you? Y'all out here trying to get me caught up with something because I what? Made some money? So what? Look what you did." She glared at Kat. "See, I told you I didn't do nothin'."

Peter deepened his tone. "We just wanted those responsible to pay for what they did to our family. We aren't killers. No one cared about Mya and who hurt her and her girls. Not until someone else died. Someone the media deemed worthy. It was the only way to seek justice for our child, our loss. We tried everything. We called the police, the media. No one would listen. If they would have listened, none of this would have happened."

Chase would be there soon, and Kat needed to know. "What about my friend Camila? Mariah isn't big enough."

"I did it," Peter said through gritted teeth. "I thought it was you. You said there was more to the investigation. The story was an exclusive, so I thought the story would die with you. Evan was gone, and Mya would be exonerated. That's all we wanted."

"You know what I look like. I was in your home, talking to you," Kat said.

"It was fast. I came at her from behind. She didn't suffer," he said as if that made it any less horrible. "I made it quick. You look similar. But when I turned her over, I realized my mistake. I should have known when I looked up your number and got a hold of her." Peter hung his head low.

Kat understood the deep-seated need for revenge and right then, she wanted Peter and Mariah to die a slow and painful death. "You couldn't look me in the eye while you choked the life out of me?" Then she lobbed a last jab before Chase got there. "How would Mya feel about ripping apart two other families just to get revenge? Would she be proud?"

Mariah pulled a syringe from her purse and lunged at TJ. "You gave my Mya the drugs! You'll pay for what you did, too."

FORTY-FOUR

VIOLA SPRUNG from the ground in front of TJ and grabbed Mariah's arm, pushing the syringe into her thigh. She used the heel of her hand to plunge the contents of the vial into Mariah's leg.

Viola let go and Mariah stumbled back, her face scrunched with pain and confusion. She stared at the syringe and let out a shrill panicked scream before collapsing to the ground. She withdrew the empty syringe and tossed it across the grass. Her breaths became shallow and morphed into a wheezing as her eyes rolled to the back of her head. Her lips turned a bluish hue. TJ ran from the cemetery.

Peter dropped to the ground and cradled Mariah's head in his arms, rocking her. He looked up at Kat, his eyes full of tears. "Please help her. Please." His pleas were thick with desperation.

Kat pulled her phone from her pocket and called

Chase. "Chase, please hurry I'm at Mya's grave. I'll explain later. Mariah took something, and she fell."

Peter said, "It was morphine from her hospice supplies. Morphine and a lot of it."

"Shit, I heard him. I'm bringing something to help. I'm coming. I'm coming. Hang on, Kat. I think I see you. I'm on my way."

She heard rustling, and he hung up the phone. Her eyes scanned the outcroppings of stones for him. His cruiser was in the parking lot and he ran toward them. His cheeks were red with exertion as he hustled toward the chaos.

Her voice was hoarse as she looked down at Peter. "He's coming. He'll help."

Peter mouthed, "Thank you," to Kat as Chase closed the final distance.

Viola spat at Mariah. "I could strangle you to show you how it feels." She lunged at her.

Peter smacked her arms away and pushed her hard. She flew back like a rag doll into the grass. Her head smacked with a thud against Mya's tombstone.

Kat yelled toward Chase, "Hurry! She's dying." She crouched over Viola, who was rubbing her head. "Are you okay?"

"No, but my head's fine," she said.

Viola watched Mariah struggling for air. Her hands trembled. "Am I a murderer, too? Am I no better than them? Is it wrong that I want her to die?"

Kat said, "No, no, we're going to save her so they can

both pay for what they've done to Beatrice and Amelia
—" She choked on her words and added, "And Camila."

Peter held his wife and whispered. "You're going to be okay. You're going to be okay." He looked at Kat standing over them, "I'll do anything, please. She's all I have left."

Chase neared them with one hand on his radio speaking into it, and his other held a small white plastic bottle Kat had never seen before.

She beckoned Chase with her hand, willing him to move faster. "Hurry!"

He ran to Mariah lying on the ground and knelt at her side. The back of his neck was slicked with sweat and he heaved for air. "I need space," he said between ragged breaths, nudging Peter out of the way. "Step back, but stay in my line of sight. If you want me to save her, you need to sit right in front of me, but out of my reach. Sit on your hands. Kat, watch him."

She nodded, and Peter obeyed. "Please save her. I'll do anything." He walked around his wife's shaking feet and sat on his hands as instructed.

Kat's desire to grab Chase's gun at his waist and kill them both was almost too much to resist, but the thought of Jillian being motherless locked her in place. She clenched her jaw. She would rise above what Peter and Mariah had become, but now she understood the temptation of revenge.

Peter rocked back and forth on his hands mumbling, "Please save her," over and over again.

Chase inserted the tip of the nozzle into one of her

nostrils and pressed the plunger. "You're going to feel better in a second." He said to her as she lay unconscious.

Kat watched as Mariah's breath returned to normal. After a few minutes, she blinked awake. He looked at Peter. "I administered Narcan, which is a temporary fix, so she isn't out of the woods yet, but an ambulance is on its way."

Peter still rocked back and forth on his hands. "Oh, thank God. Thank God."

Viola walked over to Mariah, and she spat in her face.

"Hey, hey, hey, back off," Chase said.

Viola glared at Peter. "You're both going to hell." She stumbled away from the scene and toward the parking lot, rubbing her head.

The sirens screamed louder. It wasn't long before three paramedics appeared, racing toward Mariah. They heaved her onto the stretcher and put an oxygen mask on her face. Chase gave the medical team the spent canister, looked at his watch, and mumbled something to them as the larger paramedic took a note.

Kat pointed to Peter and Mariah and said, "They're the ones who killed Camila, Beatrice, and Amelia. They admitted it."

"Yes, we did it. We didn't know Evan didn't do it. We didn't know." Peter looked up at Chase and pleaded, "Can I go with my wife?" His eyes were slick with tears from where he still sat on his hands, unable to wipe them away.

Chase walked toward him. "No, you cannot." Another police officer joined them, and he nodded at her. "She's going to place you under arrest."

Peter's lips trembled as he rocked on his hands.

Kat's jaw clenched at the privilege reflected in Peter's question and she fantasized about kicking him square in the jaw to ease an iota of her grief and anger, feeling the satisfying crack of it.

As the police officer and her partner approached Peter, Kat stepped away to let emergency services do their thing. From her vantage point, Peter appeared smaller and incapable of the atrocities he'd committed. He lay on his belly while the officers frisked him and the handcuffs were ratcheted around his wrists.

Chase walked toward Kat, his forehead wrinkled with worry. "They've got it from here. But let's get you home." Numbly, she walked beside him.

Kat's hand slipped to the shred of the baby blanket in her pocket. There was little a mother would not do for their child.

FORTY-FIVE

ON THE WAY to the car, Kat admitted her responsibility for the not-so-happenstance meeting of TJ, Peter, Mariah, and Viola. During her narrative, he blew air out through his teeth and rubbed the back of his neck.

"But why didn't you think it was Evan?" Chase asked.

"Did you study the photographs, Chase?"

"I did." He put his hand on her arm to stop her, and they faced each other. "Of course. What did you see that I missed?"

"The handprints on Mya's girls' necks. They were large. Like a man's. But the handprints on Amelia's neck were small. Plus, TJ and Evan were in a romantic relationship..."

"Which is why you assumed they were TJ's. Dammit." He blew out through his teeth. "So Evan killed Mya's girls?" They began walking again.

As they neared the car, Kat shared the abridged version of the news story. "I'll show it to you later, but I'll bet the father of that family killed Mya's girls."

He shoved his hands in his pockets. "None of that was in the file..."

"The Waltons were ashamed, never reported it. They thought Evan killed the girls and their vision tunneled. I understand. When you were working on Mariah, I wanted to kill them both for what they did to Camila. I'm no better than they are."

She told him about Steven's affair with Beatrice, and TJ's with Evan, the news story of the failed car part, and the motives and theories—both right and wrong—that she'd come to as she'd navigated the secret investigation. Each truth she told made her feel lighter.

"Wait," he said, interrupting her. "You planned to meet the woman who maced you?"

"Technically, I maced her and ended up macing myself. I knew I shouldn't have brought the mace," Kat said, stopping and crossing her arms as they reached the car.

Chase shook his head. "Whatever. You were going to meet with this woman, and you weren't planning to tell anyone? What were you thinking, Kat?" Chase repeated for the nth time since she'd started spilling her half-cocked plan. He looked at her, and hurt shone in his eyes. "Why would you do any of that? You don't understand how important you are. To Greg. To Jillian. To me. Why would you risk yourself for this?"

She shared using Camila's name and the guilt heavy

on her shoulders doubled her over in pain. Her chest squeezed tight and her vision blurred. If there was a white light, she would have run toward it to join Camila and her brother on the other side. If they'd still have her after the things she'd done.

He put his arms around her. "C'mere. You didn't do this."

She wheezed out the words, her breath tight in her chest. "I didn't put my hands around her neck, but I gave someone a reason to kill her. I'll never forgive myself."

She untangled herself from his embrace, he opened the car door for her, and she climbed in.

She realized a weight had lifted from her heart since she'd admitted everything to Chase. She was out of secrets, except for the lie about her parents, which could tear apart the very fabric of the life she'd spent over twenty years creating.

He shook his head as he climbed in beside her.

She wrung her hands. "What will you tell Greg?"

"About what?" Chase said.

It was a double-edged question.

"About what happened in the cemetery today," she clarified.

He sighed. "We're going to tell him I went with you because your car needed a jump. You had an appointment here first, and all of this unfolded by coincidence."

She blew out a breath of relief. "It's an awful lot of coincidences."

"I know, but it's the best I've got." He turned to her, placing his hand on her shoulder.

The heat of his hand and the pressure of his fingers turning her to face him sent electricity up her spine. Greg became nothing more than a shadow in the periphery of her heart. She fantasized in that moment of running away again. Starting all over, with someone new. With him. If he leaned in for a kiss, she would have. But he didn't lean in, and a picture of Jillian materialized in her mind's eye. She gulped her desire down and stared back at him.

He took his sunglasses off and looked at her directly. His hand gently rested on her wrist. The heat of his touch flipped her stomach. "Kat, let me get this out before I can't. Can we forget about everything and let me pine over you from a distance? Let's pretend you don't know I'm in love with you, or that I've loved you for years. Okay?"

He slid his hands down her wrists and held both of her hands. They were warm and her stomach swelled with butterflies. *Why did I jump into the first man's truck who would take me? Why didn't I wait for him?*

"Yes, of course," she said. "If things were different…"

"Don't." He held up his hand. "Just don't. I can't have that kind of hope. We both love Greg and Jillian."

"Agreed," she said simply. But God, she wanted him to know.

Quietly, he added, "I wish I would have met you first."

She dipped her chin to her chest. "Me too," she whispered. She put her left hand on his knee. An electric pulse shocked her, and the oval-cut diamond of her wedding ring caught the sun and blinked at her. Kat pulled her hand back.

THE SILENCE in the car on the ride back to the hardware store was contemplative, but not uncomfortable. His knuckles whitened as his grip kept tight to the steering wheel. She watched him grounding himself to a reality that if things had gone even a little differently might have been without her. Kat drummed her fingers on her thighs.

I will choose Greg more fully. A sad pit curled heavily at the base of her stomach with reality. She brushed thoughts of Chase and everything that could have been away. *Love the one you're with.* Love could not take root between them in the hallowed ground of her marriage.

He pulled up beside her car beneath the Ginkgo tree. Its filthy fruit had deposited itself on the roof of her car. She got out of Chase's car and dodged the landmines of decay as she beeped her car door unlocked and hopped in. A day ago the macing was the most dangerous thing to have happened to her in a while. That incident didn't move the needle anymore. Her car grumbled to life and Chase waved and drove off in the opposite direction.

Back at the house, she climbed in the shower to wash the confessions of the day away. The scalding water pelted her and her mind wandered to Camila. Peter killed her because he'd thought she was Kat. A third person who'd died because of Kat. Camila's death ripped the scab off the wound of her mother and brother's deaths. *Why did I think I'd outrun what I've done?*

As she toweled herself off a reminder chimed on her phone: *Reach out to Krista to help at the food pantry.* She sighed at the reminder from a few days ago. Without a thought, she cleared the notification because her hours and days to come would be brimming with mending the broken pieces of her childhood and salvaging her marriage.

Evan died of suicide by a cop because there hadn't been enough to keep him tethered to this life. TJ hadn't been enough. But Kat had Jillian and Greg. Her mind replayed Chase gently coaxing Mariah back to life. And all Kat had wanted was to unseat his gun and shoot her and Peter between the eyes and watch them die. Where would that have left Jillian and Greg?

Kat was confident the investigation would exonerate Mya and find the man whose family had died due to the bad car part guilty of the unspeakable murder of Maureen, Millie, and Mandy. To the police, it would be nothing more than a paperwork drill. No fresh arrests. There were other cases, cases where the killers still wandered the earth, threatening the lives of others. Far more glamorous than a twenty-year-old case where everyone was dead. No amount of new truths revealed would bring anyone back.

As she passed the living room, she glanced at the ashes on the mantel, and guilt pinched at her. She walked past Greg's office. His briefcase stood sentry like all the days before. Why had she snooped? For a brief time, she became Alice in Wonderland, wandering into a world where she didn't belong. Her curiosity had rocked her world on its axis and nothing would ever be the same again.

It was time to shred the papers and return to the world Kat had created for herself. She went to her shoebox and at the top sat her father's letters. Distracted, she plucked them out and traced the name Katherine written in his shaky but still-familiar handwriting. *It's time to make amends for everything.*

She picked up the phone and dialed the number she knew by heart. *Would he answer? Was the number still a working one?*

A familiar tremored voice answered, "Hello?"

"Father, it's Katherine."

THE PRODIGAL DAUGHTER
BOOK 2 OF THE KAT ELAND SERIES

THANK you for reading The Detective's Wife. Pre-order book 2 of The Kat Eland Series, The Prodigal Daughter now. I hope you enjoyed it! If you did...

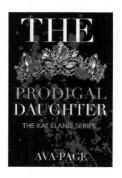

- Help other readers find this book by writing a review.
- Sign up for my newsletter, so you can find out about the next book as soon as it's available.
- Come like my Facebook page and follow me on Instagram.
- Visit my website: avapage.com

Buy at www. avapage.com

ACKNOWLEDGMENTS

I would like to express my heartfelt gratitude to the following people who have helped make this book a reality:

Hanna Elizabeth and Crystal Wren, my diligent and insightful editors, who not only polished my prose but also pushed me to dig deeper into my characters and their stories. Thank you for your invaluable guidance and for believing in me and my work.

La Jolla Press, for the stunning cover design that captures the essence of the book and draws readers in. Your artistry and attention to detail have made this book shine.

To my alpha and beta readers, thank you for your time, your feedback, and your unwavering support. Your enthusiasm and encouragement have kept me going through the long hours of writing and editing.

Finally, I want to acknowledge the love and support of my family and friends. Your belief in me and my dream has been a constant source of strength and inspiration.

ALSO BY AVA PAGE: THE RUNAWAY SISTER

BOOK 0 OF THE KAT ELAND SERIES

THANK you for reading The Detective's Wife. Haven't read the prequel yet? Get your copy of The Runaway Sister today. I hope you enjoyed it! If you did...

Buy at www. avapage.com

- Help other readers find this book by writing a review.
- Sign up for my newsletter, so you can find out about the next book as soon as it's available.
- Come like my Facebook page and follow me on Instagram.
- Visit my website: avapage.com

ALSO BY AVA PAGE: THE WATCHER

Buy at www.avapage.com

THE WATCHER

From Amazon's Hot New Release author of Thick as Water comes a gripping new novel about a mother, her daughter, and the dark secrets coming back to haunt them both.

Since her husband's death, Maggie Becker has lived to make her daughter Emily's life as normal as possible. When Emily leaves for college, Maggie is ready to live for herself again. But first, she makes one last gift, a photo book for her daughter. What she finds in the pictures makes the hairs on the back of her neck stand on end.

A killer is watching her daughter, and Maggie has the photos to prove it. If she involves the police, Emily will be dead before she finishes the phone call. The more she digs, the more secrets she finds.

What her husband kept from her may kill them all.

ALSO BY AVA PAGE: THICK AS WATER

Buy at www.avapage.com

THICK AS WATER

Ava's debut novel, published in 2021 is a contemporary fiction novel that will grab hold of the reader from start to finish.

I would like you both to come in. For Agnes and Liam, life is never the same after these words. In one afternoon, every vow in their marriage is a challenge: For worse. For poorer. In sickness.

ALSO BY AVA PAGE: ONE LAST CALL

A NOVELLA

Buy at www.avapage.com

ONE LAST CALL - FREE

Have you wondered if it's better to be born now with social media and phones, or before it was available? Read the novella *One Last Call* for free and see if it changes your mind.

PRAISE FOR AVA PAGE

THE RUNAWAY SISTER (BOOK 0 of THE KAT ELAND SERIES)

5 Stars - This is a brilliant read.

Wonderful well written plot and story line that had me engaged from the start.

Love the well fleshed out characters and found them believable.

Great suspense and found myself second guessing every thought I had continuously.

Can't wait to read what the author brings out next.

Recommend reading.

I read a complimentary advance copy of the book; this is my voluntary and honest review.

-Billie, Goodreads reviewer

4 stars

Interesting introduction to Kat Grant's story. Eager to read what happens next.

- Tikri/Letitia, Goodreads reviewer

* * *

THE WATCHER

5 Stars - Fast-paced Thriller of a Book

I just got my hands on The Watcher by Ava Page and it was a fast-paced, thrilling read! Ava knows how to create gripping tales with likable and compelling characters. Really good subject matter in this book as well, as she looks at how social media can be used among todays young people and families for both good and evil.

- Amazon Reviewer

WOW! COULDN'T PUT IT DOWN! THE WATCHER by Ava Page hooked me from the very first chapter.

- Amazon Reviewer

5 Stars - Amazing

This book has really crazy twists and turns. I highly recommend this for a quick read. I didn't want to put it down.

- Amazon Reviewer

5 Stars - Gripping Modern Page Turner exploring the wide ranges of human relationships

Gripping who-done-it page turner! Supremely crafted, interlacing the complexity of human relationships and loss with surprising twists and turns at the end. Human relationships are messy and Ava Page does a masterful job showing the beauty and heartbreak in this thriller. Highly recommend!

- Amazon Reviewer

5/5 Stars

This is a gripping, intense novel that leads the reader down a path of intrigue, horror and mystery... This is my first opportunity to read a novel from this author and I must say I was hooked from the very first page.

- Goodreads Reviewer

5/5 Stars

Absolutely loved this book. Ava Page puts you right in the story and you feel every emotion. I also read Vivian's diary and omg! I previously got a free copy of One Last Call and now I can't wait to read it.

- Goodreads Reviewer

* * *

THICK AS WATER

5 Stars - Who knew?

Thicker than Water had me on the edge of my chair and kept me quickly turning pages excited to discover what the next mystery might be. This book was both exciting and enjoyable and I highly recommend it to anyone that has the curiosity of "what if's"! Great story with a great ending. Ava Page might just be my new favorite author!

- Amazon Reviewer

Thick as Water had me on the edge of my chair and kept me quickly turning pages excited to discover what the next mystery might be. This book was both exciting and enjoyable and I highly recommend it to anyone that has the curiosity of "what if's"! Great story with a great ending. Ava Page might just be my new favorite author!

- Amazon Reviewer

...It pulls at your emotions with every turn. Have a box of tissues ready because you will need them with this book.

- Amazon Reviewer

5 Stars - You won't be able to put this book down.

Thick as Water is a real page turner. I found myself

saying I'll stop after the next page or next chapter... yet, I couldn't stop reading it.

- Amazon Reviewer

An intriguing observation of the **dangers of technology compromising privacy** told through the lens of family, love and loss.

- Sam Bland, Editorial Reviewer

5 Stars - ...It was so riveting I found that when I finally made myself put it down I looked for reasons to pick it back up...

- Goodreads Reviewer

5/5 Stars - One word...Incredible

It's hard to leave a review because I find myself speechless. I am a slow reader, slow slow slow, but I love it. This book took me two days. Unheard of for me. It was so riveting I found that when I finally made myself put it down I looked for reasons to pick it back up.

- Goodreads Reviewer

* * *

ONE LAST CALL - A NOVELLA

4/5 Stars

It was dark, gripping and I really enjoyed it!

- Goodreads Reviewer

5/5 Stars

This story is nicely written and really good, well worth reading.

- Good reads Reviewer

ABOUT THE AUTHOR

Ava Page

Ava is a veteran civil servant who has worked for nearly 20 years in the government in various roles. When not reading or writing, she enjoys walking the beaches of San Diego, which she calls home.

facebook.com/TheAuthorAvaPage

instagram.com/avapageauthor

goodreads.com/avapage

amazon.com/Ava-Page/e/B09987G5P8